THOUGH I WALK

THOUGH I WALK
Clay Anderson
Copyright © 2022 by Springer Mountain Press

ISBN - 978-1-7360898-9-7 (hardcover)
ISBN - 978-1-7360898-7-3 (paperback)
ISBN - 978-1-7360898-6-6 (ebook)

Printed in USA by Springer Mountain Press
85 East Main Street
Dahlonega, GA 30533

Cover by Clay Anderson
Interior by JW Manus

THOUGH I WALK

A Novel

Clay Anderson

For those missing but never forgotten.

Yea, though I walk through the valley of the shadow of death, I will fear no evil: for thou art with me; thy rod and thy staff they comfort me.

Psalm 23:4

Prologue

Christmas lights scattered a constellation of colors across the ceiling. Rockabilly tunes blared from the jukebox as Sam let go of a nameless man's hand and sashayed across the warped pinewood floor to the bar. As she pressed her weight precariously against the scuffed counter, her vision blurred. In the mirror behind the bar, Sam saw that her glazed eyes were shimmering pools echoing a rainbow of light at the barman. He stood with his arms crossed, examining her with dull scrutiny.

Sam raised two fingers then tapped them lightly on the bar. The barman pursed his lips and watched her closely. She was only nineteen, but that didn't matter here. As long as you were local and over eighteen, you got served at Yellow Creek Bar. Sam pouted a little, prompting the barman to shake his head and give her a toothy smile. He turned around and picked up two shot glasses that had been drying upside down on pegs.

Sam rested her chin on her palm and watched her reflection in the smoky glass behind the bar. The shelves atop were a kaleidoscope of liquor bottles. She gazed at them lustfully, her mouth watering. As she rubbed her belly softly, her face became expressionless. A vibration on the counter brought her back. In front of her sat a shot glass full of tequila along with a saltshaker and a slice of lime on a napkin.

She reached into her bra and pulled out a wad of damp, crumpled bills. She had begun to count them when she noticed the barman waving his hands in protest before pointing at a booth nestled in the far corner of the bar. There sat a solitary figure whose face was almost completely obscured under the wide brim of a black cowboy hat. Sam waved in the person's direction then held up a single finger. She turned back, poured salt onto her hand, licked it, downed a shot of tequila, sucked the lime. The liquor became a wellspring of warmth flowing throughout her core.

Personal thanks for the drink were in order. As Sam began to stagger across the dance floor, the bartender noticed her purse still sitting atop the bar. He called out to her, but the thumping music drowned out his voice . No matter, he thought to himself. He was certain she'd be back for another drink sooner than later.

Sam's unsteady gait continued to carry her across the bar.her heavy footfalls in time with the music as she dodged twirling dancers. Watching her wobble unsteadily in their direction, the figure sat with legs splayed, one elbow propped on the table, face almost completely shrouded in shadow.

Once at the booth Sam moved to sit down, but the figure quickly stood and took her by the hand. Sam observed with curiosity that the person had small, delicate fingers. Despite her best efforts, the cowboy hat's enormous brim made getting a glimpse of their face impossible.

Clasping Sam's hand tightly, the figure pulled her toward the bar exit. Sam's brain counted a multitude of reasons to tear away from the stranger's grip, but curiosity and nearly blind drunkenness spurred her to follow along obediently. She was all too familiar with the feeling of this fine line between comprehension and total blackout.

A wave of cool air hit Sam's face as she was pulled through the bar's exit and into the sparsely populated parking lot. Scattered about were trucks of various sizes, shapes, and models, all cast a sickly yellow by the weakly illuminating flood lights. Somewhere hidden among the motley crew of vehicles was Sam's ancient yellow Honda Accord.

Sam followed the bobbing crown of the black hat as her leader slinked around the side of the building. Sam just wasn't thinking. Her instincts were numbed, her brain conscious only of placing one foot in front of the other. She stumbled every few steps but was kept on course by a firm tug from the hand gripping hers.

The figure finally stopped, turning to reveal a face Sam recognized right away.

Sam smiled.

She never saw the movement. In a blur, the figure's right hand shot up and clamped tightly around Sam's throat.

Chapter 1

The pounding in Anna's head wrenched her from a deep sleep. A nonstop drumbeat of agony. She tried to swallow, but the inside of her mouth felt like sandpaper. A sticky, white film clung to the sides of her lips. As the room twisted in slow motion through her blurry vision, she racked her brain to recall the night before. The only thing she was certain of at that moment was that she had had far too much to drink.

Anna had gone out to celebrate the end of the fall semester with a group of friends. The women had agreed to each wear a black cocktail dress; Anna was excited to have found the perfect dress and matching heels at the Luxe Boutique downtown. She and her friends had bar hopped around Athens and flirted with guys for free drinks. They danced away the stress of finals and forgot about poor grades, prying parents, looming overdrafts, and bad boyfriends. The girls took selfies and savored their last night out before returning home for Christmas break. A goodbye to the freedom of college and a sad return to living under their parents' roofs. Much of the evening was masked behind a drunken fog.

Along with the misery of her hangover, Anna began to feel a sense of dread rising from her gut. She lay in bed and rubbed the tiny goosebumps that had risen on her arms, trying to convince herself that the feeling would pass. Anna watched the morning's raw light shine through the curtains as she tried to shake off the terrible restlessness.

It would not let go.

Anna rolled over to face her boyfriend, Trevor. He snored softly as she admired his chiseled jawline and high cheekbones. Like the rest of his body, Trevor's face was sculpted like the statue of an ancient Greek warrior. His presence made Anna recall texting him at some point during the night, asking him to meet up with her and the rest of the group for drinks. He had curtly reminded her that he was busy carrying out his duties as the University of Georgia's Student Council Vice President at a political function that Anna–as his girlfriend–should have attended. He had initially been sulky when she told him that she planned to go out with friends instead of with him to the function but he got over it quickly, as usual. It wasn't difficult for Anna to convince him to meet her at the Blind Pig Tavern once the UGA event was over. She had promised to work her way back into his good graces, so after a few drinks she clasped his hand and led him outside. They'd kissed passionately behind the bar, groping and clawing at each other in a fit of drunken lust. Anna remembered how they had hurried to her apartment and stripped just inside the front door. Details of the long, intense night began to unfurl in her mind.

An overwhelming feeling of thirst took over, causing Anna's thoughts to become visions of great vats of Gatorade. She slipped quietly from bed and began tiptoeing towards the kitchen when she was distracted by something on the floor. It was her special wooden picture frame that held her family photos. She and Trevor must have accidentally knocked it over in last night's drunken stupor.

The largest picture in the frame—and Anna's favorite—was of her and her twin sister, Samantha. Up until Anna went off to college five months ago, she and Sam rarely slept in separate rooms. Being away from her twin felt strange at first, but Anna eventually got used to the situation. In fact, it somehow brought them closer. Instead of fighting over silly things like the bathroom mirror, they looked forward to talking on the phone two or three times a day. Whenever Sam took a smoke break at work or Anna walked across campus to class, it became second nature to pull out their cell phone and call their sister.

The picture had been taken on the girls' last day of high school. Anna was wearing a University of Georgia t-shirt, proudly displaying the school at which her good grades had secured her a spot. Sam's black t-shirt was plain, a testament to the poor grades that meant she would not be going to college. She had always dreamed of becoming a nurse, but Sam would be staying behind while her twin left for a world of opportunities. Like the ones surrounding it, the picture showed the girls embracing, cheek to cheek, and smiling at the camera. Anna noticed for the first time what made it different from the other photos: each of the sister's eyes were tinged with a hint of sadness.

Leaving home for college had been a huge and terrifying step for Anna, and her adjustment was slow. For weeks, she had cried herself to sleep with the covers pulled over her head, hoping not to wake the stranger sharing her dorm room. Her last thought as she drifted to sleep every night was how badly she wished to see her sister.

Time passed, and it got easier.

Sam continued to live at home and work part-time at Dollar Value. Anna took Calculus, Spanish I, American History to 1865, and Organic Chemistry. She even joined the Tri Delta sorority. While Sam settled into her daily drudgery, Anna studied hard but partied harder. However, despite the widening gulf between their lives, the sisters' powerful bond never waned.

A sudden, urgent need to urinate roused Anna from her daze, and she momentarily felt out of place in her apartment. She put the picture frame back on the dresser and, instead of continuing to the kitchen, made a detour for the bathroom. Anna flipped on the light, illuminating the bevy of cosmetics scattered about the counter. A blow dryer and flatiron tangled together by their cords sat next to the sink, which was clogged with strands of Anna's dirty-blonde hair. Though it looked like chaos, Anna knew exactly where everything was. She swayed slightly as she reached over to turn on the bathroom fan. Trevor knew every inch of her body, but she always insisted on using the fan to cover the sound of herself using the bathroom.

Something kept bothering her. Anna traced the cords of her memory. Nothing troubling happened last night. One of the last things she remembered was reading the group text where all of her friends made it home safe. Exams were over. She shouldn't have a care in the world.

Yet a small voice whispered worry into her head. Anna's elbows were resting on her knees, and she leaned over slightly with her eyes closed. An imprint of Sam's face shone in her mind like a portrait. Just that image alone made Anna's stomach drop. Sweat beaded across her forehead, and she was struck with a pang of anxiety. The familiar twinge of twin intuition overcame her. Unspeakable and surreal, yet wholly providential.

At that moment, Anna knew something terrible had happened to Sam.

Anna stood and rushed out of the bathroom. Sam was scared and lost. An echoing cry for help bounced off the walls of Anna's mind. A yammering flutter from within, almost like the onset of a hallucination. A fresh wave of nausea swept over her. This wasn't a holdover from last night. It was brought about by unadulterated fear. She tasted bile. Acidic liquid formed at the top of her throat. She was going to be sick. She groped about the room in search of her cell phone. She needed to talk to Sam.

Anna's chaotic scramble for her cell phone tore Trevor from his slumber. Clothes and shoes flew around the room. A heel smacked the wall with a loud thud. She dumped the contents of her purse onto the nightstand. She turned to the crumpled remnants of last night's clothing on the floor and searched for her phone. Trevor watched her dully.

"What are you doing?"

"Looking for my phone," she said sharply.

"Right here," he said, holding it up.

Anna raced over to the bed and took her phone. She unlocked it and went to her recent calls. She hovered over the name Sam for a moment. *It was probably just an early morning check-in*, Anna thought. *I'm just over-reacting. This is nothing*. Just the remnants of the alcohol and the birth of a hangover. Sam will either laugh or be angry with her ridiculous sister. They'd chat and laugh about how silly this was, and all would return to normal. The impossibility of a twin's intuition. *It was no big deal*, Anna kept reminding herself. The hangover was making her paranoid. Solely a figment of her imagination. Yet there was no mistaking that the fear remained and emanated from the truest boundaries of her heart.

Sam was the first living being Anna had ever known. Even before entering the world, they were entwined with each other. Clutching each other in the ultrasound photo. They had an unimpeachable bond. Anna didn't know what, but no matter how much she tried to convince herself otherwise, something wasn't right.

While contemplating what to do, Anna felt Trevor's hands move up the back of her leg. She smiled at him placatingly, took a step back, and called Sam.

Sam normally picked up on the second ring. She'd answer with the same line. *Hiya, wombmate.* That silly saying they'd used for as long as Anna could remember.

The phone rang once and then twice with no answer. Trevor's hands returned, but Anna backed away. *Come on, please. Pick up, pick up, pick up.* It kept ringing. Finally, it went to voicemail. *"I've seen the missed call. I'll call you back,"* Sam's voice echoed in her ear.

Anna was hungover. Surely it was nothing more.

She hung up and stared at the phone. She held it out and exhaled slowly. She was sensing a bizarre tapestry of emotions: fear, worry, dread, embarrassment. Then Anna's hand vibrated. She looked at her phone and saw Sam's name flash on the screen. Her sister was all right. She was returning the call. Anna would talk to her after she calmed down. *Thank you, God*, she thought as she threw the phone on the bed.

Chapter 2

Anna woke for a second time to the sound of her phone ringing. She was by herself and turned to search the covers for the source of the vibration. Her head still hurt. She found her phone and stared at Sam's name on the screen. She plopped back down on the bed and held the phone to her ear.

"Hiya, wombmate," Anna said with a relieved smile. The terror from before had melted away.

"Anna," she heard through the phone. It was her mother. She sounded frantic. "Anna, is Sam with you?"

A thousand scenarios flashed through Anna's mind. "No. She's not with me . . . What's going on?"

She heard a shuddering exhale on the other end of the line. It sounded like her mother was fighting back tears of fright mingled with rage. A familiar circumstance.

"I got a call from Bud who's the bartender at Yellow Creek Bar. Said she left her purse . . . That ain't like her at all. You know she'd never go anywhere without her phone."

"But she just called me . . ." Anna's heart began racing. Her mother's words sent shockwaves of anxiety racing through her body.

"Bud said he called you from her phone. I'm up at the bar now looking it over and I'mma good bit worried. You know she'd never leave her phone behind."

Anna's breathing took on the air of a staccato, and she had to force herself to speak.

"Yeah. She'd never leave it . . . Does he know who she was with? Or when she left?"

"No, he just showed up this morning and it was on his desk. The barman leaves stuff he finds after closing. Bud said he's going to keep trying to call him for more information, but he's probably still asleep." The sound of stifled sobs came over the line. "Something's wrong. I can feel it. I know I ain't supposed to worry, but I just got a real bad feeling."

Anna nodded. Her mother was right. This wasn't like her sister. She'd have called or texted or said something if she were going anywhere but Yellow Creek. They'd talked yesterday afternoon. Anna combed through her memory for any clue as to her sister's possible location. She still had a slight hangover, and this exercise thundered her head for round two.

"I do too." Anna bit her lip. "I'm gonna come on home right now. I'll be there in about two hours. If you hear anything in the meantime, call me immediately. Okay?"

"All right, and sweetheart, please drive careful."

"I will. Love you." There was a chilling pause on the other end of the line—a rustling that sounded like her mother was moving. Her breathing increased into the phone.

"Love you too," her mother said softly. "This will be all right. Okay?"

Hearing those words, Anna knew her mom was lying. She hung up the phone and immediately searched through text messages from her sister. Anna paced back and forth and hurriedly swiped the screen. Nothing unusual about them. Just their standard silly exchanges. Anna then checked out her sister's Facebook, Twitter, and Instagram, and they were full of random postings, funny retweets, and mirror selfies. Anna scanned the dates and times of each post, but there was not a single hint of her sister's recent whereabouts.

Anna rushed over to her dresser and pulled out underwear, jeans, and a UGA T-shirt. She lost no time in getting dressed and stood in front of the full-size mirror. She tied her dirty-blonde hair into a ponytail to quickly make herself presentable. Last, she put on a pair of tennis shoes. She realized that they might have to help her really, truly search for Sam. They might even have to take to the deep pines. Anna shook her head and tried to block the thought.

"Quit this," she whispered.

A tear fell down Anna's cheek, bringing her quickly back to the quietness of the apartment. She stood and looked around. Her keys and purse were sitting on the desk. She clutched her phone—a strange, inanimate connection to Sam. At any moment, her sister might call and tell her it was all a misunderstanding. Anna found herself pleading to a god whose very existence she sometimes found suspect, yet other times not. She shook her head. Then she chucked some clothes in an overnight bag and left.

Chapter 3

Anna drove fast along the mountainous curves of Route 62. The glare from the sun caused her to slow along the sharp and winding road. Thoughts of Sam never left her mind. None of it made sense. First, Sam had never done anything like this before. Ever. Second, Sam had saved for over a year to buy her iPhone. There was no way in holy hell that she'd go anywhere without it. That phone was her most prized possession. Anna put her foot down and felt the car violently shake in protest.

Post Malone blared through the car's speakers. Anna eyed the bobbing contrast of the mountains beyond. Layer upon layer of peaks running on forever. Hollows tucked away inside their multitudes of inky black voids. The vast expanse of the North Georgia Mountains was both beautiful and overwhelming. She marveled at the incalculability of it all and shook her head. Sam could be anywhere.

Anna listened to "Candy Paint" as she formed a mental checklist of all she'd do when she got to her mom's trailer. First, she'd scour Sam's room for any missing clothes, bags, shoes, or anything that might tell if her sister had run away. Then she would comb through her sister's cell phone and look at all her text messages, calls, and voicemails for any idea of where the hell Sam might be or who she could be with. Hopefully, Anna thought, Sam's password—*wombmate1993*—was still the same and she could log in to her sister's email, Facebook, Twitter, Instagram, Snapchat, and WhatsApp accounts to find clues. If all that failed to shine any light on Sam's location, Anna would hunt every possible location in Marble Hill and hound everyone they'd ever known to find out what happened to her twin.

Anna felt the twinge of a terrible migraine. She had to redouble her concentration while driving. The pain shot like a hydraulic pump to the back of her eyes. Anna knew what was coming next. It almost always accompanied any physical pain and made her think about that day, years ago.

Sam and Anna were less than a month away from turning eight. He was sitting on the floor with his back against a milk crate. They were watching cartoons while Daddy took his "medicine." A familiar sight that the girls understood as just a regular part of their day. At the end of the show, Anna looked back and saw him grinning with his arms splayed and a needle tucked deep into his arm. She remembered thinking that he was just sleeping, and he stayed that way until their mother got home from her job at the Pancake House. Their mother's wailing and crying was the first sign that something was bad wrong. Screams, protests, and oaths toward God reverberated around the small living room and told the whole story of their father's heroin overdose. Mom sent them to their room. The girls hid beneath the covers and clutched each other tightly, dampening their shirts with tears. Anna remembered finding comfort in her sister's embrace. Maybe a memory from before they entered the known world.

She thought how Sam was put on this earth to teach charity and kindness, and Anna was a fool not to avail herself of it.

The two were absolutely alike in appearance, yet something about Sam shone beauty beyond which Anna could ever aspire. It was casual and unassuming. Sam never tried and was always so cavalier about her appearance, often picking clothes at random or whatever was closest. But mostly it was her good-naturedness. A soft heart and soul that radiated loveliness from her pores, which Anna could only try to duplicate. Never accomplishing that fact because, in truth, darkness followed Anna everywhere like a terrible shadow.

Anna's problem, she thought with introspection, was that she could never settle. Contentment was a word she knew but never quite understood. College was her escape from Marble Hill. Or Meth Hill, as it was more appropriately nicknamed. A place so small that you'd pass the town and forget it. Like the enclave was just something from a dream. In the past when marble had been good, the town flourished, but it was never truly home. Visitors were just passing through. Workers or other transients of the heart. Between jobs, wives, and whole lives.

When first leaving for college, Anna drove to Athens and never dared to check her rearview mirror, as if doing so would pull her back. Every mile of separation felt more weightless. Far behind was the ratty trailer nestled in a hollow that she'd long called home. Yet, she pondered, Athens wasn't far enough, and neither was Atlanta. Perhaps she'd find solace and serenity in exotic places such as Los Angeles, Miami, New York, or Washington, DC. Although something told her that, even then, she'd feel dislocated. Anna would yearn for the fall in the Appalachian foothills, when the mountainsides exploded into an electric scene of a billion different hues of red, yellow, and orange. Or those summer days shrouded in lush green. Fishing and drinking beers down on Bobcat Run or swimming in the deep pools of Yellow Creek.

The terrible truth Anna feared was that she'd wander the rest of her life feeling lost. What Anna envied most was her twin sister's centered-ness. Sam was always at peace in her own little world of Marble Hill and Pickens County. The wider environs weren't her concern.

Anna remembered that morning like it was yesterday. One of a few events from her childhood that stuck out in her mind. Crossing the bridge over Lake Lanier, she stared at the little whitecaps formed by the wind over brown water.

Her car struggled up the hills as she climbed higher into the pied-mont. The Honda screamed as she jammed her foot down to the floor. She wondered if her uncle Brokeback knew that Sam was missing. He'd have half the tweakers in the county looking for her. That much was a given. Promise them a bag of meth or dope for whoever found her. Anna turned off the radio just in case the phone rang. Deep down, she prayed that it would ring soon and her sister would be on the other end provid-ing a host of excuses for where she'd been.

Anna was about thirty minutes from the crossroads when she called home to tell her mother she's almost there. Each mile adding a tinge of fright to her journey. She sped on, wanting to be at home so bad but dreading it at the same time. Not knowing what to expect, but prepared for the worst.

Chapter 4

Anna turned left onto Cove Road. The road twisted and curved at the base of a river that after two miles cut off and created a natural cove inlet. A little farther past this point was the dump where people from the county took their trash. No garbage collectors in this part of the county. Every so often, Anna passed a house or trailer tucked away from the road amid the trees. Some were set off-kilter and looked like things grown out of the ossified piedmont. Or slowly dissolving into the immutable terrain. The yards thick with weeds and brambles. Bedsprings, car parts, and motley discarded bric-a-brac scattered in mighty junk richness. An aggregation of rubbish wanted by no one but the householder. The dwellings stood cantered at odd angles, as if either sinking into the earth or blown away by some enormous wind. Here and there were a few clearings that led to darkened woods of a greenish-blue hue. To outsiders, this was desolate country, but Anna called it home.

Anna rolled up her window as she passed the dump. It was a stench she had become used to while living at home, but the distance afforded by college made the aroma of spoiling waste all the more intolerable. Familiarity mingled with the foreign. Anna was almost home. Like other travelers who come to the end of a journey, there was nothing to do but see it through.

Down in the cove was a small dip followed by a steep rise in the road ahead. The sun was shining, and a few clouds created dancing shapes that migrated slowly across the flowing valley and rock-ribbed ridgeline. As her car climbed, Anna saw the white steeple first with a cross balanced on the top. Coming into view was the Cove Road Baptist Church where her father now rested. He'd been baptized, married, and buried on the same plot of land. The literal alpha and omega of his spiritual existence. The sign out front read "*And the Word Was Made Flesh*." She didn't know what that meant.

Less than half a mile farther along was the dirt road that led to her mother's trailer. Trees hung over the road that had a timeless quality bespeaking a vintage eminence. Despite desiring to leave this place from as far back as she could remember, it felt good to be driving these country roads. Her little car whined in protest as she shifted gears.

Anna saw the bent mailbox and took a right onto her mother's gravel driveway. The trailer was nestled far back enough to keep it free of strangers. You had to know where you were going. Halfway down the drive was a blackened, scorched bare spot where the yard trash went. A torn-out back seat of an '83 Bronco rested on the outskirts where you sat to watch it burn. Shards of sunlight shivered on the drive and shone up ahead from a break in the trees. Despite the chaos, Anna loved every part of this place. A flood of happy memories raced across her mind, and she momentarily forgot about the horrible reason she had to return home. Anna pulled into the clearing and parked beside her mother's car.

The dilapidated trailer was a single-wide with steel cladding all the way around. The rooftop was thin tin that banged out an orchestra of sound whenever it rained. At college, Anna missed that rhythmic disorder and beautiful melody that sang her to sleep. Window AC units were attached sporadically and were God's own blessing during the brutal Georgia summers. The sagging wooden porch held the most comfortable but ratty couch patched with duct tape, a deep freezer, and a washing machine. Strewn about the yard were bits and pieces of junked antiques that her mother believed were priceless. Next to the outdoor shed were two purposeless riding lawn mowers, which were twenty years old and held no hope of ever returning to life. There was also a lazy garden choked with weeds that always looked promising but remained bare. Her mother's old RAV4 was parked in its usual location. The brake lights on the left rear bumper were smashed and jerry-rigged with red duct tape. A clothing line hung from the porch to the shed and carried most of Sam's clothes. They ranged from her Dollar Value uniform to a waving black G-string. The scene caused an ache in Anna's heart because for her this was the most comforting place in the world.

Anna grabbed her purse and exited the vehicle. Rufus, the family's ancient and mangy mutt, came trotting out from under the porch steps. He was nearly hairless and splotchy but a damn good dog. He looked mean and menacing but wouldn't hurt a fly. He'd spent most of his life running terrified from the free-roaming chickens who found joy in torturing the terrified pup.

Anna pet Rufus, and he wagged his tail and sniffed her profusely. She heard the door slap and saw her momma on the porch smoking a cigarette. She wore a faded Atlanta Braves T-shirt atop ripped and stained jeans. Her mother didn't wave, but just stood there in a dull acceptance. Anna strode purposefully across the weed-scattered lot toward the trailer. She was trying to remain calm. Fighting against the abject panic she felt in her gut. *Stay calm*, she thought. *Don't upset her.*

"Hiya, Momma," she said. "Any word?"

Her mother just exhaled a plume of blue smoke and shook her head. "No, baby." Then she motioned for Anna to come in.

Anna climbed the rickety steps two at a time and heard Rufus scramble back under the porch. Fat and hairy flies circled a bucket full of unsnapped green beans. She waved them away as she opened the screen door.

The inside of the trailer was just as it always was. Pots and pans were piled high in the sink, and plates with caked-on food sat stacked waiting for cleaning that would occur God knew when. Half-a-dozen ashtrays filled with cigarette butts were littered about. Crushed beer cans filled a plastic trash bin that nearly overflowed. Sam's purse was lying on the coffee table, and all of its contents were spilled out. Keys, cell phone, bag of makeup, receipts, ChapStick, nail file, hair bands, phone charger, and a pack of Camels. Anna's mother lit another cigarette and was sitting down on the sofa and staring at the floor.

When Anna moved closer, she saw her mother hold up a broken

necklace. An exact replica of the one Anna wore. She took it from her mother and sat down. It was silver with a heart inside a heart. She and her sister had both received one as a graduation present. The necklaces were cheap and fake but precious beyond measure. Anna stared at it and saw that the clasp was broken. Clearly ripped apart.

"Oh God," Anna whispered.

Her mother shook her head. "I done found it in the parking lot of the bar."

"Have you called the police?"

"Yup, and you know what they told me?"

"What?"

"That we can't do no missing person until a goddamn 'reasonable time' has passed." Anna's mother held up air quotes when she said reasonable time.

"What the hell does that mean?" Anna asked.

"The officer said that 'reasonable time' meant they'd take the information down and get to it in the order that their calls come in. Unless there's a sign of violence or a crime committed, it won't be a priority. Then he had the fucking nerve to say that she's an adult and probably run off with some feller. I cussed that son of a bitch up and down."

Anna rolled the necklace back and forth in her hands. She was calculating a million variables. "Who all knows?"

"The cops, Bud at Yellow Creek Bar, and me and thee," her mother said. "I ain't told Brokeback yet. You know how he'll react . . ."

"So, what do we do now? We can't just set around and do nothing." Anna noticed within five minutes of arriving home that her country speech pattern had returned, and she felt like she was settling back into herself. The faux formality she used in Athens just wasn't natural.

"No, we can't, but I'm still kinda in shock, you know?" her mother said. She stared off into space for a moment before continuing. "I've been driving all around the Hill and checking in on where she goes. Her work, Walmart, the salon, and everywhere else I can think of. Not a damn trace. Nothing. Do you have any ideas?"

"I've thought about that the whole drive here," Anna said. "I've thought about all the guys who chased after her in high school. Jimmy is stationed over in Korea or somewheres. Last I heard of Clint, he was still locked up in Jackson. She wouldn't have a damn thing to do with Ryan after he knocked up Carla. I think they moved to Gainesville and he's driving rigs. There's always the possibility that she was seeing someone, but I doubt it. She'd have told me. She tells me everything."

Her mother nodded and lit another cigarette off the end of the one she'd just finished. "I figured as much."

They sat in silence for a few moments. Anna was going through her phone and texting every friend she knew from high school who'd stayed in Marble Hill. Just a few quick words: *Hey, I'm back in town. Have you seen Sam?* The television was softly playing a daytime soap opera, and her mother stared at it absently. Finally, she turned and faced Anna.

"You want something to eat? I ain't had nary a bite all morning." Her mother stood up from the couch and walked toward the kitchen. "I got some eggs and a little bacon that needs to cook up or it'll go to the dog."

"I can't eat." The panic that Anna had felt in the car returned. She couldn't stop her legs from fidgeting, so she stood up. Then she paced the length of the living room like some soldier's wife expecting bad news. "Look, Momma, where all have you gone to search? I've got to do something. I can't just sit around here like nothing's wrong."

Her mother took out a carton of eggs and a half gallon of milk. She unscrewed the cap and sniffed. She shook her head and returned it to the refrigerator. "I've been all over like I said," she said, fighting back tears. "But she's gonna come home, and I've got to be here. Someone has to be here."

Then her mother selected a half-empty packet of bacon and carried it over to the stovetop. She picked up a frying pan from the sink and spooned in some lard.

Anna watched her mother. She was petite and lovely, yet time had been cruel. Her hands were shaking, and it seemed like she was fighting her body to retain some form of control. Her mouth pursed with wrinkles, and her teeth were stained yellow from a four-pack-a-day habit. Her blonde and graying hair was thinning in the back, and she looked haggard. Perpetually tired from a lifetime of hard work. Raising two daughters on minimum wage had taken its toll. Yet she never complained. Even when exacerbated beyond measure at the actions of her twin daughters, Jenny remained cool. She'd never remarried or even dated after their father died. The girls had tried to set her up a few times, but that always came to naught. She said it was because she didn't want to share the remote control, but Anna knew better. Deep down, her mother had never stopped loving their father. He was a junkie and a crook, but he was hers. Something strangely romantic in that.

Anna became so entrenched in watching the shadows dance on the wall that she almost didn't hear the truck arrive. The clatter and clank of spitting gravel notified her of Uncle Brokeback's approach.

Uncle Brokeback was an enormous man who swallowed up a room no matter its size. He stood six feet six and pushed the scales at just under three hundred. Crude and fading prison tattoos covered every available surface from his waist to his neckline. A gregarious and kind man to those he loved, and a terror to anyone who crossed him. Anna had heard all of the stories from those who knew Uncle Brokeback. They spoke of him in whispers even when he wasn't around. He'd gotten the nickname Brokeback after breaking a fellow inmate's back in jail. His real name was John, yet no one called him that except for his mother, who was long dead.

"Oh God," her mother said and took the pan off the stove.

Anna was already at the door and headed outside.

The wind had picked up, and the screen door slammed behind her. She heard him cry out before he even came around the side of his truck.

"I thought that son of a bitch was lying, by gawd. I told Redbone to his face that he was a gat damn liar. That he was smoking more than he was selling and must've been hallucinating. There was no way on God's green earth that half of my favorite nieces was here and wouldn't let me know." He came into view and had a shit-eating grin on his face. He wore a pair of dirty overalls with no shirt underneath. "How are you, darling?" he asked.

Anna jogged over to him with Rufus at her heels. There must have been some tell on her face because his whole tenor abruptly changed. "What's the matter, princess? Is everything all right?"

Anna hugged him with all her might, and he rocked her back and forth. "It's Sam," she whispered. Everything spilled out. It started with a trickle and turned into a flood. She told Uncle Brokeback about the purse, cell phone, and broken necklace. The police saying that nothing could be done. Anna cried like she hadn't done in a long time. He stroked her back. When she finished crying, he let go and reached into his pocket.

"What are we gonna do?" Anna asked.

"I'm gonna call a buddy of mine down at the sheriff's office. You go back on in the trailer. I'll be there in a minute."

Anna went back inside, followed by her mother, who'd been waiting on the porch. Her mother sat down on the couch and lit another cigarette. Anna stood by the door and watched her uncle through the window. She was biting her nails to the point that they started to bleed. Brokeback paced back and forth with his cell phone to his ear. He spoke forcefully yet quietly enough that Anna couldn't hear. When her uncle hung up, Anna hurried to the couch and sat down next to her mother.

The trailer door slapped and Brokeback entered. The boards moaned under his enormous weight. He went into the kitchen, opened the refrigerator, and took out a beer. He popped the top and chugged it down in three gulps. Then he grabbed another and joined the women in the living room.

"I talked to a deputy, and he's headed this way. I got one in my pocket like a folded banknote. I told him all about the situation, and he said about the same thing as y'all did. Just like y'all said, unless she's a minor or it looks like a crime's been committed, they won't make it a priority. Lucky for us, this feller owes me a favor." Brokeback opened the second beer and sipped it loudly. "Y'all try not to worry. This'll get settled."

Anna looked at her mother, who nodded repeatedly and stared at the floor. Brokeback took a seat in a ladder-backed chair and tapped the aluminum can with his middle finger to some nameless tune. This pack of three didn't seem right. There was a hole in the family. For so long, Sam, Anna, and their mother had made this dingy trailer home. Now, that was broken. A missing ingredient that spoiled it all. Anna felt the emptiness all the way down to her gut. As they sat in silence, she was certain her mother and uncle felt it too.

They remained this way until the sound of a car's approach brought them all to the door.

Chapter 5

The deputy's cruiser parked out front and sat idling. Uncle Brokeback was the first onto the porch, followed closely by Anna and her mother. The deputy finally shut off the vehicle and got out. Brokeback turned and told them to wait while he had a word with the deputy. Anna was having nothing of it and followed her uncle down the porch steps. Brokeback tried to stop her, but Anna pushed his hand away.

"She's my twin sister, Brokeback," Anna hissed. "Don't you dare."

He nodded, and they both went on.

"How are ya, Blue?" Brokeback asked. He held out his hand, and the deputy shook it.

Blue didn't take his eyes off Anna. He looked uncomfortable with her presence. "I'd say fair to middlin."

"Wish I could say the same," Brokeback responded. "We've got a real problem here, Blue, and can't seem to get any help."

"Like I said on the phone, there's really nothing to do yet."

"I know ye did. I know ye did," Brokeback said while shaking his head. "But this is a special case. Sam's like a daughter to me, and I'd consider it a personal favor if you moved this process along. Sped it up."

The deputy was staring at his feet as he toed the gravel with his boots.

"Blue, look at me."

The deputy skittered his eyes at Anna nervously before facing Brokeback.

"Blue, you and me go way back." Brokeback placed his hand on the deputy's shoulder, causing him to recoil almost involuntarily. "I've done a lot for your career. I've given you plenty of—"

"Now, there ain't no need to be saying this in front of her." The deputy pointed at Anna and took a step back.

"She's got ever' right to hear this. It's her twin sister missing," Brokeback said. "And she sure as shit ain't gonna say nothing."

Anna nodded in affirmation. "Please, Officer. I'm begging you, help us find my sister."

"Goddamn it," Blue whispered. "All right, I'll talk to the sheriff. I can't make no promises, Brokeback. I really can't. But I'll do my best."

"That's all I'm asking, Blue. Thank you."

The deputy didn't move, clearly waiting for more. "Well, normally, you give me a little something . . . I mean, I'm taking this right to the top."

"Are you serious?" asked Brokeback. "We got a girl missing and you want me to pay you? You really are a crooked sombitch."

"I could get in real trouble on this one, Brokeback."

Brokeback spat in disgust. "Fine." He reached into the bib of his overalls and pulled out a large wad of rolled cash. He wet his thumb, peeled off two one-hundred-dollar bills and passed them over to the deputy, who stuffed them in his pocket.

"I'll let you know what happens."

"You goddamn better," Brokeback said.

The deputy got into his cruiser and reversed down the driveway. Anna and her uncle stood and watched him go. Her mother joined them. Brokeback placed his arm around his sister. "Don't you worry, Jenn. We'll find her. You guys just sit tight and keep calling around."

"Thank you."

The three went back into the trailer and waited. None of them spoke. Brokeback kept drinking beers and pacing in the kitchen. Jenn chain-smoked. Anna searched through her sister's phone, finding numbers she recognized and others she didn't. Most were friends they'd both had in high school and to the Dollar Value where Sam worked. Anna wrote down the names and numbers of who Sam had called and what times she had called them. If her sister wasn't found soon, she'd pay each and every one of them a visit.

She googled the numbers not saved in Sam's contacts. One was for the local Mexican restaurant where Sam ordered lunch every so often. Anna made a mental note to go there and ask around. Someone knows something. Another call was to Chattahoochee Technical College's admissions office. She remembered her sister mentioning in passing that she was interested in going to school. This memory combined with her sister's disappearance brought tears to Anna's eyes. Tangible evidence that Sam wanted more than a life of earning minimum wage at the Dollar Value.

The last number was for the Cove Road Baptist Church. Of them all, this was the most curious. Cove Road Baptist was everyone's church in Marble Hill. There wasn't another for miles. But Anna and her family hadn't darkened its door in years. The last time she'd been inside had to have been her father's funeral, she thought. That was over a decade ago. What on earth would Sam want to do with the church? Neither sister was religious, and Anna bordered on atheism. Compounding Anna's confusion was the fact that it wasn't just one call, or solely outgoing. There were over half a dozen in the past week alone. Anna resolved herself to go to the church and find out what that was all about. She highly doubted her sister had found God, but obviously, there was so much about Sam that Anna didn't know.

As sunlight dipped lower toward the mountains and the trailer darkened, Anna scoured her sister's Facebook page. She looked through Sam's direct messages and found that they were all deleted. Not just one, but the whole message history. Anna knew this for a fact because she'd messaged Sam a makeup tutorial on YouTube two days before. That was missing. So, either Sam had deleted them all or someone else did.

Anna searched Sam's Instagram and Twitter but found nothing of substance. Now, she gripped the phone with white knuckles. She couldn't let it go, no matter how useless.

Anna tried to think back to the moment when she and Sam diverged. What was the point of departure? She remembered as a kid fearing every dark closet or shadowed movement at night. Monsters reaching from under the bed. That same feeling had followed her all day. Yet, within these walls, Anna felt self-wrapped in her warm blanket of denial.

Brokeback's phone finally rang. Despite having consumed five beers, he stood steady as a stone wall and told them both to hush.

"Yeah," he said into the phone. "All right . . . we can do that . . . sure, right now . . . thanks."

Uncle Brokeback hung up.

"Well?" her mother asked.

"We need to bring everything that Sam left at the bar down to the sheriff's office." He ran his fingers through his thinning hair. "Blue really came through. They are going to set the wheels in motion tonight and have a press conference tomorrow morning. Y'all are all supposed to be there. No exceptions. Blue said they'd alert the media first thing."

Anna heaved a sigh of relief. For the first time all day, she felt hopeful.

"Let's ride," Brokeback said, looking at Anna. "Jenn, you stay here just in case she shows up. I'd hate for her to pop back up and no one here to greet her."

"All right," her mother said.

Anna gathered up her sister's purse and put all the scattered contents back inside. She followed her uncle to the door and across the gravel yard. The sun was waning in the west and created a glorious painting of yellow, bloodred, orange, and deep purple. An old adage came to mind: Red sky at night, sailor's delight. Anna hoped that saying worked for mountain girls too. Despite the turmoil of the past twelve hours, it made her feel at peace. The wind picked up, and the temperature cooled, bordering on cold. She hoped that Sam was someplace warm and not lost, alone, and afraid. Anna clinched her eyes shut and pushed away the thought that her sister could be in a situation more horrible yet.

She tucked a bit of wind-whipped hair behind one ear and climbed inside her uncle's pickup truck. He cranked the engine and placed a hand on her shoulder.

"Don't worry, darling," Brokeback said softly. "We are gonna find her."

Anna didn't say a word, just nodded slowly.

Chapter 6

As Brokeback and Anna drove through town, it seemed preternaturally quiet. The streets were vacant of people, and only a few cars were parked on Main Street. Twenty minutes from Marble Hill was Jasper, the county seat of Pickens County, which was only slightly larger. A small town among small towns. Dull yellow lights partially lit the sidewalk at various intervals. All along the way were mom-and-pop stores that seemed eternally on their last leg. When the strip mall opened five miles south along State Route 515, most of the city's clientele followed. Better prices, exceptional deals, and superior products were bleeding the old part of town dry. It was only a matter of time before Jasper proper consisted solely of the old courthouse.

Uncle Brokeback rolled down the windows. Despite the chill, Anna stuck her hand out and let the wind roll in a wave on her palms. She shut her eyes and thought about that time in high school when their group of friends had trekked up the banks of Pettit Creek. A quarter mile up from their cars was a narrow gorge that produced a twenty-foot waterfall. At the base was a deep pool where they'd go swimming during the blistering Georgia summers. The boys led the way up the small, worn path and carried beer and a portable radio.

Both the pool and waterfall were hidden by thick mountain laurel. The boys stripped naked and the girls down to their panties. All dove in the water and swam around the pool. Anna remembered seeing a speckled brown trout dash under a rock. She treaded water and watched her friends splash about. Her sister waded through the waist-high water toward the rock wall. The waterfall spit a white plume of mist all around. Sam entered it and disappeared for a moment. Then she started to climb.

Anna watched as Sam groped her way up the wall. Everyone else stopped what they were doing and cheered her on. The boys near the shore didn't dare stand above waist-high in the water. Sam placed her fingers and toes in fissures along the way, bracing her weight against places where the rocks protruded for a better grip. When she got to the top, Sam turned and waved at her friends below. She stood with her hand over her eyes and seemed to scan the sweeping beauty around them.

Then Sam flew.

A tinge of panic raced through Anna's mind as she saw her sister plunge toward the pool. Sam slapped into the water and sent out a shockwave as she vanished deep into the pool. A few seconds later, she popped back up to the surface, laughing all the while.

This was one of the times, Anna thought, that Sam was truly the more beautiful of the two. No matter their similarities, her sister had something more. Anna smiled softly to herself. That was okay and just fine by her.

Brokeback pulled into the parking space nearest the Pickens County Sheriff's Office, which happened to be housed at the jail. The sign over the door read "Vacancies." A piss-poo attempt at humor.

They sat with the truck running, and Anna could almost hear the gears churning in her uncle's mind. He wanted to say something but couldn't find the words.

"Yes," Anna said softly.

Brokeback sighed. "First time I was ever locked up here, I was eighteen. I was just a kid. I got forty-five days for drunk driving, resisting arrest, and simple possession—all misdemeanors. During my second week in, I had this feller who kept trying to mess with me. I was the biggest man in the place, so I reckon that's why. But really, I was scared shitless. One morning he came at me with a shaving blade melted into the handle of a plastic toothbrush." Her uncle used his fingers to try and show the length of an invisible reproduction.

"That little shank he'd configured was pretty neat if you ask me," he continued. "I remembered wondering how long it took him to make it.

What he was thinking the whole time. If he could ponder how nothing like that would take me down."

"Well, he started slicing at me, and I kept backing away. He had some books tied around his belly with torn-off bedsheets to make some protected vest or whatever. The Bible kept bobbing in and out of view each time he tried to cut me. Finally, I just stepped forward, and he slashed me one good time on my arm." Brokeback pulled up his sleeve to show a line across his bicep. Anna had seen this scar and countless others before.

"I got close, grasped him by the head with both hands, and lifted him off the ground. He'd dropped the shank and kept looking around wall-eyed for help, but no one was going to do that. Here I was, just putting on pressure until I saw blood come out of his nose. Bits of shit dribbling out of his eyes.

"By the time the corrections officer got hold of me, the guy was out. I let go, and he hit the floor like a stroke victim. He was taken to the hospital, and they fixed him up as best they could. I'd rewired his brain, and he was never the same after that. He lived out the rest of his life in a crazy house. He might probably still be there.

"They didn't charge me with nothing 'cause I was just defending myself. That incident sorta put me atop the food chain. Don't know why, but folks just treated me differently. I guess it was 'cause they saw what I could do with my bare hands." He held them out on display. "You know what's peculiar, Anna?"

"What's that?" Anna asked.

"I went to visit that feller when I got out. I'd go up to his home thing—a crazy house. I'd sit in his room and smuggle him candy, cigarettes, and pints of whiskey. We kinda became friends. We'd sit for hours and play cards. He wasn't all that bad of a guy. Not right in the head, but okay. Never remembered me, but we were connected in a weird way." He paused. "I ought to go visit him again if he's still there or alive. I ought to."

"Why are you telling me all this, Brokeback?"

"Hell, I don't know. I guess we all have that one thing we wish we could take back. His was messing with me. Mine was squeezing his head like a melon. I feel bad because I could've just knocked him out with a punch. Instead, I turned him into a retard." Brokeback ran his hand along the side of his head to wipe away the beads of sweat that had formed despite the freezing-cold car. Then he shook his head, sat up straight, and said, "Gah, quit listening to me. I'm depressing my own damn self."

Together, they exited the truck. Anna carried her sister's purse and hurried alongside her uncle's long strides. Brokeback opened the door and held it for her. She stepped into the lobby and had to squint her eyes from the blinding light. The ceiling was ablaze with rows of garish fluorescents, and the room was ice cold. She placed her hands over her eyes to help them adjust.

Brokeback laid a hand on her shoulder. "It's to disorient you. That and the cold. It's that way everywhere. Even in the cells. Gives the COs a leg up. You get used to it after a while."

He walked over to a speaker box positioned near a heavy-looking steel door. He pushed a button, and a buzzer sounded. After a few seconds a voice came through on the other end.

"Be with you in a second."

Brokeback motioned for Anna to approach. She walked over tentatively and stood behind her uncle. Another buzzer sounded, followed by a loud mechanical screech from the door panel. It opened slowly, and out sauntered a sheriff's deputy.

"How you, Brokeback? I ain't used to seeing you coming in the front door. Normally it's round back and you're wearing jewelry."

"Howdy, Leonard. Ain't too good right now. My lil' niece has gone missing, and we all real worried about it."

The deputy gave Anna a half smile. "Detective Oak told me about it. Said you're dropping off what was left from that night."

Anna handed over the purse. "I looked through it, it's just a few things . . ."

Deputy Leonard took it and placed it on the counter.

"I doubt anything has happened to her. Probably just run off some-wheres. Most of the youngerns head off to Atlanta. Sick of the mountain life," the deputy said.. Then his demeanor abruptly changed. "You know, Brokeback, did it ever occur to you that it might be in your own backyard? If she really is took or in any kind of trouble, I mean. You don't think one of your tweakers or some drug buddies mighta had something to do with this? Folks you got on the wrong side of." The deputy was speaking to Brokeback but was watching Anna with wry eyes. "When you lie down with dogs, you're liable to get fleas."

Her uncle's whole countenance changed. She saw him extend and clench his fists several times. Brokeback sneered then said gutteraly, "That's one hell of a thing to say. I don't know if you think you're funny or what. I do know one thing, you sure are lucky my niece is here right now. I'd beat your fucking face in and wait for the rest of them to take me on back." Brokeback took a step forward. "And you know I'd do it too."

The deputy stopped smiling. He collected the purse and took a step back toward the door. His heel scuffed the floor, and he had to brace himself to keep from toppling over. "Alright. Alright, Brokeback. I didn't mean nothing by it." He took out a set of keys and slid one into the lock. "I'll make sure Detective Oak gets these."

"I know you will," said Brokeback. "I know it."

The deputy left, leaving Anna and Brokeback all alone in the lobby.

Anna tugged at her uncle's arm. "What did he mean by that last part?" Brokeback walked toward the exit without acknowledging her question. She grabbed him tighter and pulled. "What did he mean?"

"I'll tell you in the car," he said. "They got recording shit throughout this whole damn place."

Anna followed her uncle to the truck and climbed into the passenger seat.

Brokeback cranked the engine and faced her. "You know what I do for a living. It don't take a college girl to realize that fact." He tapped the steering wheel with the palm of his hand. "I ain't gonna tell you nothing about it neither. Only know this. There ain't a man that works for me or, hell, knows me that would do something this damn foolish. They'd be finished. They understand that I'd kill 'em graveyard dead. All right?"

"Sure, Brokeback," she said softly.

He pulled the truck out of the parking lot. "This shit is sure hell. I never thought my heart could hurt this bad. I feel it right here." He took his hand off the steering wheel and pounded his chest several times. "You two are like the daughters I never had. I wouldn't and won't let anything happen to you."

"I know."

They drove on for a while in silence. After a time, Brokeback spoke. "What do ye want to do now?"

"I'd like to go by Yellow Creek Bar and talk to the folks there. Chat with the barman and see what he remembers."

"I think that's a damn good idea," Brokeback said. He pushed the accelerator to beat the yellow light through Jasper. They headed toward Cove Road and Marble Hill, Brokeback guiding the car through the narrow bends. The sky above was alive with stars. A billion centroids of speckled light. The moon hung low and was nearly full. Blue light engulfed the surroundings. The great vastness of it gave Anna pause. She said a short prayer. To whom, she wasn't entirely certain.

Chapter 7

The truck idled for a moment at a stop sign then turned right onto Highway 53. The last of the curves as they headed out of the piedmont. There was no oncoming traffic. The enormous truck tires gripped the asphalt and made a soothing sound like rushing water. The road so black that it looked wet. They veered around a tight bend where the guardrails were battered from countless cars driving too fast. Drunks or outlanders hitting them head-on and meeting death. A wooden roadside cross that attracted the eyes of those familiar with tragedy. Anna remembered Brokeback teaching them both how to drive. All three sitting together in the front seat of the truck, taking turns cruising around the backroads of Pickens County.

Just remember, baby girls, you gotta keep it between the mustard and the mayonnaise. You do that and you're all right.

Finally, the road straightened out as the truck cruised into Marble Hill. They hadn't spoken the whole way, and there seemed nothing to say now. None of Anna's thoughts gave her comfort. She pressed her head against the cool glass and looked out. This little alcove was as dead as always except for the bar and a Mexican restaurant run by two toothless rednecks. The Dollar Value where Sam worked was closing for the evening. Anna knew from studying her sister's calendar that Sam was supposed to work tonight. Sam's disappearance would be an inconvenience for the manager. Same with the employees having to take an extra shift. So many people whose lives were still the same.

Brokeback pulled the truck into a parking spot in front of the bar. Sam's car was still parked in the lot. It was in the farthest corner and away from the street lamps. Could the placement have been deliberate?

Anna kicked herself for not searching the vehicle before handing over the keys. She stood looking at the vast distance and thought for a brief moment that she heard Sam screaming. Maybe it was just the wind. Or perhaps a terrible afterimage stuck in the disturbed night air. Tears welled up in Anna's eyes, and she shook her head to drive that nightmare away. She turned toward her uncle, who was inspecting Sam's car.. Perhaps he'd heard Sam too?

Brokeback waited for Anna to come around, and they walked together toward the bar's entrance. Two men were outside smoking and watching them cautiously. The men whispered something out of earshot. *Why?* Anna thought. *Was it because they knew something?* Or did they recognize the enormity that was her Uncle Brokeback? Probably the latter.

Inside, the bar was lit up with Christmas lights, and country music played over a pair of loudspeakers at the rear. Anna had a continuous nagging sensation in her gut, and nothing felt right. She blinked several times in the vain hope that her twin sister would magically appear from across the room. Walk over and spill out some outlandish story of being locked in the bar's bathroom all day.

The bar was practically empty. A group of young men sat at a table and watched them walk up to the bar. Anna regarded them. She recognized a couple of them from high school and made a mental note to talk with them before they left.

The man behind the counter seemed to smile in relief as she and Brokeback approached. Anna's uncle rapped his knuckles against the wood and ordered two Coors. The barman pulled the lever and filled the glasses to the brim. Then he set them down side by side.

The barman watched Anna. "Hiya, Sam, you have no idea how happy I am to see you." He cracked a smile. "You had us all worried."

"Wrong one," Brokeback interjected.

Even in the darkness of the bar, Anna saw the barman's expression drop. "Oh no," he mouthed softly.

Brokeback drained the beer in three huge gulps and set the glass down. He pointed at it, and the barman refilled the glass. Anna hadn't touched hers.

"I've gotta ask you, Matt," Brokeback said. "What happened with Sam last night? What all do you remember?"

The barman toyed with his towel nervously. "She come in about eight o'clock or so. Looking beautiful as ever." With that last comment, he finally looked Anna in the eyes. "She came in all alone. I remember that because she was one of only two gals in the place. She ordered a couple shots of tequila and then danced with a group of fellers."

That sounds like Sam, Anna thought. "How many drinks did she have?" she asked.

"I'd say a fair amount. She tried to pay for the first two, but the boys she was cozying up to bought bought them for her. About a half dozen or so." Matt ran his fingers through his hair. "I shoulda cut her off, but she seemed all right. And it ain't like she hadn't done this before. I didn't see nothing wrong with it."

"I don't care about all that," Brokeback said. "I wanna know who paid for 'em and when she left. You had to've seen that."

"That crew over there was who she was with at first. Dancing and carrying on with 'em." The barman jutted his chin toward the table where the men sat. They were all trying to look at Brokeback without making it obvious. Which, of course, it clearly was. "But them's fine ole boys. They were just having a good time. In fact, Jim over there was the one who brought me her stuff and was real worried when she disappeared—" The barman immediately caught himself. He toyed with the towel like a nervous child. "I mean, when she left."

"Who'd she leave with?"

"I don't really know. I can't remember if it was with one of them boys, by her lonesome, or with the strange-looking feller who came in just after her. I didn't get a good look at that one's face. Spoke really soft and had this hat that was pulled way down low. I hadn't seen 'em before."

"What did that person look like?" Brokeback asked.

"Again, I didn't get a good look at their face. They were wearing this big ole black hat . . . I can't even tell you if it was a girl or boy. I do remember the person looked real scrawny. Like a real small woman, almost. Had these little hands but wearin' a big ole jacket and that hat. They was real short too.. And bought a drink for Sam. Paid cash. Sat over in that corner booth." The barman pointed across the room. Perfect line of sight for the whole place. "Am I in any trouble with you, Brokeback?"

"Not at the moment."

"All I know is that she was here and then she wasn't. I'm just as baffled as you are." Matt paused reflectively. "I wish I could tell you more."

"All right," Brokeback said. "Just be forewarned that the cops will be sniffing around here tomorrow." He turned to Anna, who was staring at the cluster of young men in the darkened mirrored glass behind the bar. "You gonna drink that?" Brokeback asked.

Anna shook her head and pushed the glass over toward her uncle. He picked it up and drained it.

"What do I owe ye?" Brokeback asked Matt.

"Don't worry about it. On the house."

Brokeback nodded. "You ready to go, princess?"

"Here in a minute," Anna said. "I wanna go and talk to those guys."

Brokeback pointed at the glass and waited for the barman to refill it once again.

Anna crossed the dance floor. There was a loneliness to it that ached her heart. Less than twenty-four hours before, he sister was twirling around the bar and lighting up the room. The thought of that stung. When Anna was halfway to the booth, the group of young men turned and watched her approach. She recognized all of them except the youngest looking one tucked in the back. Anna tried to place him, but the darkness clouded her view. At the moment, she mistrusted everything.

"Hey, guys."

They nodded or said hello back.

"Were y'all here last night? Did you see my sister?"

A lanky man nearest her spoke up. "Yeah, she was in last night. Dancing and laughing and having a good time."

"Did you see where she went? Or who she left with?"

"I was pretty drunk and don't really remember. But Billy over there was the last one to dance with her." The spokesman pointed across the table to the young man named Billy, who still hadn't taken his eyes from the table. Staring mutely at the glass of beer that sat in front of him. When he finally looked up, she recognized him. He was Billy Travis. His family owned the Universal Pro gas station and repair shop. They'd been in the same grade at school. He'd always been quiet, so his shyness wasn't a surprise to Anna. The hidden view seemed to belong to him as if he was an outcast among his fellows.

"Yes, I danced with her," he said sheepishly. "But I never seen her leave . . . I mean, I saw her leave, but never come back."

"Wait, so you did or didn't see her leave?" Anna asked.

"I meant to say that I saw her leaving with someone I didn't recognize. She walked out the door so quick, and I can't tell you who it was . . . That's to say I don't know."

The way he spoke didn't sit right with Anna. Perhaps it was all in her mind. "Alright. Well, I thank you for talking to me. If you remember anything—anything at all, please contact us."

Anna turned and saw that Brokeback was drinking a beer, his back resting against the bar. He was watching her closely. She nodded, and her uncle drained the beer and set the glass down. They both walked to the exit. Brokeback waved without turning around and held the door for Anna.

Outside, the wind had picked up. A mixture of late fall and early winter. Leaves were twirling around the parking lot. The faint smell of snow took Anna reeling back through the years with burning memories. The great blizzard of '05 had passed, and Anna, her mother, uncle, and sister were snowed in. As the storm picked up, the trailer smelled of waiting and wet fires. Her mother feared the roof might cave in, but Brokeback reassured her that it was alright. Anna remembered him speaking in an almost foreign language. He used words like plumbness, ceiling joists, rafters, and unsagging steel. Several times, Brokeback went out into the storm to clean what he called the air intake and exhaust vents. Anna and Sam huddled in fear that he wouldn't return. Yet, each time he walked back through that selfsame door, covered in snow and smiling.

Anna remembered that, when the storm had finally passed, she and Sam went outside to sled down the hill behind their trailer.. Both carrying trash can lids and stepping carefully to keep from falling. Anna reached for the purchase of a small branch sticking out of the snow. As she gained a handhold, the flimsy branch slipped seamlessly from the ground. She was knocked off balance and tumbled down the hill. The world turned upside down, and everything went white. Anna hadstruck her shoulder on a buried rock. Pain raced through her body, and she howled. Tears burst from her eyes as she rolled. After what seemed like forever, Anna came to a hard stop against a huge pile of snow built up into a drift against the trailer. She clutched her injured shoulder and sobbed. Suddenly, Sam appeared by her side and held her close. Her sister had ridden down on her trash can lid like some storybook hero.

Whenever it snowed, Anna remembered those moments. Even the smell of snow brought her back to a time when the world was made up of inconsequential events. A reminder that everything you needed came from those you loved. Yet, on this cold and dreadful night, the suggestion of snow constructed in Anna's mind the terrible trajectory of a nightmare moment that either hadn't arrived yet or passed unnoticed some time ago.

She shuddered at the thought and hurried to Brokeback's truck. Anna looked up to the heavens and saw where the clouds were moving in and blocked out the stars. The dark tableau was dimensionless and uncaring. Anna's world was misaligned and beyond any hope of commiseration. Brokeback asked if she wanted to look inside Sam's car and held out a flashlight, and she said absolutely. The car was parked at a slant and taking up two spots. Like Sam had been in a hurry. They walked over, and Anna noted the faint glow emanating from the parking lot light overhead. Enough darkened shadows for someone to hide. You'd never see the person before it was too late.

Anna turned on the flashlight and placed it directly against the glass. The passenger-side floorboard was filled with Monster Energy drink cans, McDonald's wrappers, crumpled receipts, Pall Mall cigarette packages, Sam's Dollar Value uniform, an old pair of Nike tennis shoes, and various other bits and pieces of trash.

The middle console was equally covered in trash and crumpled paper, and an assortment of lip glosses spilled out of the cupholder. Nothing looked out of place, though.

The back seat was a different story. It was clear of clutter save for a hoodie pushed against the side door like a pillow. She'd never seen that sweatshirt before, so sheshone the beam of the flashlight directly at it. There, among the folds, was a design that looked like the outline of a football. Something clicked in Anna's mind, and she recognized that type of hoodie. They were handed out to Pickens High football players at the beginning of every season. She remembered that it was tradition for the athletes to give them to their girlfriends. But Sam had never dated a football player. Where had she gotten it? More importantly, Anna thought, who gave it to her?

Chapter 8

When Anna woke the next morning, it was still dark outside. She felt like death warmed over. Anna laid in the bed she'd shared with her sister for years; now it felt enormous and lonely. She'd slept fitfully but didn't dream. She could almost see and feel the shadow of her twin. Everywhere she looked was her sister's ghost. The whole room felt off, like something all but unaccountable. The bed she'd shared with her sister for years felt enormous and lonely. Although alone, Anna stayed on her side of the mattress. It didn't feel right to lie in the middle.

Memories of Sam flooded Anna's mind, each more precious than the one before. Anna felt a strange fear that she needed to be careful. Perhaps drawing on these memories might ruin their origin. After a while, she rose and crept out of the bedroom. She walked down the narrow hallway with a blanket wrapped over her shoulders. The floor creaked like an ancient wooden ship. She'd decided to watch the day break. No point in trying to go back to sleep. She feared nightmares.

The morning was cool and smelled wet. No sign of life. She wasn't wearing any shoes and hurried over to the ratty couch that was pushed up against the trailer wall. Anna sat with her legs tucked under her. The couch stank, but it always had. A mixture of the woods, sweat, and cigarette smoke.

Anna stared off into the distance. Silent lightning flared and momentarily silhouetted the black spine of a far-off mountain chain. The ridgelines seemed to shudder and were sucked away into the blackness again. She heard an owl call. It sounded enormous and loud amid all that silence. It was amplified by the nothingness. She felt very bleak, everything askew. Anna searched for order in her mind. She was doing everything in her power to forget the present by chasing the past. Returning to good memories of Sam might allow her to escape all of this. It didn't matter how painful or utterly heartbreaking.

The first bit of gray light appeared atop the mountains. The light shone just enough to turn the world pale. A cauterized terrain. A sea of skeletal pine and oak. She studied the country to the east, and it was barren and silent. It seemed ashen and burnt. The sun continued to rise and for a few moments looked opaque. She stared at the jaundiced birth of day. Anna heard the mournful call of a dove from deep in the woods. Then she whispered softly, "Where are you, Sam? Are you lost? Please, don't be afraid. We will find you."

Anna heard her mother's cell phone ring from inside the trailer. It sounded like an evil thing, and her heart stopped. She rose quickly and went inside.

Sheriff Jeffrey Haskins was telling her mother through speaker-phone that he would open an inquiry for her missing daughter. To begin, though, he needed a recent photo of Sam and wanted to have a short press conference to help get the word out to members of the commu-nity. Hopefully, Sam didn't know she was missing. Once that informa-tion reached her, she'd get in touch. If she was somewhere held against her will, then the press conference might put pressure on her abductors and lead to Sam's release.

Anna's mind went to the inevitable dark place. If Sam's captors got scared, there was always the possibility that they might panic and hurt her or do something even worse. Yet Anna kept those thoughts to her-self. Her mother didn't need to know that.

The Pickens County Sheriff's Office looked different in the light of day. Anna and her mother stood behind a podium out front and faced the parking lot. The sheriff had hinted over the phone that it was probably best if Brokeback stayed at home. He was a known fixture in the county, and his presence might produce the wrong impression. Surprisingly, her uncle fully agreed and waited at his house for more news.

The sun blazed overhead, but the wind produced a biting chill. Anna clutched her mother tightly for warmth, comfort, and strength. It tore at Anna's heart to see her mom go through this. She'd lived a life full of disappointments, literally from the start. Her own mother had died in childbirth. Complications that would've easily been taken care of in a hospital, but beyond all hope when occurring on the dirt floor of a shack. Her father had gone off to fight in the Korean War but never really returned. He did in body, but his mind was gone. Storms and other loud noises took him back to the harsh realities of war. Then, when Anna's mother was nine, a tornado rolled through the piedmont, and they'd found her father's lifeless body the next day. He was clutching his Bible and rifle and staring frozen in fear toward the heavens. A soldier to the last. Later, Anna's mother left school at seventeen because she was pregnant. When starting out life in poverty, a child often makes matters worse. Two at the same time compounds the issue. Yet Anna knew that her mother wouldn't have changed having them for anything. That in the here and now, half of her heart was missing as well.

Sheriff Haskins was talking to one of his deputies and guffawed at something the subordinate said. After what seemed like an eternity, the sheriff checked his watch and approached the podium. Several local news agencies from Atlanta were in attendance, as were members of the concerned citizenry.

The remote sun was nearing its zenith. Anna felt the earth was speeding away from her. She spied the audience. Several official-looking people were holding out cell phones to record the press conference. A solitary cameraman had taken up residence in the back. There was also a group of older men that Anna recognized as members of the VFW. Standing shoulder to shoulder were a couple of staff members from Pickens High School. Mr. Jameson, the PE teacher, stood watching Anna with an unnerving intensity. He was known to leer at the girls, and rumors abounded. Others were curious onlookers who'd heard about this unusual turn of events and wanted to be part of it. Front and center of the small crowd was a noisy knitting circle of old crones who might've thought this was the most exciting thing to happen all year. Perhaps it was. Standing in the back, almost hidden, was Pastor Hinson from Cove Road Baptist Church and his son. Anna couldn't remember the son's name, but he was wearing the distinct impression that he wasn't listening. Or he was listening too closely. Remembering her sister's call history, Anna made a mental note to talk to them before they left.

It seemed that news of the press conference had spread like wildfire. All of it was so surreal. Like something out of a movie. The looks on the people's faces spelled out absolute astonishment that something like this could happen, especially in the sleepy town of Jasper.

Anna held her mother around the shoulders and squeezed her tight. She looked distraught but strong. Her skin was pale blue, and she occasionally dabbed the corner of her eyes with a tissue.

The sheriff checked his watch again and turned to Anna and her mother. He spoke to them softly, "I won't rest until Sam's found." They nodded their heads in acknowledgment, and Anna exhaled heavily with a shudder. The sheriff hugged her mother, who embraced him tightly. A bizarre formal affirmation that everything wasn't all right but was, perhaps, okay.

Anna watched him stand before the microphone very stoic and austere but seemingly out of place like a reticent man amid all things. Yet she could tell that this wasn't a task he relished or was ready for. He was clearly a man of law and order, but press conferences were an obvious source of discomfort for him.

She saw him shift the microphone to just under his mouth. He cleared his throat, and a screeching noise reverberated out of the small, hastily set up PA system. Anna held her breath.

"Good morning, everyone," the sheriff said. "I'd like to thank you all for coming out on such short notice. Thirty-six hours ago, Samantha 'Sam' Renfro went missing from the Yellow Creek Bar around ten p.m. After a preliminary investigation, the sheriff's office has deemed this a possible criminal missing person's case. There is evidence to suspect foul play and that Sam was abducted against her will."

Anna heard her mother let out a mournful wail and clutched her tightly around the shoulders. A tangible vestige of sorrow that was irrevocably concrete. Her mother buried her head against Anna's chest. Anna's shirt dampened, and she couldn't help but cry too.

"We are asking the public to stay vigilant and be on the lookout for anything suspicious," the sheriff said. "Look for any abnormal behavior. Changes in someone's behavior since Sam's disappearance to today. Something as simple as shaving of their face. Could be changing of hair color. Cutting of their hair. Change in their mood or personality. Even parking a vehicle in their garage when they've always parked it in the driveway. We suspect that someone in the community knows this individual or individuals. We are asking the community for support."

The sheriff continued. "This is just preliminary. But we are taking this extremely seriously. If you see Samantha, contact us immediately, or again, if you notice any suspicious activity. We are providing flyers with her picture, and the same will be put on social media. If you know anything or suspect something, please call us or 911."

A reporter who looked completely out of place amid the crowd raised his hand. He wore a green tartan three-piece suit and held out an expensive-looking recorder. The sheriff pointed at him.

"Sheriff, do you think she might have run away?" the reporter asked.

"That's a possibility, but none of the evidence points to that. We are fairly certain that she didn't leave on her own. She left her cell phone, purse, keys, and car at the bar. If she were to have run away, we believe Samantha would've at least taken her wallet. But, of course, we can't be entirely sure. That's why we as a community need to be vigilant. Any other questions?"

A scruffy-looking man with a POW/MIA shirt hollered out, "You want us to set up a search party? We can get a big ole group of veterans together. Trust me, we'll find her."

"I appreciate that, Lester, and I know y'all would. We will set something up this afternoon. But as of right now, we just need folks to be attentive and keep their eyes peeled. Just . . . anything out of the ordinary. We don't know all that much right now, but our department will keep y'all informed. Our Twitter and Facebook will post updates, or you can give us a call here at the jail." The sheriff adjusted the microphone again. "Are there any more questions? All right, thank you all for being here, and have a good day."

The crowd mulled about uncertainly for a moment. There was a great awkwardness that became such rare events in sleepy Pickens County. Anna watched the sheriff closely, and he seemed to note it all. Finally, he turned back and motioned for her mother. "Jenny, can I talk to you in private?"

Anna cut in. "I need to hear this."

The sheriff looked very serious and stern. "No, you don't. And you won't." There was absolute and utter finality in his voice. He gently took Anna's mother by the arm and walked her away. She seemed to step woodenly, like she wasn't all there, as if in some form of fugue state.

Anna clenched both fists tightly. This was her sister. Her best friend. Huddled in their mother's belly, the two knew of each other before anything else in the world. Holding on for dear life against the unknown. She glared at the sheriff and her mother, who spoke softly to each other with their backs turned. Anna exhaled and looked over the crowd. They all held Sam's missing person's flier. The news media had dispersed, but the others stood around and chatted. Almost like a usual country gathering. Folks asking, *How's yer momma-n-them?* All that was missing was a table piled high with food.

She saw the pastor and his son walking toward the rows of parked cars. Anna made a beeline for them. She pushed her way through the crowd, apologizing profusely as she went. Out of the small mass of people, Anna set off after them. Her feet slapped the pavement. The sound was unmistakable. Hinson and his son stopped and turned around. The pastor was smiling. His son looked away.

Here, Anna remembered his name. It was Daniel. Named after a boy hurled into the lion's den. Sentenced to his death for some reason that she couldn't remember. Unlike most Old Testament epics, she thought, that one had a happy ending.

"Pastor Hinson!" Anna called. "Can I speak with y'all for a moment?"

"Absolutely," he said. "What can we do you for?"

Daniel looked sadly at Anna. One of those inescapable expressions where a deeper abiding pain was locked within. She knew it well.

"Firstly, I want to thank you for coming out," she said.

"No problem at all. I am here to serve the community. When I get back to the church, I will call the congregation to spread the news about Samantha. We will set up a prayer chain." He gently laid his hand on her shoulder. Anna couldn't place it, but that small gesture was incredibly reassuring. Like the laying on of hands for the afflicted or a tradition passed down by the unevolved. Yet Anna felt real power in his touch. Almost like an electric current running down her body. Her world shifted focus, and the hairs prickled on the back of her neck.

She looked down and saw that he carried several copies of the flier. The words typed out in bold red letters with Sam's senior class picture underneath.

"Pastor Hinson," Anna said, "I was going through Sam's phone and saw that she'd been calling the church. If you don't mind me asking, what was she calling for?"

He smiled. "Yes, she's in regular contact with my wife. Samantha's looking for spiritual guidance. She's exploring her spirituality."

Anna was a little taken aback by this. Neither had ever been religious and hadn't thought of church since their father's funeral.

He continued. "I don't know the details of their conversations, but you are more than welcome to talk to my wife, Ruth. She is in Atlanta this morning but should be back soon. Please, feel free to drop by the church this afternoon or tomorrow."

"Okay," Anna said. "I'll do that. Again, thank you for coming."

"Our pleasure."

Daniel finally looked up. He stared into Anna's eyes. It was an expression that she couldn't place. At first, she thought it was condescension. But there seemed too much sadness for that to be the case. Then his eyes watered, and he averted his eyes and stared down at his feet.

Pastor Hinson gave Anna a curt smile and then took Daniel by the shoulder and led him away. It seemed like there was something the young man wanted to say. His father walked across the parking lot with his hand firmly pressed against his son's back.

Anna stood and watched them go. Ever since her sister went missing, a chaotic story was falling into place. There were different perspectives and characters who orbited Sam's world. Anna kept attempting to fill in the gaps with some sort of narrative that made sense. Yet a picture was forming that she couldn't believe.

Could her twin sister have been living a double life?

Anna felt a sharp pain in her gut. A physical manifestation of a cold and unmistakable truth. Sam was getting on with her life. Just like herself. Despite looking exactly the same, the twins were diverging along different paths. The fork split when Anna went off to college and left her sister behind. A terrible moment of clarity struck Anna as she stood in the parking lot. She understood exactly what was going on. Her personal role was clear. In Anna's own cruel way, she'd abandoned her sister. By embracing her new life, she'd pushed her sister away. More like shoved.

All of this might've been averted if Anna had only remembered where she'd come from.

Chapter 9

After the press conference, to say Anna and her mother got into a fight would've been a gross understatement. Anna hadn't felt this redneck mad in a long time. She wanted to snatch a handful of her mother's hair and scream in her face. Anna exploded into unbridled fury. She thought she'd known anger before. Believed that she'd experienced rage. Yet, on this day, Anna learned that clearly she had not.

This was all because her mother wouldn't tell her what the sheriff had said. She claimed that it was a personal conversation and that it didn't concern Anna. None of her business. This hurt her. Almost like her mother had smacked her across the face. Dug her nails in and drew blood. When her mother said that Anna was on a need-to-know basis and that she didn't need to know, one of the glass ashtrays flew across the room and shattered against the wall. Cigarette butts and dust plumed. The trailer was too cramped, too hot, so Anna left.

She went without a coat. The air outside felt cool and prickled her skin. It produced a memory that she couldn't grasp.

Outside, Anna's car kicked up a flurry of gravel rocks as she floored the engine and sped off down the driveway. Her hands were vibrating as she white-knuckled the wheel. The outline of her tunneled vision turned red, and despite the cold, her face felt hot. Perspiration beaded on her forehead, and she felt a line of sweat run down the back of her neck. Anna cracked the window and let the car fill with crisp mountain air.

As she drove down Cove Road, Anna played over in her mind each conversation she'd had since finding out about Sam's disappearance. Lingering suspicion that felt like a whisper in the night. Scenes flashed and words echoed, but these seemed like a foreign language. Anna held them like a photograph caught between moments. No odd or intangible connection went unnoted. She froze each one in time and pondered the multitude of possibilities that existed at once.

She drove down Steve Tate Highway toward Marble Hill. The tiny intersection that designated a blip on the map. Nowhereville, North Georgia. With each passing mile, Anna felt lighter. The rage that boiled fiercely just minutes before slowly simmered away. Yet the fear remained. It had entered her heart and seemed like it would never leave. The feeling was parasitic. Like a malevolent thing that incubated in her soul. Fed off her until there was nothing left, and Anna was just a shell. She swallowed hard to drive those thoughts away. There were more important things to do than stew over her mother's stubborn incompetence.

At the four-way stop, Anna turned left onto Highway 53 and took an immediate right into the Dollar Value parking lot. There were a few cars parked outside, and she noticed a dilapidated Chevy Nova parked around back that belonged to the manager, Victor. Besides running the Dollar Value, Victor cared for his aged and ailing mother. She'd been sick for decades, and he was her constant companion. Took her to the grocery store, the doctor, and church every Sunday. They were each other's world.

Anna parked and walked quickly toward the store. The door was heavy, and a bell jingled loudly when she pulled it open. The inside of the Dollar Value looked like a place in chaos. Everything was arranged in ways that evoked ordered insanity. It seemed a store locked forever in some Sisyphean curse whereby shelves were never full and the workers were forced to stack until the end of time. No one was behind the register, so she stood in the empty line. There was a little dog toy with the words "Squeeze for service" written on the side in black magic marker. Anna grabbed the toy, and it let out a shrill squeak.

She was about to squeeze it a second time when Victor hollered, "Right with you," from somewhere in the store. Anna turned and saw him dragging his uncorrected clubbed foot toward the register. He was straining and breathing heavily. His face was a blistering bright red.

When he got closer and he saw Anna, his whole expression changed. "Great God Almighty," he said with a strong country twang and a slight lisp. "Great God."

Victor held both arms out and tightly hugged Anna. He kept repeating his petition to the Almighty as he rocked Anna back and forth.

After a few moments, Anna let go and stood back. "I guess you've heard."

"Yes, sweet child," he said softly. "And I'm sick to death with worry."

"Me too."

"When your momma called up and told me, I knew something was bad wrong. Sam would never miss a day of work. Just ain't like her a'tall."

There was a gap of silence, and Anna watched him. Sad dolls eyes that glimmered with a baleful hope of providing comfort. She hugged him again, and he rubbed her back gently.

"It's all right, child. It's all right. She'll be found, and all this will be just a silly story we joke about. I just'a know it."

"I need to know, was Sam acting weird or different in the past few days?"

Victor shook his head. "A detective came by earlier and asked the same thang. Nothing out the ordinary. Just same ole Sam. Bubbly and full'a life."

"Was anyone hanging around?" she asked. "I guess, acting suspicious?"

Victor laughed. "You mean outside the normal fellers?"

"Yes," Anna said.

"Nobody new. Just the usual guys coming in to talk to her." He sighed. "She's beautiful, but you already know that. Just ask the mirror."

"Please, Victor, can you be more specific? What are their names?"

"Well, that Billy boy for one. He was always dropping in for cigarettes whenever Sam was working. Never came in when she wasn't here. But she never gave him the time of day. Then there's that pastor's boy, Daniel. He'd been coming in more often. Chatting Sam up . . ." Victor paused and squinted his eyes. "Come'te think of it," he said. "Lord, how can I just remember this?" He sighed heavily. "Daniel came in sometime this past week—I can't think of the day just now—and was talking with Sam real serious like. She was stacking toilet paper at the rear of the store. I walked by, and they was arguing about something. Or at least that's what it looked like. I mean, they were hollering in whispers, which has never made sense to me when people do that. Why not just talk normal like? It sounds the same—"

"Wait, okay!" Anna nearly shouted. "What exactly happened?"

"Right, well, they was doing that and stopped when I went by. Both kinda glared at me, so I went on. Do you think I oughta call up the detective?"

"I'm not—" Just then, Anna's phone started to ring. She looked down at the screen and saw Trevor's picture with his name and number blinking. Anna smiled at Victor and held up one finger. She stepped away and answered. "Hey, Trevor, this isn't a great time. Can I—" Anna was quickly interrupted.

"I saw the news. Gosh, I had no idea this had gotten so serious. Why didn't you tell me?"

Anna was a little taken aback by her boyfriend's tone. His inflection a mixture of annoyance and frustration. Was he really berating her? "It was serious enough for me to come home immediately," she said.

"I mean, I didn't think it was that big of a deal. But then I saw you on TV. This is huge. I'll be there in about two hours."

This was a confusing turn of events. She was dealing with too much to worry about Trevor. "Yeah, okay. Just call me when you get in town. I'll meet you."

"Sure, sure, sure. I'm going to start Tweeting and posting on Facebook about this. Really spread the word. I'll send out an email blast, and we can get this trending on social media. Let me be in charge of talking to the media. I'm made for this type of thing—"

"Look, I've gotta go," Anna said and hung up the phone.

A cornucopia of anger, confusion, and desperation flashed through her mind. Was her boyfriend seriously trying to control the situation?

Her whole body trembled. Ideas were colliding in her head. Perhaps Anna was just trying to find meaning in her twisted thoughts. A feeling of unease coursing through her veins. Too much was going on to worry about that now. She was hardly keeping her shit together.

Anna took a step toward Victor and tried to steady her hands. Her vision was out of focus, and she stared at the tiled floor to gain a sense of equilibrium. She noticed dirt and wondered if it was Sam's job to sweep.

Anna sucked in her breath and hugged Victor. His hands were pressed tightly against her shoulder blades, and he rocked back and forth very gently. He had a way of calming anyone just by his presence. Some people are just born that way. Sam fought back tears. She was uncertain as to how much more she could take. Her nerves felt shot, and she was drifting precariously near a breaking point. She kept hearing an echo. Was it Sam, her ghost, or another version of herself from a different dimension, pleading for relief?

The farthest they'd ever been from each other was when Anna was at UGA. Yet being home with Sam missing made the distance feel like an unstoppable gulf that kept growing. Each second the space between the sisters lengthened into a vacuum filled with darkness. Very appropriate for a woman in self-imposed exile. For as far back as Anna could remember, she had wanted to get away. One foot perpetually out the trailer door. Always going. In the here and now, Anna was struggling but could still breathe. She hoped Sam could too.

As Anna was leaving the Dollar Value, she saw her old friend Melissa Jefferies exiting a minivan. Just a year older than herself and already roaming around with a small brood. Three kids at eighteen-month intervals and another on the way. When the eldest caught sight of Anna, she pointed and held her hand over her mouth. She instinctively clutched her younger siblings for dear life, perhaps seeing her as the one who'd disappeared. Her childlike fear spotting danger of what she couldn't understand. Melissa saw all this and swatted the little girl, who wailed and scurried off toward the store entrance.

Melissa mouthed sorry and rolled her eyes in exacerbation. Anna smiled and half jogged back to her car. She unlocked it with the key fob and slid behind the wheel. She looked in the rearview mirror and watched Melissa and her scion enter the store. She tried to erase from her mind the universal truth that when things are gone, they're gone. Anna placed her head on the steering wheel and cried. She sobbed like she'd never done before.

Chapter 10

Anna drove down Cove Road toward the church. As she went, she thought about Victor, Melissa, and everyone else in Marble Hill. How the spread of gossip in a small town acted like a virus. Infectious and something Anna understood all too well. Even the smallest transgressions spread. The talk was dangerous. It wasn't just the communicable nature of lies. No. Gossip always carried with it a grain of truth.

An eighteen-wheeler sped past on the curvy mountain road, and it made her car shudder and reel like a nervous colt. The eighteen-wheeler had a malignance about it that she couldn't place. She viewed the world as a projection of her fear. She'd hope to conjure some recollection of strength, yet such reserves were exhausted. She thought about her sister and the secrets between them. The transiency of those claims. The world to come, the world past.

Horror kept eating at her. A primogenitor coming down the pike. Anna drove slowly and cautiously with her hands at ten and two. *Mustard and mayonnaise*, she thought. Anna looked out the corner of her eye and saw a line of seemingly endless fence rows. Off to the right, a group of deer leapt the bar ditch as her car approached. A small doe lost her footing on the damp clay. She scrabbled wildly and sank onto her hindquarters, then rose again and vanished into the woods with the others. Further on, Anna noticed the blocked-off entrance to the old McClintock driveway, which disappeared into the woods. Still haunted if the stories were true. The ghosts of the family the farmer hacked to death. Anna detected a childish desire to see it again. She imagined taking the path and never looking back.

Anna pulled into the church parking lot. It was surrounded by a short wrought-iron fence. There was a sleek black Cadillac parked next to a badly used old church bus. Anna sat with the car running for a long time. She passed her hands across the top of the steering wheel twice as if she were making smooth something unseen before her. Finally, Anna exhaled with a quiver and exited her car. She walked to the side entrance of the church where an outdoor light burned listlessly overhead. The cracked pavement reminded her of things that she'd once known, which held her in good stead. Thoughts of the past to shield her from grim portents of the present. Twin sisters holding hands wearing matching dresses going to Easter service. Sneaking candy to eat during the sermons. Mom doling out pinches as they giggled through prayers. Moments almost forgotten.

Now, Anna knew that she cut a strange figure of a heretic trudging across this hallowed ground. She concentrated on moving in a straight line and putting one foot in front of the other. She tried the door, but it was locked. She banged on the entryway with three loud slaps from the palm of her hand. She waited a few moments, then pounded with her fists.

Nothing. Not even an echo.

Anna went around to the front of the church and climbed the steps. It was quiet in the churchyard and quiet in the country. She was unnerved and didn't know what to make of it. The door was unlocked, but the inside was dark. It gave her an uneasy feeling. She propped it open to light up the vestibule. Just inside the sanctuary was a long row of switches that Anna pondered. She had no way of knowing which to flip, so she turned them all on. The whole interior lit up. The nave was nicely kept, and the sacristy had a plain elegance that was strangely beautiful. Anna walked down the aisle toward the pulpit.

As she neared the altar, a noise sounded to the right, and in walked a woman wearing an ankle-length dress with long sleeves. It was a yellow flowered print that became her. She was beautiful in a plain way. Her hair was pulled back in a taut ponytail. She wore no makeup. Meek and unassuming. Almost like she hid her own attractiveness. Perhaps something that made her ashamed.

Ruth stood with her hands clasped at her waist. "Hello, Anna," she said soberly. "What can I do for you?"

"I need to talk to you about my sister."

"Certainly," she said. "Come with me."

Anna followed the pastor's wife out of the sanctuary. They walked down a long hall that was cheaply tiled. Ruth's shoes tapped out a rhythm that echoed loudly. Knockoffs of great biblical works hung on both sides of the walls: *The Transfiguration of Christ, The Creation of Adam, The Last Supper,* and *The Return of the Prodigal Son.* Anna knew them from her art history class. Ruth stopped in front of an open door that led into an office. Above the entranceway was a framed cross-stitching that read *Do not be afraid, do not be discouraged. Be strong and courageous.*

Ruth motioned for Anna to enter. Inside was a large sofa and two plush-looking chairs that faced a big desk. The room was empty and evoked an anxious blankness. As if a tribunal could be called at any moment to pass some uncomfortable judgment against the accused. In the corner was a dusty plastic plant. Along the walls were various types of religious iconography. Some made sense, such as Christ ascended and Jesus crucified on a cross, while other pieces were strange. There was a framed picture of Jesus in a robe and sandals playing basketball with a group of young African American boys. Another was a cartoon of a shirtless Christ wearing sunglasses and talking to a group of girls in bikinis. Above the sofa was a large poster with the words *Christ is risen* written in neon pink. Anna stood in the middle of the room, uncertain of where to sit.

Ruth placed a hand on Anna's shoulder and gently led her over to the couch.

"Firstly," Ruth said, sitting down next to her, "I want to let you know that I'm praying for your sister's safe return. We all are."

"Thanks. We are hoping it's just a wild hair and that she'll be back."

"Yes, yes, of course. Now, what can I do for you, Anna?"

"Well," she said. She wiggled her hands uncomfortably. "I looked over my sister's recent calls, and several were to the church. I talked to your husband earlier, and he said that they were to you. I was wondering if you might tell me what your conversations were about. Might shed some light on all this."

"Certainly," Ruth said. She sat rigid and stoic like a stone. "Sam came to me several months ago and wanted to know more about God. She was having some very intense personal problems and needed guidance. My husband felt that I should be the one to talk to her. We had many pleasant conversations. She was very curious about God and Christianity. Living a more spiritual life. She'd drop by once a week or so. We'd sit in this very office and chat. Right like we are now. It's strange with you being here . . ." Ruth paused. "You are both exactly alike."

"Yes, we are identical twins—"

"No," Ruth interrupted. "What I mean is that your eyes are the same. Both of you have the same fire. With monozygotic siblings, you often find discrepancies seen in the sclera. There are little differences. Flecks or slight variations. Due, of course, to the environment and not genetics. These are reflected in the epigenome. You both started out with one set of genetic instructions, but once you are born, the copies begin to change."

"How do you know all this?"

"I graduated from Emory University pre-med. I married Thomas, who was getting his doctorate of divinity from Mercer. Somehow, we ended up here." She waved her hand absently at the world about.

"You mentioned problems. What sort of personal problems?"

"I normally wouldn't share conversations had in confidence, but this is a special case. We discussed issues related to sinfulness and whether she might be forgiven. Sam discussed some relationships and how she felt deep shame for her actions."

"What actions?"

"Sex," Ruth said matter-of-factly. "She was having sex."

Abruptly, the office door swung open, and Pastor Hinson entered. He looked panicked and disoriented. His face was covered in sweat.

When he recognized Anna, he gave her a startled grin. "Oh, I'm sorry. I'll leave you two alone."

Anna's phone vibrated, and she looked at the screen. It was a call from her mother. "It's fine," she said. "I've got to get going."

"Are you sure?" Pastor Hinson asked.

"Yes." Anna stood.

Ruth remained seated and held out a hand. "It was a pleasure speaking with you, Anna. Please, feel free to drop by again." Anna shook it softly.

Just as she was about to leave the office, Pastor Hinson spoke up. "You know, Anna, we'd sure love to have you here on Sunday. We are going to be talking about keeping on that straight and narrow in the face of sin and horrible temptation. Traveling that road to salvation and finding happy destiny."

Perhaps it was stress, tiredness, rage, or fear. But Anna stopped at the door and faced them both. "Road to salvation? A road is difficult to travel," she said. "Everyone has their own reasons for going one way or the other. It has benefits and costs, and all that anyone can hope for is that on judgment day the ledger evens out."

"You must know the road to salvation," Pastor Hinson said with conviction. His eyes were huge and burned with religious fervor.

"Maybe so," Anna told him. "For things at a common destination, there is a common path. Not always easy to see, but there."

Before Anna left the office, she saw the pastor's brow furrow, and, in the corner, Ruth was smiling.

Anna's phone rang again, and she answered it while walking across the parking lot to her car. "Mom, I really don't want to talk to you right now."

"Why haven't you been answering your fucking phone!" her mother screamed. "They've found Sam's dress and underwear."

"Oh God," Anna said.

"Someone found them on a trail in the Pickens Wildlife Management Area. I'm on my way out there."

Anna started to run. "Okay, Momma. Me too. I'm sorry . . ." She was going to say more, but her mother had already hung up the phone.

Chapter 11

Anna's foot hardly left the accelerator. She gunned the engine and straightened out the curvy mountain roads. Her little car hiccupped and strained as she overtook slow-moving vehicles across double yellow lines. She surged past the enormous gated community of Big Canoe, a mountain retreat for the wealthy of Atlanta. When the mineral plant shut down, the whole of the tiny town of Marble Hill was hit hard. But with the construction of Big Canoe, the residential neighborhood became the new employer. The rich outlanders needed house cleaners, tree cutters, street sweepers, trash collectors, and other professions of the lowest common denominator. But it was a blessing for the town.

Anna pulled into the Pickens Wildlife Management Area and saw several police cruisers and half-a-dozen cars parked near the trailhead. She left her car catty-cornered, exited the vehicle, and stood by the door. The wind in the cove moaned with a long, wet sound among the deepening sky. She noticed a small crowd a ways off from the deputies who stood around her mother. Her mother had been crying, and her face was bloated and splotchy. She rocked gently on her heels and held her jaw. A signature of sorrow. Anna jogged over to them.

As she drew closer, she saw Sheriff Haskins holding an evidence bag with a black and red dress stuffed inside. Even from across the parking lot, Anna recognized it. The dress was Anna's until a month ago when she hit the freshman fifteen. It was low slung and exposed the arch of her back and had a long slit that rose from the hem up to her thigh. She'd bought it from an expensive boutique in downtown Athens. Sam had begged her for it, so she'd mailed it home.

Bitter bile retched up and hit the back of her throat. She saw a vision of her twin lost somewhere and afraid, huddled in a cove and trying to stay warm. Where the cold cracks the stones. A wasteland trellised in shadow. How sweet to be merely in exile. To long for what is. At least, that was the best-case scenario. A more horrible nightmare flooded Anna's consciousness. Sam's naked body dumped beneath freshly turned earth. Rigor mortis setting in as insects lurked to find fresh places to burrow and call home. As Anna hurried across the parking lot, she dug her nails into her palms to break from that terrible vision. *Sam's safe*, she forced herself to think. She's run away or been kidnapped, and this is a ruse to keep them off her scent.

"That's it," Anna whispered. "That's it."

The small crowd made way for Anna to join the sheriff, her mother, and the deputies.

Haskins held up the clear evidence bag with Sam's dress stuffed inside. "Does this look familiar?" he asked.

Anna nodded. There it was. Another substantive piece of the puzzle that made Sam's disappearance tangible. "Yes," she said. "That's my dress. Well, Sam's. I gave it to her about a month ago."

The sheriff nodded. "Do you know if this was what she wore?"

"I have no idea, but it's hers."

The sheriff turned toward a deputy and handed him the clear plastic evidence bags. "Take these to the barman over at Yellow Creek. See what he remembers."

"Yessir, Sheriff," the deputy said.

Anna was shaking and wasn't sure if it was from fright, adrenaline, or both. A fresh wave of nausea rolled up her esophagus, and she swallowed several times to keep it down. Her mind pounded and sent painful shocks of hypothetical possibilities. In a flash, Anna had lost all semblance of everything she'd tried to keep together. Panic pulsed and gave her an almost debilitating headache.

The sheriff spoke to the group. "Y'all listen up. Our investigation shifts to this location. The clothing was found about a quarter mile or so up the trail. The hiker was Jacob Stallings. He went to take a leak and found it sticking out of some leaves. Thankfully, he didn't piss on it or we'd be up shit's creek." The sheriff removed his hat, ran his fingers through his thinning hair, and replaced it on his head before continuing.

"Since the clothing was found in a wildlife management area, the GBI will be heading up this investigation. In the meantime, I want to search the path and surrounding areas. We've got volunteers lined up, and I want an officer with each group. Some of these helpers are elderly, so keep that in mind. Just be careful, be vigilant, and keep the radios clear unless you've got something. All right?"

There was a collective response in the affirmative.

"Good luck, men," the sheriff said.

The two dozen members of the search party broke up into small groups while Anna and her mother stood awkwardly. A couple of them stared at Anna as they went, and it chilled her to the bone. Anna knew those looks. Recognition of rumors and how they always start from something. Or how gossip turned to stories that weaved into facts. The sheriff watched his men talk with a group of citizens congregated by the trailhead. After a few cautious moments, he cleared his throat and addressed Anna and her mother. "I want y'all to head on back home—"

"Like hell!" Anna exclaimed. Her mother clutched her hand and gave it a slight squeeze. Not out of anger, but pleading understanding. The early morning fight felt like years ago. They were, yet again, each other's strength.

"You will," The sheriff said sharply. He spoke with rigid conviction that made you fear and want to trust him. "You will do like I tell you. I can't have you off in these woods when the GBI comes around. They'll want to talk to y'all first and foremost." The sheriff exhaled heavily, and his tone changed to something almost fatherly, but Anna wasn't sure. "Now, I want you two to go on home. It's important that we know where to find you. This thing is minute by minute. The second we find out anything, you'll be the first to know."

Anna listened intently, but her mind was going haywire with possibilities. Each one worse than before. Her anxiety was such that she couldn't stop shaking.

The sheriff adjusted his belt. "A couple more things," he said. "First, don't give any details out to the news media. I'm sure they'll come sniffing around, but keep the particulars to yourself. If it gets out about her underdrawers being found with the outfit, that'll hurt us when we get to questioning a suspect. If that feller knows about them and it wasn't released to the public, then bingo, we got 'em. Does that make sense?"

Anna said she understood, and her mother nodded.

The sheriff spat and toed it into the dirt with his boot. Then he looked off into the distance. "Don't y'all worry, though. It's going to be all right."

Anna stared at him. Something about the sheriff's cool demeanor seemed off, yet she didn't care. Not at this moment. All she wanted was to find her sister. Bring Sam home safely and forget all about this nightmare.

"Don't forget what I said, Jenny. About Brokeback—"

"Tell me," Anna said. She watched as the sheriff's face darkened. She reached out and gently placed her hand on his arm. "Please, she's my twin sister."

The sheriff took a step back and exhaled. He looked her dead in the eyes. Anna saw herself reflected in an almost mirrored image, and it unnerved her. She thought he was about to turn and leave, but instead he said, "It ain't no secret what your uncle does for a living. I probably know him better than God Almighty. The only reason he ain't collecting dust down in Jackson is because so far, he's stayed one step ahead. That ain't gonna last forever. You can take that to the bank. That being said, my dislike for Brokeback won't take away from this investigation. He's just moved several seats closer to the front."

Anna grew angry as she listened to the sheriff discuss her loving uncle. Was Haskins just piecing together a formula or puzzle to assign blame to Brokeback? Someone had to be the villain, she thought. Or at least take some part in the blame. Perhaps everyone in this tiny town played a part.

She tried to speak, but the sheriff raised his hand. "I know you know that," he said. "But let's talk turkey about your uncle. You don't cook and sell dope without making a few enemies. And the fact of the matter is, you need friends as well. But not entirely good ones. Do you see what I'm getting at?"

"Yes, sir."

"Good. Best-case scenario, your sister has run off or gone somewhere without letting anyone know. That happens all the time. Hell, sometimes I wish that I could get away for a few days." He paused as if waiting for a nervous laugh that never came. "In all likelihood, that's it. But we are keeping all options open. No stone left uncovered. That means we gotta think of everything, which includes the worst case. That being Broke-back getting on the business end of some bad folks. Well, bad don't even begin to say it. I told your momma all this earlier. And that we're gonna be looking in on him real close."

The sheriff went on. "But don't think we've got blinders on. This is a missing person's case, and we haven't had one in a long time. This is highly unusual considering she's one of our own. We are tracking down every lead. I promise you, we'll find her."

Anna nodded and took a few hesitant steps back. She felt her mother's hand on the small of her back. The faintest bit of pressure. Anna wasn't sure if that was meant for reassurance or what.

"Thank you, Sheriff," her mother said with weakening inflection. "We'll head on home now. We're much obliged."

"Take care and mind what I said."

"Yes, sir."

Anna and her mother returned to their cars. Anna's feet felt heavier with each step. Each one you take is forever. Like walking away from the search party euchred impending doom. For the first time in her life, she felt a real distance separating her from her sister. It was nothing like what she felt going off to college. This was a tangible and awkward gulf that was still growing. There was a nagging sense of irritation that she tried to hide. When they were little, Anna swore that she could tell what her sister was thinking. Sam believed the same thing. Each tried to conjure or summon the other with just a little concentration. Sitting back-to-back with their legs crossed in the middle of their mother's bed. Anna's eyes clenched tightly as she visualized treats or toys that Sam would try and guess. As children, neither was very successful at reading the other's mind. And yet, during periods of true distress, Anna always felt something.

Stamping across the pavement, Anna pondered again if that was real or childish flight of fancy. Perhaps they had never really delved deeply into each other's psyche. *You are hungry*, as suppertime approached. *You are tired*, as night fell.

Anna got in her car and gripped the steering wheel for dear life. She shut her eyes and focused on her sister with all her might. *Are you scared? Are you lost?* Anna felt nothing. Not even the slightest tug. Even though she knew this was all hocus pocus, she kept on. *Are you alive?*

With that last introspective question, a violent spasm ruptured in her chest. Her heart felt stretched, and a burning sensation welled in waves of fire. A pit opened in her stomach with seemingly no end. Dark thoughts fired from every direction. Her mind wanted to wander down a rabbit hole, but she knew that only led to another, and another, and another.

"Oh God," she whispered. "Please, no."

Chapter 12

Before Anna drove away from the wildlife management area, she saw that she had seven missed calls and thirteen text messages. Trevor was in town, and Anna couldn't shake the feeling of dread. The circumstances were complicated enough without adding him to the equation. Trevor micromanaged everything. He always tried to interject himself into every situation. Paint a picture where he looked like the one in charge.

Yet that wasn't always a bad thing. In many ways it was an endearing quality. He had no fear and stood up for his principles. It didn't matter how unpopular. He always helped those who couldn't do it themselves. Teaching and molding others. Like any leader, Trevor evoked a certain magnetism when he spoke. You would stop everything you were doing and listen. It reminded her of Brokeback, but without the intrinsic undertones of mindless violence.

Anna turned into the grocery store parking lot and found Trevor's Prius in the far corner. She pulled up next to it and rolled down her window. He was typing on a laptop and didn't look up. When she hollered out, Trevor lifted his hand and continued typing without looking at her. Anna felt her face flush with anger. This was the other side of her boyfriend. Cold and impersonal. Measured indifference when she needed him most.

Anna slid the car in reverse and was about to back away when she heard his car door open. He placed his elbows on her car's passenger-side windowsill and smiled at her. Their eyes met. He wore a stock and almost impenetrable expression. Something akin to artificial concern. Yet she'd grown accustomed to the silent communication and mock depredations.

"How are you holding up?" Trevor asked.

"Aboveground." Once those words left her mouth, she wanted to swallow them back. She'd been home for forty-eight hours and already reverted to using hickisms and country speak. Anna's heart sank deeper. She even noticed a little twang. The things she'd worked so hard to leave behind.

"Any word on your sister?" he asked.

"No . . . well, there is something. Get in the car and I'll tell you."

While sitting in the empty parking lot, Anna let everything flow out. From start to finish, including the dress and panties tossed away like trash. As if the owner was nothing. She shared with him fears, secrets, suspects, and scenarios surrounding her sister's disappearance. It rolled off her tongue. The shell of the car seemed like a bubble of safety. For the first time, she admitted what terrified her. That Sam might be hurt or worse. Shaking as words spewed, Anna painfully vomited her true feelings. Doing so made her feel better. She was no longer alone with the weight of the world. By the end, she was crying uncontrollably.

Trevor placed his hand on her shoulder and whispered, "There, there. It'll be all right. Don't worry," he said softly. "We'll find her."

"Do you really think so?" Anna asked. Her vision was cloudy, and she wiped her eyes with the sleeve of her shirt.

"Yes," Trevor said reassuringly. He took out his phone and showed her the screen. He scrolled through lines of tweets regarding her sister. "Look, hashtag 'Find Sam' is trending in Athens and Atlanta."

Anna felt a rush of relief. The thought of it was so comforting. Trevor was actually doing something helpful. That momentary release changed when Anna leaned and looked closer. She saw his original post and nearly screamed. He'd used her picture instead of Sam's. It was of her and Trevor at one of his Student Council events. "What is this?" she asked.

"Oh, well," he said matter of factly. "I didn't have a photo of her, so I used the next best thing. You are identical twins."

Anna rested her head against the seat back. Her shoulder muscles tensed. "I need to get on home," she said flatly and through gritted teeth. "I've got to help Momma. You can follow me. It ain't far."

"All right," he said.

Anna waited until he exited her car, and then she cussed him up and down. Trevor was the smartest man she'd ever met, but he could be dumber than a sack of shit. Incompetence that was infuriating. Didn't he understand how much that would hurt her? How could he be so stupid? He had messaged and shared across the internet a fraudulent copy of her beloved missing twin. Not only was Sam gone in real life, she had been purged on the web.

"Stop it, Anna," she said aloud to herself. Be calm and rational. He's just trying to help. Atlanta or Athens wasn't Marble Hill. Outlanders couldn't tell the difference like the folks back home. A retweet or share might solve everything. "You're just looking for a reason to fight," she whispered.

Trevor's horn sounded, and Anna put her car in reverse and drove away. She went slow and made sure he was right behind her. Normally, if a driver blinked, they'd miss the turnoff, but not today. There was a WKB news van parked at the entrance of the driveway. They'd given just enough room for Anna's car to squeeze past. A reporter was using her reflection in the window to fix her hair. Anna looked in the rearview mirror and saw Trevor inches from her bumper. She detected a momentary flash of an excited smile.

Anna pulled up in front of the trailer. Her mother was sitting on the porch steps. She looked haggard and aged beyond her years. The past two days had taken their toll. Anna met her mother halfway up the steps.

"I can't talk to them people," her mother said. She pointed vaguely toward the road. Or perhaps the world at large. "They came up to the house, and I panicked. I believe I mighta threatened to kill 'em, but I ain't entirely sure. I just got to hollering. My nerves are shot to pieces." She lit a new cigarette with the end of the old. "Are those news people still down there?"

"Yes, Momma," Anna said. "I'll go talk to them."

"That your little boyfriend?" her mother asked.

Anna turned and saw that Trevor was standing by her side. He approached her mother with an extended hand. She hesitated slightly but shook it.

"Pleasure to meet you, Mrs. Renfro. I'm terribly sorry that it's under these circumstances." Trevor returned to Anna's side. "We will gladly go speak to the news media on your behalf."

Her mother nodded. "I thank you."

Trevor took Anna by the arm and practically dragged her down the gravel path. In truth, Anna was just as circumspect as her mother. This wasn't a story, but a reality. What do you say under these circumstances? The media had an unyielding drive to gain viewers. Sharing the news ended up being solely a secondary issue. The distance between the known and unknown was turning substantial. Gaining a semblance of the unreachable.

When the news van came into view, Anna saw the reporter and cameraman jump into action. The newswoman strode purposefully toward the approaching couple with her hand extended. Then her ankle buckled. She nearly fell when her high heels slipped on the gravel drive. Trevor rushed forward and helped catch her. The reporter looked embarrassed and smiled at Anna's boyfriend. She brushed loose strands of hair behind her ear and blushed. She was just a kid herself, Anna thought. Probably her first gig.

"Hello, my name is Elizabeth Peters, and I'm a reporter with WKB-TV. We've read about Samantha Renfro's disappearance, and we'd like to interview the family for the five o'clock news. I'm guessing that you are her sister, Anna?"

Before Anna could respond, Trevor said, "Yes, twins to be exact. Identical."

The woman's eyes lit up and flashed with excitement. Now this was a story. "Yes, I noted the resemblance almost immediately. Perfect," she said a little too enthusiastically. "You guys just stand over there near the mailbox. Stand with your backs to the road, and we'll begin here shortly."

The cameraman picked up the tripod, and the reporter fixed her hair. She smiled at Anna, but there was something hollow in her eyes. Perhaps just her own reflection. Trevor clasped Anna's hand and led her toward the mailbox. "Don't worry," he whispered. "I'll do all the talking." She tried to release her hand from his grip, but he squeezed tighter.

They stood with their backs toward the road as instructed. Above were rolling clouds that altered the light. Shadows passed through the dead and twisting trees. They created a haunting vision of blighted waste that hinted at indecipherable configurations. A car passed slowly on Cove Road, and the driver gawked at the unusual sight. Anna felt weak with hunger. She hadn't eaten anything all day. There was no time for that. Maybe Sam experienced the same. Anna's chance at camaraderie, perhaps.

The reporter held out a microphone and began a countdown. At one, she started to speak. "Good afternoon. I'm Elizabeth Peters reporting from Pickens County, Georgia. A Marble Hill woman has gone missing, and the story has gone viral on social media. 'Find Sam' has been retweeted hundreds of times and is trending throughout Georgia. I'm here with her twin sister, Anna, and the young man behind the post. What can you tell us?"

Despite the chill, Anna felt sweat bead on her forehead. "Um . . . my sister went missing on Thursday night from Yellow Creek Bar. She left all her possessions and hasn't been seen since. I, um . . . just want to say to Sam that I love you. We all love you and miss you. Please come home."

"Do you believe that she's run away or been taken against her will?" the reporter asked.

Anna's mouth felt like sandpaper. "I . . . I can't imagine she's run off."

"We've heard that something was found at Pickens Wildlife Management Area. Are there any updates since the press conference this morning?"

Before Anna could answer, Trevor spoke. "Yes, there are updates. Sam's dress and underwear were found at the scene . . ."

Anna was mortified. She'd expressed to Trevor what the sheriff said.

That no specifics were to be reported to the press. She'd told him that information in confidence. He'd single-handedly fucked it all up. Well, that wasn't true. It was her fault for telling him.

Anna grabbed his shoulder and forcefully spun him to face her. "What the fuck are you doing?" He looked shocked and embarrassed, even a little confused. "I told you what the goddamn sheriff said. Jesus, what the fuck is wrong with you?"

She looked over and saw that the red camera light was still flashing. They were capturing it all. Fuck them, Anna thought. And fuck him.

"I apologize, but y'all get the fuck off this property. Now!" she shouted. Then she stormed up the driveway. As she doubletimed around the bend, she heard the quickening sounds of Trevor running to catch up. I'm going to hit him, she thought. I'm going to punch him in his stupid fucking face.

"Wait a second, Anna," he said. "Wait."

Trevor caught up to Anna in the front yard. He took hold of her elbow, and she spun quickly to release his grip. "What the fuck, Trevor? Don't you realize the damage you've caused? They're going to report that shit. The sheriff specifically said to keep that information a secret. If someone has Sam, they might panic now. God knows what they might do to her. If something happens to her because of this stupid stunt, I'll kill you graveyard dead."

"Look, Anna," he said with his politician's smile. "Breathe. Okay? Just hear me out. If we didn't give them something, the news wasn't going to run the story at all. Now they'll probably lead with it, okay? The sheriff's thinking about what they'll do with a suspect once they find one. I'm just thinking about finding Sam. The more people who know she's missing, the more will be looking for her. We need to get out there on every channel. NBC. Fox. CNN. I've got a list of reporters in my car we can call. And if you don't want to go on TV anymore, that's fine. I can do it."

"Is that all this is about to you? A chance to get on TV?"

"It'll help us find Sam."

"You just want the publicity for your stupid campaign for Student Body President."

"Listen. The publicity won't hurt, that's for sure. I'll be—"

Anna cut Trevor off by punching him in the face. Struck him in the mouth and felt the grooves of his teeth on her knuckles. This surprised her as much as it did him. She'd never hit anyone before, but it felt so good. She reared back and hit him again, this time on the nose. She threw one final blow that struck him in the cheekbone, followed by a crunching sound. Blood poured through Trevor's nostrils, and he held his face with both hands. Tears sprang to his eyes. He was whining and cursing simultaneously.

"You white trash bitch!" he yelled. "How dare you touch me. I'll call the police."

"Do it!" Anna hissed. "I'm sure the sheriff would love to hear about it!"

He backed toward his car, his shirt covered in blood. "You are nothing but trailer trash. Always have been and always will be. To think I was going to save you from this." He pointed a bloody finger in the direction of her home. "I'd have raised you up. Made something of you. But not now. You'll forever be white trash!"

Anna took two steps toward him with clenched fists. There was real fear in his eyes. "White trash?" Anna asked. "You're goddamn right I am."

With that, she turned and stormed off toward her trailer. Tiny shocks of pain raced from her knuckles to her forearm. She heard him scream something indecipherable, but Anna kept on. She didn't feel sorry for hitting him. It needed to be done, she thought. Walking up the steps, she felt a wave of tiredness overtake her. Her strength was zapped, and she felt an enormous weight atop her shoulders. All Anna could muster was a single-fingered grand gesture as she walked inside.

Chapter 13

That night Anna had a horrible nightmare that would haunt her the rest of her days. In it, the trailer's hallway seemed to shrink and undulate like something out of a mirrored funhouse. Anna walked in a trance toward her room. The floor rocked wildly like waves on a windswept sea, and the lights above exploded in a prism of rainbow afterglow. She felt a stinging cool breeze strike her as she opened the door. The first thing she noticed was that the window was ajar, and a neon-green mist billowed into the room. The next was Sam sitting cross-legged on the bed. Almost like she was waiting for her sister. She wore an enormous T-shirt and black basketball shorts. Her feet were caked in mud. The girls had matching tattoos of birds taking flight, which started out small by the ankle bone and wrapped twice around to the shin. Sam's tattoo was nearly obscured by red clay. Leaves and dirt clung to her legs. On each wrist were handcuffs. The chain connecting the manacles was separated in two. Her arms were covered in dried blood. Tears in her skin where the metal bit down to the bone. Sam's hair was disheveled and ripped in clumps. Anna stood dumbfounded and completely mute. "Hiya, wombmate," Sam said. "Bet you weren't expecting me."

Anna opened her mouth, but nothing came out. She was hardly breathing.

"Well . . . that's fine," her sister responded with a sigh. "I'm just glad to be here. I'm happy to see you. It feels like forever." Sam looked down at the comforter and the mess she'd made. "Sorry." Sam laughed. "Didn't mean to dirty it up."

Anna broke from her trance and took a single step forward. There were tears in her eyes. "Where have you been?" she croaked. "Are you okay?"

"Me? I've been around. Just needed a break."

"What about those?" Anna pointed at her sister's wrists.

"Ha!" Sam giggled dramatically and slapped herself on the shoulders like some guffawing ape. "Long story."

"Please, let me take you to the hospital."

"No," Sam said. Her smile disappeared. "I will not go. Wouldn't do any good."

"How can I help you? What do you want me to do?"

"Stand right there and listen," Sam said with quiet ferocity.

"Okay."

"Good." Sam's smile returned, yet it was sarcastic, false, and cruel. "I'm so happy you are here. Amazing, though, what it took. You ran off to college and never looked back." Sam shook her head. "My darling sister," she spat. "If you forgot, we had plans. Since we were kids, we'd planned to move to Chattanooga. Get jobs together and share an apartment. But you decided you were too good for that. Too good for me. So, don't you see? All of this had to happen." She lifted her bloody and bruised arms. "I had to go through so much for you to give a damn."

"You've got it all wrong—"

"Shut the fuck up!" Sam screamed. "I'm talking." She sighed and rolled her eyes, then continued. "For years, we'd planned on Chattanooga, but in the end you abandoned me. Now, you know how it feels. Yet even still you've managed to make it about you. I saw the internet post. I can't even go missing without you interjecting yourself into the situation." Sam shook her head slowly. "It's unbelievable. Absolutely unbelievable."

"I didn't do that."

"I'm sure," her sister said. Sam raised her right hand, and Anna saw a small and lethal-looking blade that reflected a blazing light like a million unpierced suns. Anna was forced to shield her eyes and momentarily look away. "It's always about you," Sam said, waving the knife back and forth. "You are the most selfish person alive."

This is insane, Anna thought. "Please give me that—"

"No!" Sam screamed. "You aren't paying attention. You never pay attention. But you will now. You'll see. It's not about you anymore." Sam took the knife and ran it across her throat. The silver blade disappeared and reappeared dripping with blood. "It's not about you!" Sam garbled. "It's not about you! It's not about you! It's not about you . . ."

It's not about you. It's not about you . . . It's not about you . . . It's not about . . . It's not . . .

Anna woke with a start. Her face was drenched in sweat. She sat up and looked around her little bedroom. The window was shut, and she was alone. The bed was dirt-free but sopping wet from her waist up where she'd perspired.

She got out of bed, stripped out of her soiled clothes, and put on an extra-large T-shirt. Normally, her nightmares dissipated to nothingness once she woke. Yet she had a feeling that this one would nag at her forever.

The hallway was back to normal, but she found little solace in that. Her mother was snoring loudly, so Anna crept on her tiptoes toward the front door. It reminded her of high school and sneaking out. Knowing exactly where to place her footfalls to remain undetected. One wrong step and the floorboards sounded like shattering glass. Sam always right behind her, reluctantly tagging along.

Anna went outside in just her short sleeves. The mountain chill revitalized her. She thought about how it had taken forever to fall asleep. Home was distinctly different with the heavy aura of absence. She'd worried herself sick straining to find some clue, sign, or anything she'd missed. Now she realized that not even her dreamscape was safe. The difference between her nightmares and existence was questionable at best. Just more discomfort in horrible possibilities that eternally grew into abject terror.

Anna sat down on the couch and watched the loose porch light sway in the breeze. It created dancing ghosts in silhouette across the gravel drive. She saw two dark shapes darting around. The bats were silent except for the faint flap of wings. The pale moonlight above draped the yard with shadow and faint reflections, morphing it into something foreign to be set right only by the bringing of day. Like twilight turned the familial landscape into another dimension.

Looking up, Anna stared at the enormous pale moon and watched the running clouds pass in front. Faint stars of muted light. Her mind jumped erratically, and she thought about how humanity gets swept away in legends or myths we don't understand. The mountains full of painters, haints, or boogers. But these are often real, and the monsters are us. Perhaps the old stories were true. That the untamed wilderness was full of witches or sprites. Foolish mortals finding doom through curiosity after being led deeper by fatal inquiry. The provinces of blind destinies.

Anna remembered that as a child there were rumors of panthers spotted in the hills around her home. Traveling south from the Smoky Mountains to carry away small animals or domesticated dogs. There was a time when a child went missing and the community was in panic. The mother claimed that a panther had stolen her little one away. But the truth came out later. The mother had killed her own child. She'd cleaved her daughter's head in with a rock and thrown the tiny body off the side of a ravine into the churning Etowah River below. Proving that humans are the vilest creatures on earth. Kill and torture for reasons beyond proper knowing. Selfish beings who bring death for pleasure. The world was perilous, and the image of it we tried to create was more dangerous still.

Yes, mankind was the true animal here.

Anna stared into the ink black world that was the wilderness. There were secrets in the woods outside the curious wildlife and unknown terrain. It was an overlapping past of nightmares that were just beyond the tree line. A sinister mumbling or slight whispering to come closer and take a look.

She lay down on the couch with her arms tucked under her head and closed her eyes. The wind shook the trees and created a light cacophony of straining wood. The sound like the shepherding of ghost voices. A vision of her twin's dirty feet flashed through her mind. Lots of places to go in the forest, she thought. Plenty of locations to hide. Paths leading to nowhere. Ascending the hills or descending into the hollows, one might walk into a wall of thickets and be lost forever. Or you'd come upon the ruins of a house with no road or path leading anywhere. Decaying and strangled with vines as if being dragged back to its natural form. How did it get there? What became of the residents who once called this home? Almost fairy tale mountain folks with Scottish surnames found throughout the Appalachians, Ulster, and the Highlands and Lowlands of Alba.

Dispossessed, dead, and nevermore. All things heretical against the known world. The ode of the Appalachians.

The woods were full of mysteries and more that called you further. Wandering into the deep pines, you didn't just vanish. You acted like memories drifting further away. You slowly disappeared in fragments. Bits and pieces until you were completely gone.

That was Anna's final thought before she drifted back to sleep.

Chapter 14

The Georgia Bureau of Investigation showed up at the Renfro trailer first thing that morning. Rufus's barking woke Anna just as the car came into view. Two dark-haired and serious-looking agents exited the vehicle and approached. Both seemed to take in everything but her. A short conversation followed. The GBI needed to scour the trailer for clues and asked Anna and her mother to leave. What sounded like a request was clearly an order, so they went into Marble Hill to eat breakfast at the Pancake House where her mother worked.

Sitting in the booth, Anna shrank and kept her eyes on the plate. She pushed the eggs around and watched the yolk break and run over everything. Her grip on the fork was tight and unyielding. The shock of her nightmare still burned deep in her psyche, ate at bits of her soul.

"You okay, Anna?" her mother asked, holding back a sob. "I know I can't be much help to you, but do you need anything?"

"Momma, I need all the help anyone can name."

"Lord, help me too." Her mother shook her head. "I keep hearing her. Crying out to me, like when she was little. Screaming out, 'Mommy, Mommy.' Driving me crazy 'cause I know it's in my head, but it seems so goddamn real." She reached out and grabbed Anna's hands forcefully. "Don't you do nothing like this, you hear me? Don't you dare."

"Of course, Momma," Anna said. Her mother dropped her head and cried softly onto her plate. Anna told her mother that she loved her and that she'd be back to take her home when her shift was over. Then Anna rose and left the restaurant.

She sat in her car and tried to imagine the world as Sam saw it. A place of goodness, where the bad parts existed solely as an aberration.

For Anna, though, she couldn't get past the universal truth that this world was no good and that was all it would ever be.

She couldn't just sit around and wait.

She knew of one person who might know where Sam was and shed light on her disappearance. His name was Luke, but everyone called him Spud. He got the nickname back in high school because he had terrible acne. The pustules broke out all over his face and looked like sprouts on a potato. Instead of shying away from the moniker, Luke embraced it, which gave him a bizarre sense of power over his bullies. Now, the tag was so widespread that hardly anyone remembered his given name.

Spud was a dope dealer who worked directly for Brokeback out of the Main Street Inn just south of Jasper. Anna was desperate for any news, sign, or crumb of information. It was no secret that Spud had his pulse on the underbelly of Meth Hill. He was the county's number one peddler for pills and crystal. He prided himself on having or getting anything you needed.

Anna drove north on Highway 53 toward downtown Jasper. Just before the city limits was the seedy motel. The sign out front flashed "Vacancy," but in truth, it needed no such signifier. There were only two cars in the lot, and one had two flat tires.

The Main Street Inn was one of the last remaining vestiges of an older time. A time before the chain motels popped up along the highway. The motel was crumbling to pieces and shaped like a giant, lopsided U. The motel needed a fresh coat of paint a decade ago. All pretense of respectability was dropped. With corporate hotels a dime a dozen along the interstate, this privately owned enterprise had lost practically all its customers and fallen into disrepair. Now it served as a refuge and way station for itinerant degenerates—exactly who Anna was going to see. She didn't think so, but perhaps Sam was among their number now.

Anna pulled into the pockmarked parking lot and scanned it for anything that might forewarn a police presence, such as cars too fancy or clean-cut patrons. An old Ford Ranger with a mix-matched paint job was parked by the motel office. The only other car was Spud's rusted purple

Cadillac, leaning to one side on two flat tires. It was parked directly in front of Room 7. After deciding the coast was clear, Anna turned off her car and walked to the motel room. She knocked on the door and waited. She kept glancing side to side in the guiltiest manner possible. Suddenly, the curtain pulled aside and she saw Spud's wild eyes staring at her. He was walleyed, and he wore a nearly toothless and bizarre smile. Anna heard the chain unlatch and the door opened a crack. Spud's jaundiced face registered recognition, and he opened the door wider.

He stood wearing filthy boxer shorts before Anna and opened his arms wide. "Hiya, Anna!" Spud exclaimed. "Come on in. How are you doing?"

She entered the darkened motel room. It was the color of moth-balls, suppressed rage, and permanent regret. The small area was filled with cigarette and caustic meth smoke. She saw Spud's longtime girl-friend, Tristen, sitting naked and cross-legged on the floor. She'd been in Anna's grade in high school. Another strange woman wearing nothing but a thong stood in front of the mirror, critiquing her skeletal body. The room was trashed, and it looked like this bizarre trio sharing their lives together were the last people on earth.

"This is unexpected," Spud said. His eyes were like glass, and his jaw was grinding like a thing set on wobbly gears. "Whatcha need, girl? Whatcha need?"

A mound of baggies was piled up on the bed next to a computer and pistol. Anna saw an enormous mountain of goods heaped in the corner. Electronics, garage tools, household appliances, mounds of gold and silver jewelry, and other various bric-a-brac were stacked waist high. If the junkies had no money, Anna guessed, Spud would take certain things in exchange. Most of it looked stolen, but that didn't seem to matter. He'd probably later fence those goods for cash.

"I was wondering if you've heard anything about Sam. Anything at all."

Spud's eyes skittered about, and he began rubbing his hands together nervously like some petrified child. "Sam, Sam," he repeated. "Sam?" He reached both hands behind his head and rubbed his neck. "Does your uncle know you're here? Does he know?"

"He doesn't," Anna said. "I'm here on my own."

Spud looked like he was on the verge of having some sort of epileptic fit. Anna wasn't sure if this was the drugs, her presence, or the fact that he was hiding something. "You know, your uncle is like a father to me. I'd do anything for him. Anything at all."

"That's great, but I need you to think. Have any of the people you deal with said anything, hinted at something, or acted different?"

A bizarre-sounding laugh seemed to come up from the inner reaches of his gut, and he started to dance crazily from foot to foot. "I deal with characters all day, every day." He wheezed. "Hell, I'm one myself."

"Please, just try," Anna said. She turned to face the two women. "What about either of you?" she asked. Neither of the women seemed to be paying attention. Both were frozen in attitudes of indifference, resigned fear, or pain at the enormousness of their trying existence. As if each new moment wrought more evidence of life's cruel realities.

Anna stared at Spud with a new intensity. Perhaps he was aware she knew he was lying. Something seemed to switch in his mind. Anna could also see the twisted calculations in his head that she took for the lies he spilled. "I haven't heard. I haven't seen her since we was in high school," he said.

Anna's whole expression changed. She'd seen Sam's call log that showed they'd talked. Anna knew he was lying. Now, she shifted her questioning and took a step forward. "Brokeback doesn't know I'm here," she said while raising her phone. "But he will. Unless you tell me the truth."

Spud looked at her and then quickly averted his eyes. The whole atmosphere of the motel room seemed to change as if the air had been charged with an electrical current.

"I have her phone records. She called you seven times. Seven. So, again, tell me the truth."

Spud began to bounce up and down erratically like a fretting and squirming child. "I haven't lied to you. I really haven't seen her."

"But you talked to her. What did you talk about?"

"I'll tell you here in a second, but just let me smoke. Okay? I need to get high. Then I'll spill it. Okay? Okay?"

Anna nodded, and Spud walked over to the nightstand, picked up a black leather toiletry bag, and reached inside. He quickly pulled out a baggie and dumped half its contents into a glass pipe. It had a bulb at one end with a hole in the side and a long, circular tube that ran out from the bowl. Spud grabbed a butane lighter and sat down next to Tristen on the floor. He reached up to the bed, grabbed the gun, and laid the pistol on the filthy carpet in front of him with the handle in easy reach. He never looked at Anna.

"Barbs, get your ass over here," Spud hollered to the woman standing in front of the mirror.

The woman walked over to the others, and Anna noticed the jagged line that ran across her emaciated stomach. Suture dots on either side that looked like a resting giant centipede. She joined the small circle of lost souls. Spud flicked the butane lighter, and the perfects shards of ice began to sizzle in the glass. He pulled on the lip at the same time and inhaled the wafting smoke into his lungs. Spud repeated the exercise a second time and passed the pipe to Tristen. The circle remained completely silent during this act of solemn occasion. Like some latter-day pilgrims before a shrine. Each taking turns bowing as penitents before an altar.

Tristen passed the pipe to Barbs, who hit it twice and passed it back to Spud. They'd gone full circle.

"Did you know, Anna, that the earth is actually flat?" Spud mentioned between his two hits on the pipe. "I read all about it on the internets . . . Look at the fucking pictures supposedly taken from space. Flatter'n hell. And the damn moon landing was faked. Why the fuck does the fucking ocean look so damn flat? It's because it is." His eyes bugged and morphed into the zealous sheen of some crazed acolyte of a cultish order. Like two glazed and bulbous orbs of tonsured insanity.

Suddenly, Tristen set to chittering. "Guess where we're going next, Anna girl? Down to the big city! I ain't never been to Atlanta. Lived here my whole life and never gone southerner than Ball Ground. I wanna go someplace fancy like Canton or Woodstock. Hey, maybe even Marietta!"

"You just wanna leave me!" Spud cried out.

Tristen's eyes went wild with vexation. "Never, Spud! Never ever."

"I'll kill you if you ever do," Spud said. "Just remember that!"

"I'd deserve it, baby. I'd just plain deserve it," she said with a huge smile. "That's why I just love you! I don't know what I'd done if I hadn't ever met you—"

Spud interrupted, saying, "I don't know why the government wants to perpetuate the lie. I figure that feller in charge now—that, that man is amazing. Gonna drain the swamp faster than a jackrabbit with the squirts . . ." He cackled, apelike.

"I'm gonna kidnap her," Barbs interjected. "It ain't no kidnappin' if the kid your nappin' is your own. Right?"

"This moon, though, that was all done on stage. They had this director, Stan Kubrocks or something, make it all up. He did that movie with Jack Nicholas about the evil hotel. It was The Overwatch or something," Spud said while picking at a bloody scab on his face.

The pipe was back in Spud's hand. The bowl was jet black and bubbling. He was leeching out the final vestiges of residue. Not allowing any of the ice to go to waste.

Anna spied these comrades in misery. Each with a story to tell. Children gone, loved ones lost, abuse, and a host of other tragedies that highlight the complexity of life. Some can deal with it, while others can't. It didn't make them weak or less of a person, she thought. They were just lost with seemingly no place to turn. That was the problem.

A cell phone chimed from across the room. Spud smiled and stood up. He stretched his back, and the thundering clap of cracking bones and ligaments filled the enclosed space. Tristen put her hands over her ears, and Barbs picked at some form of anonymous life buried in the folds of her skin, her emaciated frame protruding sharply. Looking like coat hangers in a trash bag.

Spud spoke into the phone. "Yeah, motherfucker ... Of course, motherfucker . . . All right, motherfucker." Anna heard a strident and strong voice come out of the speaker. The conversation was brief and calculated. Yet at first it sounded all wrong. Not what she expected. There was a voice in the back of Anna's head that told her to go. Something seemed off. She'd never felt such an overwhelming urge to flee.

Anna was listening intently to Spud's conversation. "Sounds good, motherfucker . . . Thanks, motherfucker . . . You're the best, motherfucker . . . I owe you, motherfucker."

Spud hung up the phone and returned to the circle. He had a big smile on his face. "All right, ladies, we've got some folks coming in soon. That was Derek, and he needs a few baggies."

Anna took Spud by the arm. "Tell me about Sam. What did y'all talk about?" Anger rose in her chest, and she stared him down. His eyes looked like mirrored glass, and his capillaries exploded from his enormous irises like vicious-looking jagged lines. "Where is she?"

"Who?" he asked absently.

Anna's heart sank because she knew he was gone. This was a complete waste of time, and anger welled up inside her. The women hurried about the place, while Spud stood by the draped window and peeked out into the parking lot. He was picking at his skin and scratching until he bled rivulets that coursed down his arm.

"Tell me, goddamn it," Anna said angrily. "What did y'all talk about? Tell me or I swear to fucking God I'll call my uncle."

"She," he stammered. "She was setting up a sale. Some guy. Always wears a Pickens High football shirt." Spud coughed and spittle flew. "He wanted dope, and she was the go-between. Gave him my number and that's all."

"You're lying!" Anna barked. "She called more than once!"

"Yes, because I told her no at first, because of Brokeback." Anna stood back, but Spud stayed cowed in the corner. "Finally, I said okay. That's all. I didn't talk to her again."

"Who's the person?" Anna asked.

"I dunno who he is. Just some white dude. He came here and I sold to him. Bought a couple times since then. Just a weird guy. Weird fucking guy . . . Look, I think he was giving her a finder's fee. Seemed like she was trying to get some money put together for some reason. I never asked why, and she never told."

Just the thought of this made Anna shudder. She turned away, cursing under her breath. Was Sam getting money so she could run away? How much could she get for something like this? And most importantly, who could that guy be?

Spud made some noise behind her, but she didn't turn around. She opened the motel room door and walked swiftly across the lot. She hurriedly entered her car and cranked the engine.

Anna looked in the rearview mirror and saw Spud watching her from the window. He had his phone to his ear and seemed to be speaking to someone with great earnestness. She cranked the engine and put the transmission in drive. She drove over the concrete parking partition and heard the unnatural agonies of metal scraping. It nearly rattled the meat from her bones. Swearing, she punched the accelerator and screamed out of the parking lot.

Chapter 15

Now there was only one person left who Anna needed to question. Jacob Stallings, whom everyone called "Old Man Stallings."

He lived somewhere out by the Dawson County line. She'd never visited him, but everyone knew which mailbox was his. It was a homemade University of Georgia bulldog whose mouth opened to swallow good and bad news. The bulldog wore a red football jersey with the letter *G* stenciled garishly on either side. It gained a bit of local notoriety because he dressed it up for special occasions and various holidays. Soon, the UGA football mascot would wear a Santa hat and be strangled with lights.

Old Man Stallings was loved in the community. An old World War II veteran who picked up trash on the highway, volunteered at the food pantry, led Bible studies at the county jail, helped with the trails committee, and generally looked out for the less fortunate. Now, a man who possibly held insight into Sam's disappearance.

Anna headed east on Highway 53. "Shut Up and Dance" by Walk the Moon was playing on the radio. Normally a song that Anna loved, but not today. It was a happy track that Anna wanted no part of. She needed everything to match her sorrowful heart, so she hit the power button and shut the system off. She listened to the sound of the road. The minor clanks and soft clamor of the engine.

Anna hugged the curves. Electric lines ran parallel that crossed the road every so often. The mountains along the edge of the valley peaked in ever-increasing intervals. She passed alcoves of rocky fields with outcroppings of spruce trees and small loblollies. The sky was overcast with a few breaks in the clouds. These created dancing shapes of light that

migrated slowly across the flowing valleys and baleful ridgelines. Everything had a tinge of gray like her heart.

It took her ten minutes to get there. She was filled with a strange
sense of panic and nervous energy. So much was going on, but eventually her body would shut down. Like living with a powder keg of guilt
stacked on top of the weight of her own sins. Adrenaline only lasted for
so long. Soon, it would be all over.

Anna turned onto the dirt driveway and followed the fresh tire
tracks. The bottom of her car groaned as the undercarriage scraped
against ruts. Tiny evergreens and calico bushes added bits of color to the
dead-looking world. There was a steep dip farther into the hollow, and
then the house came into view. An ancient pickup truck was parked in
front. Smoke billowed out from the tall chimney. It was an old log cabin
that looked impenetrable. The walls were shorn from the strong wood of
the region. Simultaneously, they looked ageless and harbored beautiful
antiquity.

She pulled up next to the truck and got out. There was a bluetick Lab
mix lying down on the porch. He lifted his head and regarded Anna with
a sort of dull insolence. He quietly huffed twice. Then the dog lay back
down and went to sleep.

Anna walked across the dirt yard. When she was halfway to the
wooden steps, the front door opened and out stepped Old Man Stallings.
On his face was a comforting grin, and he held a steaming cup of coffee
with both hands. Craggy lines were deep-set into his face. A white beard
and thinning tufts of matching hair. He wore an olive-green army jacket
with badges sewn on the arms and a lumberjack flannel underneath.

"Hidy, darlin," he said. "I's expected to see you."

Interesting statement, but not unlikely. So many of Anna's recent
movements seemed preordained and out of her control. "Good morning, Mr. Stallings."

"Morning. Now come on in. Get yourself out the cold." The old man
looked at the dog. "Don't work too hard," he said with a shake of his head.

Anna climbed the stairs. Old Man Stallings held the door open for her. The inside of his house was dark but cozy and warm. The walls were filled with interesting bric-a-brac and old signs. Advertisements for objects or products long gone with these as their lasting memory. Rusted adverts for Fire Chief Gasoline, Joe Louis Hair Pomade, John Ruskin Cigars, X-Ray Headache Tablets, and Dad's Root Beer hung scattered throughout the living room. Things of promise and life's work, living out their days as mantelpieces.

"Have a seat on the couch. Would you like some coffee?" he asked.

She shook her head.

"I don't blame you. I take it strong. Almost the texture of soup. Tastes plum awful but'll wake you up. Puts hair on you where it ain't supposed to grow. Pardon me for saying that. I can't seem to mind my manners. I'll pretend that it's old age."

Anna walked over to the couch and sat down. The warmth of the fire tingled her cheeks. She gently rubbed her hands together. Anna hadn't realized how cold she'd been. Nothing seemed to matter at this perilous moment. "No, you're fine," she said. "I prefer it strong, but I've already had my fill. Thank you, though."

Anna heard a steady vibration off to her right. She turned and looked out the ancient and sagging window. A light winter mizzle clung to the distorted and warped glass that blurred out the world.

The old man sat down in a wicker chair next to the fire. His knees cracked in a cacophony of snaps, and he winced in pain. He slowly set the coffee cup down on the floor and held out his hands toward the flames. The dancing light twisted her vision, and she thought Old Man Stallings looked like an old Grecian sage from her history books. Erect posture like a god made from stone. Perhaps he was in another life.

She continued to rub her hands together slowly and looked uncertainly at her feet. She shuddered and exhaled. After a few awkward moments, she spoke. "You said you were expecting me. Can I ask how you figured?"

"Sure. Well, I knew you'd come on. Smart girl such as yourself. Going to Georgia. It ain't no Ivy League, but I don't think we've had one go there in a long time. I knew you'd do some investigating."

Anna hadn't thought about that. Perhaps she was the smartest person in Marble Hill. She was valedictorian of her high school class. "How did you find my sister's clothing?"

Stallings picked up his coffee cup, swallowed, and responded. "I'm a member of the trails committee at Pickens Wildlife Management Area. I clean it up, pick up trash, that sorta thing. Make sure the paths are maintained. Watch for overgrowth. You get what I mean. Easy stuff. Basically, it gives me an excuse to wander the hills. I get a lot outta it. Keeps me young and from using this." The old man pointed to his head.

He paused here as if to ponder her query for another moment. Almost like he forgot the question. Then he continued slowly. "Yesterde, I was doing my walking and had to pi—use the toilet something awful. Too much of this stuff," he said and lifted the mug. "Well, I took a couple steps off the trail and started going. While I was, I noticed something strange. Black material poking outta the leaves. I woulda stopped what I was doing, but you understand. So, when I finished, I wandered on over and picked it up. Well, you imagine my surprise. A black dress and little underdrawers aren't exactly what you find there."

"Yes, sir," Anna responded.

"Well, so, I remembered hearing about your sister gone missing. I kindly put two-n-two together. I dropped 'em real fast and took off down the trail. Ass and elbows, you know? Pardon my language."

"That's fine. Go on."

"I got to my truck and went on into town. I don't have one of them cordless phones folks carry with them. Now, I kinda wish I did." Stallings took another sip of coffee and shook his head. "I didn't see much else. I told all this to the sheriff."

Anna leaned forward and squeezed her hands together. Little ticks of pain from her fingertips. "Did it seem like they were hidden? I mean, purposefully."

The old man squinted his eyes in contemplation and looked out the window. Almost struggling with himself. It seemed like this was a conversation he didn't want to have. An old code where men hid troubles from the fairer sex. He shook his head and continued. "No, I don't think so. Maybe. There were leaves covering them, but that might've been from the wind. I figure if someone was trying to hide 'em, they'd do a better job. Plenty of places for that." He tapped his knee. "I didn't see no sign of trouble. Well, besides clothes being in the woods. That's trouble enough, but you get what I mean."

"Yes, I understand."

Anna looked long and hard at Stallings. Old even when her mother was young. As if he'd skipped some discernable in-between and woke up one morning eternally aged. She knew most of his life, as what happens in a small town where everyone knows everything. He had lost his wife ten months after returning home from the war. A child born dead who took with it the one who sought to give it life. Both buried together in a single grave behind the Baptist church. The old man never remarried. Wore his wedding ring still to this day. She looked at it hanging loosely around his finger.

"I," she said reluctantly, "I just feel so guilty."

"Why's that, darlin'?"

"Leaving and going off to college," Anna said. She felt comfortable with the old man, so she opened up. "If I'd never gone, she'd still be here. I'd have looked after her. Instead, I was selfish, and all this happened." She waved her hand in the air. "I don't think I've ever felt so bad."

"Darlin', we've all done things we regret," he said solemnly. "But going off to college shouldn't be one of 'em."

Anna stared at the floor and spoke softly. "Not you. I can't believe you've done anything bad."

"That's not true," he said. Anna looked at him intensely, trying to read his mind. He sighed and continued. "You want to hear the worst thing I've done? Or, I mean, what I'm most remorseful about? Eats at me, same as you say."

"Yes, sir."

"All right. Hold on a minute." Old Man Stallings stood and walked into his little kitchen. She heard glass clank and the shuffling of his feet as he returned. "You want some of this here mulberry wine? I made it myself."

"Please."

The old man held a large mason jar filled with a dark purple liquid. In the other hand, he carried two empty glasses. He poured both halfway and handed one to her. Anna took the glass and tasted it. The wine was tangy and sweet. It burned slightly going down her throat. She drank more and felt the blood rush to her cheeks.

"I tend not to drink this early, but I'mma share something that I ain't talked about in years. But I think about it all the time. Hopefully telling it now will be a comfort to you. But I dunno. I've not spoke about it to someone else in ages. Maybe God in prayer, but he don't really count. At least in my view. He knows it already."

Anna leaned forward and regarded him.

He took another sip of the homemade wine and told her a story.

He'd been a lieutenant in the Seventh Infantry Division formed in the V Amphibious Corps under General "Howlin Mad" Smith, he told her. "We was on the Mariana Islands campaign, and God, was it hell. I'd fought in many tough battles, but Saipan was something new. We had them Japs against the ropes, but instead of giving in, they just fought harder. We was on that island less than a month, but it felt like a lifetime. It weren't a battle of miles. No, it was of inches. War to the knife."

Stallings paused, drank, and wiped his mouth with the back of his hand. "Not only did the Japs build fortifications, but the whole damn island was full of caves. I saw for myself a platoon pass by just a regular ole spot, only for a load of the enemy to jump out. The smell of gunpowder was choking, but trust me, you'd not dare wish it away. After the first week, bodies stank and bloated in the heat. We couldn't carry 'em away." He shook his head. "It was really nasty stuff."

Stallings stopped and swallowed a mouthful. He licked his lips and continued. "We were slow going but had the upper hand. I only lost two men dead out of my unit, but we were all injured. I got hit by shrapnel that stuck into the meat of my arm. I weren't gonna leave my men, so I told the medic to do his worst. He told me to bite down and that this would hurt like hell. Which, it did."

He rubbed against some phantom pain in his arm. "The whole battle was horrible and seemed like it was never gonna end. We'd kill a bunch and more'd show up to take their place. At the end, they'd just charge us with bayonets and we mowed them down. Even the wounded would banzai instead of surrendering. I saw a Jap on crutches rushing our line with a damn sharpened piece of bamboo under his arm. He was a hobbling and a hollering bloody murder. We shot him down." Stallings paused and looked up. "What else could we do?" he asked. As if querying God himself.

"But the worst was the civilians." His inflection seemed to shift, and his words took on a coarse and weighted tone. "Old men and young boys would come on after us with all sorta stuff. I personally clubbed one feller with the butt of my pistol who rushed at me with a spatula-looking thing. He was whapping my face and clapping me on the arms. So, I smashed him one good time and he dropped it and calmly walked away. Others weren't so lucky. We lost a few soldiers when civilians turned on us. Horrible business all around. At the end, many of 'em just kilt themselves. I reckon they thought we was going to torture them or something. Many went and jumped off cliffs to their death. Helping their elderly mothers go and them jumping after. Young women holding their babies and diving headfirst. I heard of elderly grandfathers shooting the household and then dispatching themselves. We saw evidence of families lying in bed together and then setting off a grenade. No one was sure, but seemed the case."

Anna sat immobilized and transfixed on the heaviness of the old man's story. "That's just awful," she whispered.

"Yeah," he said, putting his empty wine glass down. "But what I did was even worse." Old Man Stallings sat up a bit and took on an atavistic manner. "My unit came upon this little village at the base of Mount Tapochau. It was like many others we'd come across and looked deserted. Some figured they'd headed into the hills to hide, but my instinct told me otherwise. I ordered them to fan out and check the place for combatants. Or anyone. I had my sidearm out and went into this one hut and the sight chilled me." He extended his forearms and showed her the prickly goosebumps tracked along both sides.

Stallings cleared his throat. "Lying on the floor was a boy, maybe ten, with his throat cut. Well, more like he was decapitated. His head was at an odd angle and blood was everywhere. It's plain horrible to think about now, but I could see the pearl-colored bones of his spine. I heard a noise to my left, and back against the wall was a young woman. She was about your age. She stood behind a crying boy with a bloody knife to his throat. The kid was maybe four and dressed in rags with his mother little better. She was just a dern kid herself."

The old man shook his head. "We stood staring at each other for what seemed like a long time but was more like a second or two. Then she started sawing away at the boy's neck. I shot her in the head, and she fell stone dead. I went to the boy and applied pressure to the wound. A medic burst in and fixed the boy up. She hurt him bad, but I kilt her before she done got to the arteries. That boy was very brave, but I never heard nothing else 'cept that he lived."

"That's not a bad story," Anna said. "You saved that boy's life. You're a hero."

Stallings poured more mulberry wine into his glass. He looked out the window and drank. "No, no," he said. "You don't hear me. That boy lived. If I was a hero, I'd have let him die. Can you imagine the life I gave him? By saving him, I sentenced him to an existence that I can't imagine. The gash on his neck a reminder of a mother's twisted love. His family wiped out in a manner of moments. Maybe he was too young to remember what happened, but that there scar won't lie. That's forever. Every time he looks in the mirror, he'll see it. Plain as day. He'd be in his seventies by now, but that scar won't ever go away. Each morning, he'll know how his mother tried to end his life. If I live to be a hundred, that'll always be my biggest regret."

"You did the right thing," she said softly.

"Perhaps . . . I tell you what, though. I fear for you youngerns. The way this world is headed. Folks seem to think that all this craziness is takin' us by surprise. No. Every disaster and atrocity was predicted. Hell, often our barbarism was first heralded by the yearning for some imagined good. Best intentions are our undoing and that life is a misfortune without measure or bound."

"Yeah, well, you've certainly made up for any past sins. I've never met a more selfless person in my life."

He waved his hand at her. "Well, I hope so . . . I guess I told you all that to let ya know that we've all got regrets. There was something else . . . I don't regret it, but it was pretty bad. Happened around here, but I'm tired. And that's a story for another time."

"Yes, sir," Anna said.

Old Man Stallings sat back in his chair and looked at her with a sort of fierce sadness. "I reckon I said all that for some more reasons."

"What's that?"

"To warn you that we've all got a capacity for meanness, and don't trust no one."

Chapter 16

The GBI had turned the bedroom upside down. When Anna entered, she was shocked to find so much out of place. The closet was open and empty with clothes scattered everywhere. The dresser was upended, its contents strewn about the floor. The only thing left untouched was the small bookcase attached to the wall. It appeared a tornado had descended on the bedroom, and they had inspected every nook and cranny. Which, she thought, was certainly a good sign. None of the agents shared their findings with the family. When asked directly, they were purposefully vague and carried away a few bags of possible evidence. As if Anna or her mother were possible suspects. The GBI kept the information confidential. Doubtful the Pickens County Sheriff's Office was in the loop. Anna imagined scenes like out of detective movies. A no-nonsense, chain-smoking gumshoe from Atlanta riding north to crack the case. It was only a matter of time.

Since meeting with Old Man Stallings, Anna realized she needed to stay hypervigilant. Be wary of everyone. She thought long and hard about her uncle. How even he was perhaps part of the puzzle. Not a suspect per se, but those connected to him certainly were. The web of degenerates related to his line of work.

Everyone knew Brokeback cooked and ran meth. Worked with Mexicans bringing weed and guns to North Georgia. Fear of Brokeback's wrath kept friend and foe in line, yet anything was possible. Just like Stallings said: we've all got a capacity for meanness, and don't trust no one. Their uncle's love and affection might have inadvertently been her sister's ruination. Brokeback had been conspicuously absent recently, and that didn't bode well.

When Anna returned to the living room, her mother was half out of her mind crying on the floor. She was surrounded by photographs of Sam and whiskey drunk. A half-empty bottle of Evan Williams Green Label sat between her legs. Her mother's hair was unkempt and wild. Eyes bloodshot from both liquor and tears. When she saw Anna, she let out a simple wail. In front of her was a handwritten missing poster. A reward scrawled across the bottom that was just for show. The number was so outrageously large that it almost made Anna laugh. Her mother held up two photographs and stared inquisitively at Anna.

"Please, help me," her mother said while fighting back tears. "I can't figure out which one to fucking use." Exacerbated, she tossed the two back into the pile and unscrewed the lid on the whiskey bottle. She took four massive gulps and slammed the bottle down. Her mother had been so composed just the day before, yet now had completely lost herself. Like her very willingness to be brave for Anna had reached the end of its tether, and unquenchable sorrow took its place. She exhaled with a spastic shudder. "What do you think?"

Anna sat down on the couch, picked up the bottle of whiskey, and took a sip. It was nasty and cheap liquor, but the burning sensation was soothing in its own way. She felt every ounce of whiskey travel down her esophagus and tear into her empty stomach. Soon her cells would expand, and the alcohol would permeate her bloodstream. The tribulations of the day evaporating along with her feelings of sorrow. At least that was the hope.

She thumbed through the collection of pictures looking for a photo to use that was different from the police flier. One stood out from the rest. Anna reached down and picked up Sam's senior yearbook photo. She faced slightly to the left and showed her right profile. Always with a radiating smile for the camera. Yet, for Anna, the snapshot carried with it a tinge of sadness. The story behind the picture raced back. Another bitter memory that burned her heart. She sipped the cheap whiskey and stared at the portrait.

Anna and her sister were always fighting over clothes. Anna worked at the Boho Boutique in Ball Ground their senior year of high school. With her 30 percent employee discount, she was never short of faux fur vests and floral dresses, lace bralettes, and last season's UGGs. Sam bought most of her clothes from Walmart. Anna was always protective of her expensive outfits and hated the fact that her sister often borrowed them. Especially without permission. The day of senior portraits was no different. Sam had taken Anna's new blouse and hidden it in her book-bag. It was pricey, and Anna had spent all summer saving up to buy it. When it came time to take the class photos, Sam changed in the bathroom and wore it for the shoot. Anna found out about her sister's theft and flew into a rage. It was a fight of epic proportions. Hateful and cruel words were said between both parties. Finally, Anna slapped her sister. Just one terrible, loud concussion that froze the sisters in an attitude of horror. They'd never been physical before. When the dust settled, they collapsed into each other's arms. Tears were shed and apologies made.

Up until now, Anna had harbored anger. Faced with the photo, she realized that was insignificant. Her bitter feelings withered away.

"This one, Momma," she said, holding up the class photo. "I think it's the one."

Her mother took the picture and looked at it for a long time. "Yes," she said with a sigh. "That's perfect." Then she started to cry again.

Anna joined her mother on the floor. She wanted to embrace her, but couldn't. Something blocked her ability to provide affection. The words of the old man reverberated. *Don't trust no one.* A thunderous echo of warning. What role had her mother played in all this? *We could all be held accountable*, Anna thought. *Perhaps we should be.*

Anna's role was clear. She'd abandoned her sister and run off to the University of Georgia. She could've gone to the University of North Georgia or Kennesaw State and lived at home. Commute and still receive a fine education. Instead, she took the first opportunity to flee. On the surface, Sam never complained, but that didn't mean resentments weren't there. While Anna was off doing bigger and better things, Sam remained. She might've gone to a local community college, but she was paralyzed with inaction without her sister around. She was stuck in a shit town, with a shit job, and shit prospects for a better life. These truths were highlighted with absolute clarity by Anna's absence. Sam might've felt the weight of the world and the toxicity of living in a shadow.

And what of their mother? A woman of abounding love for her children and heroin. In the past, gone for days with itinerant boyfriends who plied her with dope, used her for sex, and abandoned her when bored. Now, coasting through her addiction on the whiskey and marijuana maintenance plan. Maybe she figured anything was better than following her husband to the grave from an overdose. Her sorrowful path laid bare. Still working at a dead-end job as a waitress at the Pancake House and living in a barely habitable trailer. Working daybreak to backbreak for minimum wage. A mother's whole existence an example of what not to do. Perhaps Sam saw her mother like someone trapped in mirror glass. Only age separating the two.

Please, Anna silently prayed. *Please have just run away.*

Anna collected Sam's senior picture and the homemade reward sign. She looked at her mother and felt a stinging hurt in her chest that was a cocktail of sadness and anger. Try as she might, there was nothing to alleviate her mother's pain. Not even heroin would drive it away. Some things just can't be helped.

"I'mma take this to the store and make copies," Anna said. "And I'll start putting them up around Jasper."

"Okay," her mom whispered. Her soft voice cracked and waivered like a wholly frail and fragile thing. Like she was totally boundless to this horrible desperation.

Anna stood. Before leaving, she said, "I love you, Momma."

Her mother didn't respond. Not even a whisper. She raised her hand in farewell but didn't even look up. Only stared transfixed on a mysterious stain on the carpet. One of many that the girls had created throughout the years. Spills and splashes in their multitude. Their mother screaming in rage at each transgression. Perhaps now playing them over on a loop of regret. She faced the same torturous guilt and feelings of culpability that might never go away.

Anna nodded solemnly in understanding and walked out the door.

Chapter 17

The raw, cold breeze ripped through the mountains and bit into Anna's fleece. She held a stack of missing person posters in one hand and a roll of duct tape in the other. The temperature flashed 40 degrees Fahrenheit on the bank sign, but the bitter windchill made it seem much worse. Anna's fingertips tingled and turned blue, but she continued attaching the posters, one on each side of every lamppost. It was slow going and took the better part of an hour to finish one side of Main Street. Several cars passed and slowed to watch but sped away when they recognized her and the situation. The bizarre aspect of southern hospitality where a respectable distance is paramount to butting in.

Anna crossed the street and started on the other side. A gust of wind picked up and ripped the flyers from her numb hand. The stack of papers flew into the air and scattered across the main thoroughfare.

"Fuck" she shouted and ran after them.

Thankfully, over half of them fell flat in the middle of the road, while only a few kept skittering across the street. Anna collected nearly all of them, but one danced in the breeze just out of her grasp. She chased it, bent over in a half crouch and swearing all the while. Then her twin's missing poster came to an abrupt halt when a dirty work boot stamped square in the middle. Anna looked up and saw Billy Travis standing there in the same outfit he wore at the bar two nights before.

Then he looked down.

"Oh God," Billy said with a tinge of panic. "I'm so sorry." He quickly picked up the poster and tried to dust off his boot print. "I didn't mean to step on that. I thought it might've been trash. Not, well, that." Billy straightened the paper out as best he could and handed it to Anna. His cheeks were pink from either the cold, embarrassment, or both. He seemed very awkward and unsure.

"That's okay," Anna said as she shuffled the missing poster with the others. "I've got plenty." She held up the ruffled stack. For some bizarre reason feeling the need to mollify him.

Just then, the wind picked up again and whipped loose strands from her ponytail. Anna tucked the unruly hair behind her ear and took a step back. She felt the temperature drop and was far from finished.

"Well, thanks," Anna said. "I've got to keep putting these up." She turned to leave.

"Do you need some help?" Billy asked.

Anna stopped and thought about all she needed to do. She wanted to be alone with her thoughts, but she knew she needed any and all assistance to get this done. Precious time was slipping away. Every second counted. "Yes, please. That would be a big help."

He smiled. "All right, let's do this."

They jaywalked across the empty street. The few working establishments on Main Street were open, but no one was about. Jasper felt like a ghost town. Swallowing and strange. She'd always felt indifferent to the county seat. A tiny town full of pretention. She'd take her Marble Hill enclave over it any day.

They walked over to the unfinished streetlamp, and Anna handed Billy the tape. "I'll hold the poster up and you tape it."

"Sure," he said and unfurled a length of duct tape. He bit into it and tore it free. Billy adhered the top and repeated for the bottom. As a team, they were quick going. They hardly spoke, and Anna actively set her mind to other things. Anything to help her forget for a moment. At one point she began hauntingly mouthing just above a whisper "Cake by the Ocean," and was taken aback when Billy joined in. A song that didn't exactly fit the country-boy mold. Despite her initial reticence, his presence evoked a strange yet calming sense of security. She had misjudged him. Anna felt a little at peace knowing that he was there.

It didn't take long for them to finish placing the missing posters on each side of every streetlamp. Anna looked down the main thorough-fare at the green posts. There was her sister, Sam, for everyone to see. A constant reminder for the people of Jasper that the Renfros needed their help. In a sense, one of their own. Maybe she was hiding out at a local motel or holed up out of sight. Hopefully, if someone knew something, they'd make a call.

Anna turned to Billy. "I've got to ask local businesses if they'll let me put flyers up in their windows. Thanks for helping me out. It would've taken a lot longer without you."

"Would you like some company?"

She paused and considered this. In high school, they were strangers. Aware of the other, but that was all. He was an outlander from Tate. A blip on the map that made Marble Hill look cosmopolitan by compar-ison. Anna regarded him for a moment. Short in stature, but thick and strong. At first glance, a little scary. Yet now he seemed harmless. Kind of cute in his own way. It wouldn't hurt to have him tag along. She might even learn something about the night Sam disappeared.

"Yeah," she said. "That would be nice."

He flashed her a toothy grin. "All right. Want to take my truck?"

Anna hesitated and hoped he didn't see the expression of trepida-tion on her face. She had let her guard down. The words of Old Man Stallings played over in her head: *We've all got a capacity for meanness, and don't trust no one.*

"How about you ride with me. I'm parked just down the street."

"All right," Billy said. There was no hint of disappointment or anger. No sense that this foiled some diabolical plan. Just someone who wanted to help in any way he could. A refreshing change from her boyfriend. Or, ex-boyfriend.

The day waned, and the sun burned opaque through the clouds in the west.

Anna unlocked the car, and they both got in. She cranked the engine and waited for it to warm up. Billy tapped his knee soundlessly with his index finger. She rubbed her hands together to fight off the cold. The missing posters sat in her lap. Sam was smiling up at her. A tangible and false derivative that hurt her heart.

"Where all do you want to start?" Billy asked.

"That's a good question," Anna said with a sigh. "I was thinking about beginning at the Rite Aid and heading north."

"That'll work," he said with a smile. "Let's roll."

All of the business owners were more than happy to oblige. The two hit every location with an open sign. Each shop seemed to chip away at bits of her armor. Sapped Anna's strength. Most of the proprietors or workers shied away from looking Anna in the eyes. As if doing so might inaugurate them into this tangled web of despair. She didn't exactly blame them. Were this anyone else, she'd probably do the same.

Thankfully, Anna had help.

Billy did most of the talking. He seemed to morph before her very eyes. She recalled him as a shy and quiet kid in high school. Both known and unknown by everyone. From the looks of Billy's greasy hands, Anna surmised that he'd taken up the family trade working at the auto repair shop.

After an hour, she drove her car north across Main Street, but instead of stopping at another business, Anna parked along a side street with the engine running. The radio played softly through her speakers, and the two sat quietly for what seemed like a long time. She glanced over at Billy. He contemplatively stared out the window. After a few moments, he looked at her and smiled. Neither said a word. Their silence orchestrating a great deal.

Finally, Anna broke the spell. "This is all a bit surreal. I never thought I'd be doing this. Never in a million years. Especially not with . . ." She reached over and touched his arm. "No offense. I really am grateful for your help."

Billy nodded. "I know what you meant."

More silence, but less awkward. "So, what brought you all the way out here?"

"I was seeing my probation officer."

"Oh gosh," Anna said with a half laugh. "What did you do?"

"Nothing breaking the law or anything," he said. "I got a DUI here a while back."

Anna smirked. "I've got some bad news for you, Billy."

"What's that?"

"Driving under the influence is against the law."

"Smart ass." He smiled. "I meant that I didn't do something all that bad. A dumbass thing to do on my part. Didn't hurt anyone or anything. Just myself. That son of a bitch was expensive, let me tell you. I'll be paying that shit off for the rest of my life. Dad basically owns me. He never paid me much to begin with. Now, I work for free."

"Where are you living?"

"Well," he said with a little trepidation, bordering on embarrassment. "I've got an old travel trailer that's on the property. A 1974 Winnebago around back of my folks' place. It ain't much, but it's home. Better than staying under my parents' roof."

"That's cool, though," she said. "It's still your own place. I'm sure some hipster would pay a fortune to live in it."

"Yeah . . ." He paused and shifted his weight. The car radio was playing softly in the background. "Can I ask you something?" He rubbed his thigh with both hands. "You don't have to answer."

"Sure," Anna responded. She knew the question he would ask. "It's fine."

"What do you think happened?"

Anna sat back and looked out the window. She waited for her mind to create some coherent response. This was something she'd asked herself a thousand times yet never fully expressed to someone else. After a time, she turned and looked at Billy. He watched her with sympathetic and concerned eyes.

"Hopefully, she's just run away," Anna said. "Got tired of life here and split." She gave a muffled sigh and continued. "We used to share dreams about getting away. Often staying up all night living out our fantasy in a make-believe world. The stories changed as we grew up. But our imagination had one constant theme, and that was escaping Marble Hill. Getting out of North Georgia and creating a better life. Never living in a trailer again. Owning one of those mansions near the governor's house. Hell, just getting the fuck outta here."

"I believe everyone in the county wants that," Billy said.

"No, I know," Anna said with tears coming to her eyes. "But I was making it happen. By heading off to college, my dreams were coming true. I was on my way out. Maybe she saw the writing on the wall."

"Yeah."

"That's not what happened, though. I can hope, but I know that's wrong. Call it twin's intuition . . . Someone has her. She didn't leave on her own. Sam would never do that. Something horrible has happened. I just pray it's not as bad as my imagination tells me. I don't think she's dead." She took several deep breaths to keep from losing her composure. "We've always had a cosmic connection. If one of us was hurt, the other would feel it. Like in the movies, but this is real . . . I know she's still alive. At least for now."

"Hold on to that," Billy said. He clasped her hand and squeezed. A soft reminder that someone else cared. She needed that. Anna rubbed the back of his hand with her thumb.

"I'm trying, Billy. I really am."

The overcast world shifted slightly with the setting of muted light. It would be dusk soon. Another night with Sam gone.

There was still so much to do, Anna thought. Yet just sitting in the running car and listening to the radio provided a much-needed respite. She had found someone to talk to. An outlet to vent her stinking mind-set. Flirting with the possibility she's gone. Anna looked at the clock on the dashboard. It read 4:45. She'd spent all afternoon putting up missing posters.

"I hope I'm not keeping you from anything," she said.

"No, I've got nothing on my plate. It's fine—"

Just then, a voice interrupted the song on the radio. "This is an update from WKB radio. During the five o'clock news, our reporter Elizabeth

Peters will have an exclusive interview with the sheriff of Pickens County regarding the missing Samantha Renfro. Turn to Channel 2 for more details."

"Fuck," Anna said. "I've got to go. Where are you parked?"

"Don't worry about that. I'll walk. It's not far. Just get home."

"Okay . . . Billy, talking to you has been so helpful. I don't think I can put it into words."

"Do you want my number? For if you need more help? Or just to talk about anything."

"Sure, that would be nice." Anna took out her phone and handed it to Billy. He punched in his number and "A Country Boy Can Survive" played from his pocket. He handed back her cell phone.

"Thanks," she said.

"No problem . . . Now, get out of here. And be safe."

The second he shut the door, Anna sped away.

Chapter 18

Anna raced home, straightening out the curved roads and crossing double yellow lines. Brokeback would be disappointed, she thought. Not keeping it between the mustard and mayonnaise. Ahead was her driveway, and she slammed on the brakes at the last minute. Tires screeched, and Anna heard the gravel spitting the wheel well. Racing up the steps, she cleared them in two successive bounds. Boards creaked in agony with her footfalls. It was one minute to five o'clock. She couldn't miss the news segment.

Anna nearly tore the clapboard door off the hinges. Inside, Rufus lay on the couch and didn't acknowledge her presence. Her mother was passed out on the floor with the empty bottle of whiskey serving as a pillow. Pictures of Sam scattered all around.

Anna was irate. To say anything different would've been the understatement of the year. Her cheeks burned, and she felt sweat despite the stinging cold. Her hands wouldn't stop shaking. The fucking sheriff wasn't true to his word, she thought. He had promised that they'd be the first to know, yet Anna had to find out about the news segment from a third party. All he needed to do was make one phone call.

Perhaps the sheriff assumed the same about her. Probably repercussions from that disastrous interview with Trevor. After it had aired, Anna's social media exploded, and she'd had to shut them down. "Damn him," she whispered. "Damn them both."

Anna flipped the channel to WKB. Live and in living color was the selfsame news reporter from the day before. She was standing in front of the Pickens County Sheriff's Office. A huge smile plastered across her face.

". . . our exclusive interviews with Sheriff Jeffrey Haskins and Georgia Bureau of Investigation Agent Michael Lafferty."

The scene cut to the sheriff.

"What updates can you give us regarding the missing person's case of Marble Hill resident Samantha Renfro?"

"Well," the sheriff said, "we went to a scene yesterday where we found evidence that Samantha Renfro might've been abducted. We're hunting down every lead that we've got. Uh, we've called in different agencies, we've got tracking dogs, helicopters, everything we could get to help in looking for the young lady. As of this time, we have found some evidence, but our office don't know about any suspect or whom that might be. We ain't sure if it's an enemy or a friend. I doubt we'll have much more until we get additional things together. We're still doing preliminary investigations here at the sheriff's department. To help us, though, we've got a captain from the highway patrol here and several members of the GBI."

"This seems like a huge investigation," the reporter said. "I've never been to a missing person's case of an adult and seen this type of response. So quickly, that is. Is there something else behind this? Or, what I mean is, why the influx of so many officers?"

"We are not sure at this time. We are taking every precaution that we know to take. Whatever it might be. That's what we're trying to prepare for."

"What's the search area of operations?"

"The initial search area we were looking at was five miles square from Marble Hill," the sheriff said. "Since then, it has been expanded. Specifically, into the Pickens County Wildlife Management Area. Don't know exactly how far in there. We've got volunteers in the area that are doing foot and horseback searches. We've got everything that we know to bring."

"Do you believe that Samantha might still be in the woods?"

"We don't have any idea. Our assumption is that she might be. But we have no proof beyond a few articles of clothing."

"Has something like this happened before?" the reporter asked.

"The small rural community that we live in, we never dreamed that this would happen. Um, but, it has, and I guess big city things are coming to our areas. It's very disturbing for the residents of the town, and for law enforcement. We are praying for the family and the young lady. It's our hopes and our prayers that we find her alive."

Anna watched as the screen panned over to an official-looking man wearing a nicely pressed suit. Pale skin and fresh-looking. Almost like he'd never worked a day in his life. It was a far cry from the sweat-stained and dirty uniform the sheriff wore. She was unsure what to make of that.

"Agent Lafferty, what is the GBI doing in this case?" the reporter asked.

"We are working with the Georgia Wildlife Resource Division to deploy site imaging technology in the Pickens Wildlife Management Area," Agent Lafferty said. "These are specifically looking at isolated areas and places that are difficult to reach on foot. Also, covering specific waterways to see if we can develop some leads. We also have a helicopter in the air with infrared thermography. The GBI is directing law enforcement and volunteer efforts for neighborhoods and surrounding woodlands. We are hoping that with all of this combined, we will find some evidence of Samantha Renfro's whereabouts. Additionally, special agents from the GBI are piecing together a narrative of her last known movements and where she might be. Overall, we ask that everyone in North Georgia and the rest of the state remain vigilant. She might be anywhere. Please, look on the GBI website, our Facebook, and Twitter for more information. You never know what might help us solve the disappearance of Samantha Renfro."

The scene changed to outside the Jasper Diner. The reporter was standing beside a girl who looked vaguely familiar. Anna tried to recognize her but drew a blank. Then she remembered. Her name was Cassady something-or-other, an acquaintance from high school. She hardly knew Sam.

"I'm here with a close friend of Ms. Renfro. What can you tell us about Samantha?"

"She's beautiful, sweet, and a good Christian girl. Kinda shy and quiet until you get to know her. And then, she's just funny and kind. Samantha's amazing."

"Have you spoken to the family?"

"Oh yes. Right now, they're just trying to be strong. You know, it doesn't seem real. It's the last thing anyone would ever expect. Saying that, they're a close family who're trying to hold it together. Everyone just wants her back."

The camera panned back to the reporter. "Here in this small North Georgia town, a mystery is brewing. We at WKB will keep you up to date on the latest. This is Elizabeth Peters, signing out."

Anna sat back with her mouth agape. *That lying bitch.* She shook her head in disgust and turned off the television. The room seemed locked in a vacuum. Yet her mind wouldn't hush. It whirled with indigestible curiosity. Words echoed that Stallings said just before she drove away: *Life is a misfortune without measure or bound.*

Just when she thought it couldn't get worse. If Sam had run away and she saw this, there was no coming back. Anna felt affronted and guilty for her own part. Her whole world crashing down and all Anna could do was watch it in wonderment. Like a thing happening to someone else.

She looked at her mother on the floor and watched her chest rise and fall irregularly. Anna stood, went over, and leaned down. She raised her mother's left eyelid with her thumb. The capillaries were blistering red and surrounded the pupils like a spiderweb. The lines retreated down a terrible vortex of darkness. Anna pushed the eye shut and opened the other. It was the exact same.

Anna sat back on her heels and stared across the trailer at nothing.

They shut her out, Anna thought. But she wasn't done by a damn sight.

"We'll see about that," she whispered. "And we will. You better believe it."

Chapter 19

In her dream or dreamer's dream, it was night in the canyon. Out there in the dark, the chatter of a nameless river sounded enormous. The sheen of moonlight bouncing off the limestone walls. It flooded the rocky edifices and filled Anna's vision with light of an unfamiliar color not seen elsewhere. She carefully tested each step on her way down and felt the pure embodiment of a nonbeliever. Anywhere but a dreamscape and she'd know this was nothing more than a solipsistic trial.

Anna reached bottomland and walked through the woods carrying a lantern. Shadows from it swinging among the dense and tangled trees. She wore a flowing white dress that created a wraithlike silhouette behind her. Ahead was an opening that led to a field. Her faint lamp illuminated a thin fog coating the ground.

Though she walked through the valley. Above, the stars were brilliant and shone like a perfect planetarium painted upon the night sky. Anna cast a glance upward to check for inclemencies. Nothing but the severity of her heart. The weather was cold. As she continued on, the tall wheat on the ground parted before her. Magnetism pulled her forward.

She entered the woods on the other side. She'd gone a good mile into the forest when Anna found the body. It was placed not to be seen or found. Anna stopped and stood for a long time. Finally, she walked forward and knelt over her sister.

Sam's skin was so pale, and her golden hair contrasted enormously against the dark tableau. A bit of color in the gray desolation. Anna's lantern flickered mirrored light against her twin's enameled eyes. Blue lips and tinged skin. Limbs stiff and wooden. Anna placed her hands together in prayer.

"Saver her, Father," she whispered. "At the hour of her death."

Anna understood that the world was a mystery without limit or measure. She felt entrapped in this implacability, the ever-expanding universe held no prescription of her soul. She considered the need to purge herself from jurisdictions that assaulted her existence.

Anna woke. She'd been crying in her sleep, and tears had dampened the pillow. A burning sensation in her chest. Anna's soul ached in a way that she didn't understand. Existing only in dominions that lay claim to the dead. Some sort of subconscious atavistic rage and loathing.

In the deepest regions of her heart, she knew that Sam was truly gone.

Chapter 20

Anna knew what the knock on the door was about before getting out of bed. She walked down the hallway with muted footfalls. Her mother was passed out on the couch and didn't hear the loud banging. Her inconsistent snoring reverberated around the tiny trailer.

Cold beads of sweat tracked down Anna's forehead, and she whispered one last prayer.

The Pickens County Sheriff stood on the front porch with hat in hand. He nodded in some perverse and cursed ritual of acknowledgment. The first light of morning crept above his shoulders, and he looked gutted. A struggling pilgrim weighed down with terrible news. The gray dawn morphed him momentarily into a chimera from a fevered nightmare. Anna didn't know why, but she felt immediately sorry for him. As if the information he harbored plagued his heart just as much as it did hers. They stood facing each other for a long time.

He closed his eyes like a man in quiet meditation. Then he opened them and spoke. "Good morning, Anna. Do you mind if I come in for a moment?"

Anna shook her head. "Momma is asleep, and I don't want to wake her. Not yet."

Here, awful defeat set in. Wretchedness of spirit took hold. Despite the morning breeze, Anna felt blistered as if some inward fire blazed mightily. She looked away and bit her lip, fighting back a flood of tears. The neutered winter landscape bleak and unsettling.

Finally, she collected enough courage to ask. "Where did you find her?"

The sheriff didn't respond at first. He took a step back out onto the porch and pointed at the ratty couch. "Please, sit."

Anna did as she was told.

He leaned forward. "I wish I knew what to say . . ."

"I know she's dead. Where was the body?"

He sighed. "Toward the back end of the Pickens Wildlife Management Area. About a mile or so past Copperhead Valley. A couple of old boys searching on horseback found the remains."

There it was, Anna thought. Her dreamscape molded into a nightmarish reality.

"Little more, though," the sheriff said. "We're gonna need you to come down to the coroner's and help us identify the body." He shuffled his hat uncomfortably from one hand to the other. "We've got us a situation."

"What?" Anna asked. A torturous flash of panic raced up her spine and sent stinging shots of pain reverberating from her prefrontal cortex into her cochlea. An endemic pain true to twins. *Jesus fucking Christ*, she thought, *how can this possibly get any worse?*

"Well . . . I just want to say that I hate to ask you to do this thing. If you don't want to, nobody would blame you . . ."

"I know it, Sheriff. But you ain't answering my goddamn question."

Anna saw a chink in the armor. Tears filled the sheriff's eyes. "We found her body, but not all of it. Her head and hands are missing. Us down at the department are fairly sure it's her. We were hoping that you could identify her anyway, for official purposes."

Anna looked at the floor in complete shock. It seemed like the sheriff was speaking in slow motion. Her brain struggled to keep up.

"Do you understand what I'm saying?" he asked.

She stood up but wobbled a little. The sheriff reached out and took her by the arm. He steadied her as best as he could. She smiled at him weakly and took a cautious step. The next planted more firmly. "I'm all right," she said. "Just let me get my coat."

"Do you want me to come in and tell your momma?"

Anna shook her head. "No, Sheriff. Best let her sleep. Give her a few more hours of hope. She might be having a good dream."

"You know, I hurt for you and your momma."

Anna paused. She wanted to tell him that we all lack the ability to share another's pain. We can imagine it, but it's something we can't feel. Instead, she gave him a slight nod and went inside.

Chapter 21

Anna counted the single yellow marks in the middle of the road. The sheriff drove in complete silence, and Anna was grateful for that. The only noise was the occasional bleep through the radio attached to his shirt. It was full light. In the sky, the clouds created shifting specters of baleful mosaics just above the ridgeline. She watched a hawk plunge and crest against the mountainous backdrop. Then it spun and disappeared apparently into the sun. The gray winter trees looked like the inner workings of something yet to be built. There wasn't any traffic either way. The engine revved powerfully as the sheriff hugged the curves headed into town. Instead of driving through Jasper, he turned off and took back roads to the station.

The sheriff drove around to the back of the building and stopped in front of a tall chain-link fence topped with razor wire. He spoke into the radio, and the gate slowly opened. The sound of it faint and flat. The cruiser pulled slowly into an open bay made of concrete blocks. The sheriff shut off the engine and got out. Anna followed.

Two deputies stood by a heavy steel entryway and nodded in acknowledgment. One of the officers used a strange-looking key to open the door then stood back and held it for them. He purposefully averted his eyes from Anna as she passed. She didn't blame him.

The sheriff led her down a long, brightly lit corridor. She shivered in a way that transcended cold. Each footfall was a step closer to uncovering the terrible truth.

Anna's heart hammered in her chest. Every cell vibrated in pain. It was amplified and repeated into a single drumbeat and frequency of unbelievable anguish. She felt a bit like a madwoman stalking a carcass.

The nightmare made tangible. The unmistakable truth that her twin sister—her best friend—was now nothing more than a headless corpse. Up until then, she prayed it was just conjecture. She already knew what to look for. The matching tattoo of birds growing larger as they sailed upward. Sailing away with the simple hope that their hearts might be somewhat restored. In hindsight, it pained Anna to think just how wrong they were.

They had been identical in almost every single way. Yet that was no more. Her twin was dead. That part of the mystery, now over. Another one just beginning. They'd finally found her. No longer lost. At long last, Sam was coming home.

The sheriff led Anna toward a door marked "Coroner." He removed a big set of keys from his belt and unlocked the deadbolt with a heavy clank. He stood back and held the door open. Anna entered and saw a set of stairs leading into the belly of the building. With each step, she felt the temperature drop. That was all right. It matched the slow thunder of pounding sorrow in her heart.

At the bottom of the stairs, Anna reached for the door handle but the sheriff stopped her. "Look, I know this will be hard. But we've gotta find who's done this."

"I know," she said.

The sheriff nodded and opened the door.

An even colder splash of air struck Anna. It bit down deep to the bone. The room reminded her of a meat locker, and perhaps it was. Inside the middle of the room sat a metal slab table where there lay atop a human mold covered in white cloth. She took two steps forward and noted how the outline of the body was deformed and strange. A figure like something out of a fun house. A pile of wire hangers under a sheet. A wave of nausea washed over her. Anna thought she was going to be sick.

In the corner stood Dr. Pollard, family physician for most of Marble Hill and also the Pickens County coroner. He wore blue scrubs, a green smock, and latex gloves. Anna looked at him, but he shied his eyes away.

He, too, was impacted by the horror of the situation. Perhaps everyone was.

Dr. Pollard had brought both girls into the world. Took care of them as children. Saw their progression into young women. Never charging their mother full price for checkups. Knowing that many in the county would go without medical care otherwise. Now, he was responsible for ferrying Sam off.

Pollard stepped forward and waited for Anna to approach. She did so cautiously.

"Anna, I want you to tell me if this is your sister's tattoo," Dr. Pollard said. He pulled back the cloth and delicately tried to move the ankle into clear view. Sam's body was stiff with rigor mortis. The bottoms of her feet were stained with dirt. Indelible signs that Anna didn't fully understand beyond the horrible truth that her sister had met a terrible death.

But there they were. Birds in flight. "Yes," Anna said and stepped back. She reached down and pulled up her right pant leg. The sheriff saw the replica imprint that matched the corpse. He nodded and motioned for the coroner to cover the body. Dr. Pollard did so. Finally, the old man looked at Anna. She saw tears in his eyes. One wide streak down his cheek. He wiped it away with the back of his latex-covered hand.

"I'm so sorry, sweetheart," the doctor said. "I'll take good care of her."

"I know you will . . . Can you tell me if that happened before or after she died?" Anna pointed in the direction of Sam's neck. A grisly question, she thought. But the time for being a meek and scared little girl was over. She wanted to know what the fuck had happened. Fear and sadness dissipated. Those futile emotions were replaced by unadulterated rage. Hot bursts of fire flashed to her cheeks, and she saw red. Someone had brutally murdered her twin sister. And Anna would make it her life's work to see that the murderer was punished. She would tirelessly fight to ensure that they died for what they did.

"I don't know at this time. Don't even have a time of death. I think around thirty-six to forty-eight hours. I've only given the body a preliminary look. The autopsy will start here shortly. Just waiting on a medical examiner from the GBI to arrive. They have their own separate investigation that I'm not privy to." He crossed his arms awkwardly behind his back. "After that, I'll tell you what I can. What the sheriff will allow . . ." Dr. Pollard cut his eyes from Anna's. "I'm afraid we won't be able to release the body for some time."

"I understand," Anna said. She turned to the sheriff. "What now?"

"Now, we get you back on home," he replied. "This stage of the investigation is over with. From here, we find the killer."

That last word stiffened her back. "I don't know what I'll tell Momma."

"Don't worry," the sheriff said. "I get paid to do that sort of thing."

"Okay . . . thank you."

The trip home only made her angrier. As they drove through Jasper, Anna looked both ways down Main Street. She saw her handiwork from the day before. All the effort put into getting the word out had come to naught. Dozens of worthless missing posters dotted the lampposts. The lost now terribly found. She dared not delve too deeply into her conscience. There resided the fleeting murmur that such pressure fostered the rash act. Perhaps her best efforts incubated Sam's destruction. No, Anna thought. This brutality was beyond anyone's control. That fact just hardened her resolve. Chiseled oaths in her heart that only blood would legitimize. A sort of primal rage. Revenge creating things from the simple hope that hearts might thereby be somewhat restored.

When the sheriff turned onto Cove Road, he broke the stalemate of silence. "I'm gonna tell you some things that might or might not surprise you. Either way, I feel it's my duty as your elected official to share it. I'm charged to look after the folks of this county, and I can't help but hurt knowing that I've let your family down."

"I don't think it, Sheriff."

"Well, I appreciate you saying that . . . Look, I'm gonna shoot straight. Your uncle is gonna come under a lot of scrutiny. Specifically, from me and the GBI. Do you understand what I'm getting at?"

"He had nothing to do with this . . . Brokeback loves Sam." Anna winced like she was struck dead in the chest by an invisible force. "I mean, loved."

"I don't disagree with that point. At all. But you don't cook meth and run dope without making some pretty bad enemies. I know for a damn fact that your uncle has run out of the county a couple of serious players. Stopped gangs from coming into Pickens and takin' hold. Which, if I'm honest, I might be half-grateful for. Trust me, it ain't a stretch of the imagination to see that this is probably an act of revenge. The Mexicans are known for doing this sorta thing to make a point . . ."

The sheriff paused as if divining another thread and continued. "Now, I hate to say it, but there's more. The GBI wants your uncle dead to rights. This whole mess is only gonna get worse before it gets better. I just want you to be prepared."

He stopped to wipe his brow with the back of his hand. "Your momma will need you. Don't get caught up in all this. Let me take care of it. You're a smart girl with her whole life ahead of you. Please, know how serious this is. I don't want you sharing a spot on that cooling slab with Samantha. You and your family might be in danger. Just stay safe. All right?"

Anna felt a quickening boil of rage rising in the pit of her stomach. At her uncle, not the sheriff. The words he spoke rang true. Practically every day, the news was filled with the barbarous actions of the cartel. Killing and maiming in acts of unspeakable brutality. As if hacking off limbs with dull axes was a casual pastime. Torturing because they had nothing better to do. Murdering Sam to get at her uncle. That made perfect sense.

The sheriff pulled his cruiser into the driveway. He drove very slowly, and Anna wondered if he was hoping to extend the time before sharing the awful news with her mom. The car rounded the slight bend into view of the trailer. Anna saw her mother leaning against the deck and smoking on the porch. The sheriff parked in front. Once they exited the vehicle, Anna's mother's face froze into a painful frame then twisted

and contorted. A terrible agony in understanding. She let out a piercing scream that echoed through the valley like the chorus of a thousand
broken hearts. A wretched multitude of indubitable sorrow crying out in
protest that sought to reach God himself.

Chapter 22

Anna gave her mother three pain pills to help her sleep. Or knock her out. Meant to waft up a haze of narcotics that would erase the terrible truth. At least for a short time. Her mother was inconsolable. Anna had never seen her so upset. Not even when the girls' father lay cold and dead with a needle in his arm. Her mother kept howling that this was all her fault. Screaming about being a terrible mother. Anna just held her and whispered softly that it was all right. Sam was in a better place. Reunited with her father. They didn't need to worry anymore because she was found. No longer lost and eventually coming home. Bitter sweet affirmation that she was singing with the angels and holding hands with Almighty God.

All of that was bullshit, though. Anna was just trying her best to comfort the only family she had left. Her fleeting belief that Brokeback was innocent in all this slipped away. He was dead to her. Brokeback's eternally maladroit life had led to this, and his hands were soaked in Sam's blood. Might as well have done the deed himself. Practically carried her to the executioner.

She knew the drugs were taking hold. Anna watched as her mother's eyes turned to glass, followed by slurring words. Eventually, she stopped crying.

"This was all preordained," Anna's mother said. "I should've known."

"What do you mean, Momma?"

"The reason I had twins. For why there were two of you. God made this happen to allow for failure. So I weren't left all alone."

"Please don't say that," Anna said.

"The Lord works in mysterious and fucked up ways," her mother said.

A strange calmness rinsed her voice. It seemed entuned with a momentary flash of clarity. "I finally see it all now. God is obsessed with causing us pain. And he loves inflicting us with agony." She shook her head. "Yes, the very same Almighty, which we're supposed to praise without question. Why, God, why? What is it about humanity that only through our misery can we be redeemed? What is it the Lord expects to hear in our anguished cries? Is it love? If it's excruciating enough, will the Almighty finally answer? If this is all a test, well, damn him. I want no part of this betrayal . . ." Her voice trailed away into intoxicated oblivion.

Then her mother started to hum a familiar lullaby. The selfsame one that she crooned hundreds of times to put the girls to sleep. Anna gently rocked her back and forth. She listened to her mother's voice until it dissipated and was no more. After a few moments, she laid her mother down on the couch and covered her with a blanket.

Anna stood and watched her mother sleep. Then she shook her head slowly.

You are wrong, Momma, she thought. *It's not God who loves inflicting pain. It is us. Humanity fears it more than anything else. Pain is our foremost undesired. As a result, our obsession with it can never be satisfied.*

Anna fled the trailer and descended the porch steps two at a time. She was on a mission. Family loyalty be damned. She headed straight for the small aluminum shed that held various discarded junk, tools, and random knickknacks they'd accumulated for over twenty years. The door creaked as Anna pulled it open. The sun lit up the small enclosure, and she was hit by the smell of decay. An animal of some kind chose this place to die. Up against the wall was an axe handle without a head. Anna snatched it and headed toward her car.

Her face was red hot, her mind filled with visions of murder. Brokeback set all of this in motion. Her twin sister dead and her mother inconsolable. The incubator of all this led straight to him.

Anna pulled her car down Highway 53 with the axe handle sitting in the passenger seat. She turned on the radio and heard the breaking news. Sam's body had been found, and the police had started a murder investigation. Person or persons unknown. Anna rolled down the window and spat with disgust. She couldn't get the bitter taste of betrayal out of her mouth. She knew exactly who was to blame. The sheriff was right. When someone engages in benighted activity, they never know what's coming down the pike. The illegality of her uncle's life's work provoked unspeakable pain. Now, it had come home.

Damn him, thought Anna. *Damn him to hell.* This man who betrayed his family. His very own flesh.

She took McClintock Drive, which ran parallel to Yellow Pass. There were many animals in the valley. Running through the middle was a river that ballooned into something sizable. The water swept past huge and ancient boulders that created various deep pools. These held bowfins, spotted bass, and yellow fins that year-round supplemented food stamps or pantries for the many Appalachian poor. All around, small colorful birds swooped from tree to tree. Evergreens and calico bushes speckling bits of color against the dead-looking ridge side. Not a single thread of order in this confused tapestry. Everything alien and beyond the kindred reaches where beasts inhabited. She was too enraged to bask in the beautiful and bizarre cognate desolation about.

Anna struggled to take charge and dictate the terms of her own fate. Her life felt completely out of control. As if she was hanging onto a slick and jeopardous precipice, her grip slowly slipping. A phantasmagoria of sensations bled into her mind and told her to just let go. *Not yet*, she thought. *Not fucking yet.*

She knew where Brokeback cooked. A place secure because it was so obvious. Only an idiot would shit where they ate. Her uncle, the police thought, was too smart for that. And he let them believe it. So, he manufactured meth right there on his property, and no one in law enforcement was ever the wiser.

Anna fishtailed onto the dirt road that led to Brokeback's dilapidated house. She drove on until reaching the locked gate that offered a bit of protection. Her rage seemed to welter up from someplace beyond the pale. Like a woman possessed with some new form of nameless rage.

She'd known anger before, but this was something wholly different. She paused briefly and looked at her reflection in the mimicked rearview. What stared back was a mirrored image she didn't dare recognize. Anna grabbed the axe handle and jumped out of the car. She ran to the gate, climbed up two bars, and hopped over it. It was a short jog to his house. She continued at a fair pace, swinging her weapon by her side as she went.

Brokeback's house was partially lopsided at one end, as if the earth had tried to swallow the den of sin into the very depths of hell. The porch sagged like a teardrop. The house was held up by jacks to keep it from toppling over. All as before, but haltingly changed forever. Anna saw Brokeback's jacked-up truck out front.

The son of a bitch is home, she thought. *Good.*

She'd not thought fully about her next move. Just that it contained the promise of mindless violence.

She headed for the large aluminum building tucked in the back of the property. Hidden in plain sight. Despite the sun overhead, thunder mumbled somewhere in the distance. The loose dirt showed signs of crossed and recrossed tracks. She stood ready by the garage and looked about. She saw nothing. Stark silence but for her steady breathing. No wind or birds or any sign of life. Anna yanked at the handle and pulled the door up. It made a terrible racket, but she didn't care. Let him come and find her. There'd be a fight. Her youthful truculence feeding a taste for ferocious rapacity. Anna wouldn't stop until she broke every damn piece of dope-cooking equipment he owned. If he tried to stop her, she'd beat his ass too.

The interior of the aluminum shed was ordered chaos. Just enough calculated insanity to serve its purpose. Making it look like nothing at all. Yet Anna knew better. She remembered as a little girl watching her uncle dig out the hole. She and Sam eating popsicles and watching their uncle work incessantly with a shovel and hauling away the dirt in a wheelbarrow. The twins anxiously waiting to see the storm shelter. Brokeback swore them to secrecy. A place to hide from torrential weather. Safety from whatever the skies might bring. The girls closely guarded their clandestine salvation. Little did the twins know, the shelter was a hiding place to bake untold misery.

Anna pulled back the blue tarpaulin that covered the trapdoor. It was little more than a wooden door set on bulky hinges. A lock mechanism secured the other end. Anna yanked on it several times and swore loudly. Calling out curses toward her uncle and God indiscriminately. She felt strength in rage like never before. Practically swaddled in it. Taking the axe handle, Anna raised it above her head and smashed it against the hatch. She repeated the exercise over and over. Her muscles burned with each new blow, but she did not let up. Long about the tenth strike, she heard the distinct sound of wood splitting.

"Fuck," screamed Anna.

She dropped the handle, which made a dull thud when it hit the hollow concrete. The wood was nearly split in two. The hatch showed no sign of giving in. Anna looked around the shed for a replacement. Atop a workbench was a rusty crowbar. She snatched it up and started prying at the padlock. Sweat beaded across her forehead, and she wiped it away with the sleeve of her coat.

"What the Sam Hill are you doing?" Brokeback asked as he . . . .

"You!" Anna screamed. She turned sharply toward the doorway. There stood the creator of her sister's demise. Half of his face blanketed in sunshine. She gripped the crowbar tightly in her right hand. "You motherfucker! You killed her!"

He tried to speak, but Anna saw no need in discussing the matter any further. Instead, she took three quick steps and swung the crowbar at her uncle. He backed away from the doorway and moved into the yard. Anna followed and chopped at him twice more. Despite his enormous size, Brokeback moved lightly, resembling a cat. For a moment, they circled each other like primitive apes. After a full rotation, Anna charged and swung the crowbar at Brokeback's head. He easily feinted and snatched the crowbar from her hands in a quick, fluid motion. Then her uncle slung the metal instrument as far as he could into the woods. Anna's eyes followed it as it disappeared into the trees.

That didn't stop her. Anna ran at Brokeback, screaming bloody murder. She started punching him in the chest and slapping his face. Clawing wildly for his eyes. Suddenly, Anna felt two huge arms wrap around her. Her uncle hugged her tightly. A comforting embrace. She squirmed and twisted, but he wouldn't let go. Finally, she quit struggling and buried her head in his chest and wept. What began as muffled cries soon morphed into uncontrollable sobs. She shook like a terrified animal and cursed his soul to hell in soft whispers. Brokeback rocked her back and forth ever so slowly. It reminded Anna of her childhood. When the world about was terrifying and new. The twins existing with a dead father and absent mother. Brokeback was one of the few constants in their lives.

Now, Anna tried to comprehend what her life had become. A seemingly turbulent exercise that she wanted no part of. The only certainty was that she didn't know what to do.

"She's dead," Anna cried. "Sam's dead. They mutilated her."

"Oh God," he whispered. "Oh God."

Anna pushed against her uncle's chest with all her might. He reluctantly let go. The rage returned. She embraced that comfortable shell. Anna stepped back and glared at Brokeback. His face was wet, and tears tracked down his face. His expression a reflection mirroring the endless complexity of utter sorrow tabernacle therein. A man among men, hurting like any other.

"I had to go identify her body. Our tattoos . . . that was the only way." She noted Brokeback's eyes were glowing red as if the reflected light of coals burned in them. "They chopped her fucking head off. And her fucking hands . . . She's gone, Brokeback. My twin sister is dead. Murdered." Her voice tightened. "And it's all your goddamn fault."

He ran his hands through his hair. "I'm sorry, sweetie, but that's not true. Not a bit. Why would you say that? I love you girls. Yer like daughters to me. You know that."

"The sheriff said this was revenge. Something the Mexicans do to prove a point."

Brokeback breathed heavily and stared off at some unknowable point in the distance. He clenched and relaxed his fists. The veins in his neck pulsed. She practically heard the calculations churning in his head.

After some moments, he spoke. "The Mexican cartels wouldn't do such a thing . . . They are blood-thirsty savages, but those bastards aren't stupid . . . They'd never kill a blonde-haired, blue-eyed white girl. Bring too much heat."

"Then who murdered my sister?"

"I . . . I," Brokeback stuttered. "I don't know."

"Why would anyone hurt her?"

"There ain't anyone around here who'd be so fucking stupid," Brokeback said. He started punching his palm. Softly at first, then harder. He kept looking about. His eyes skittering all over the place. Finally, Anna grabbed him by the shoulders and he focused on her. He was crying, and his knees buckled.

"But I swear on my momma's grave, they are dead." He spoke with fiery intensity. "I'm sure as shit gonna find out. I'll kill the son of a bitch, by gawd."

A phone rang from the bib of his overalls. He struggled for a second to remove it. Brokeback held out one finger and answered. "Yes, Blue?" He said a few hums and yesses. "All right. I'll be down by the street." He paused. Anna tried to hear the conversation, but the wind picked up and drowned out the sound. "Okay," her uncle said.

He hung up and shook his head. "That was Blue warning me that the sheriff and an agent from the GBI are on their way over here. They want to interview me. You head on out. I don't want you deeper into this shit than you already are."

"Please, let me stay. I want to listen—"

"Absolutely not," Brokeback said, cutting her off. "Go on and be home with yer momma. She needs you right now. Once I'm done talking to these fellers, I'll drop by and tell you everything I know."

"Okay," Anna said softly and turned. She took a short stutter-step and turned back. "I don't think I've ever felt so lost. I'm completely untethered. There's nothing in this world for me. Not anymore."

Brokeback stepped forward and hugged her again. "Don't say that, please. I'll find out who done this, and trust me, they'll wish the cops got to them first." His voice started to shake, and blood flushed his face. "You can take that shit to the bank . . . Now, you go on home. I gotta fix that shed up before the cops get here."

Anna nodded in acknowledgment. Her uncle turned to leave, but she stopped him by taking his hand. "I'm sorry, Brokeback. For all of this." She waved her free hand about.

"Don't," he said, gathering Anna in his arms. "I understand."

She clutched him tightly. Her uncle continued to tremble. Brokeback lifted Anna's head to regard him. She stared into his eyes and noticed that he seemed lost in his own thoughts. Predacious in attitude. Like a man in serious reflection and standing in judgment. He swayed on two unsteady legs and weaved slightly.

"My heart hurts so bad right now that I can hardly stand it," Brokeback said. "But don't you worry. This has awakened something that was better left sleeping."

Chapter 23

The sun was well up when Anna pulled out of her uncle's driveway. All about, the barren oaks and few evergreens created an apparition of haunted autumn. A world devoid and desolate that fit her well. Half a mile down the road, Anna passed the sheriff's cruiser and a black Crown Victoria screaming in the opposite direction, morphing into a blur in her rearview mirror. Anna jammed her foot down on the pedal. Her car lurched, surged, and sped onward.

With each mile, she grew regretful and morose. A lifetime of wrong, both old and new, arrayed her troubled mind. She punched the steering wheel and fought back tears.

She kept on at speed and hugged where the road angled through switchbacks down the hill until it broke free from the woods and straightened out into a valley. Clear and stark meadowlands. A creek marked its course, and Anna slowed down to cross over a little bridge in the middle. The planks groaned with the sound of lasting resistance. Along the side, Anna watched the current swirl and pool and carry on. Ebbing slowly in perpetuity. Moss attached to chunks of limestone beneath the surface danced wildly. Follow the creek south and you'd come to faster-moving water occasionally fragmented by deep pools perfect for swimming. Eventually it formed a small river that broke over a waterfall into amber depths below. The same one her sister flew from a lifetime ago.

"Samantha," Anna whispered. "I pray you didn't suffer."

Yet she knew in her heart that this entreaty was meaningless. That was the terrible truth. Sam suffered in ways beyond human reckoning.

She pulled onto Cove Road toward home. Eventually she saw the small steeple of the Baptist church. Half schemes racked her mind, and she pulled into the parking lot, turning the wheel almost inadvertently. Like someone propelled by actions set forth in a fevered dream or somewhere in the inner recesses of her mind. The sign out front proclaimed a Bible verse: "For you were continually straying like sheep, but now you have returned to the Shepherd." A collection of words that Anna didn't understand yet rang strangely true.

There were two cars parked near the entrance of the church's office. The pastor and his wife. Anna had no idea what she was doing here but felt drawn to this holy place by some kind of otherworldly magnet. Driven like a multitude of others by sorrow and unrequited questions to a house of God, seeking certainty like a lost soul for an eternally allusive answer or a gullible mortal trampling along in a transitory state of mourning. Perhaps Anna longed for an escape from the temporal and was searching for salvation in the ethereal void. Hoping to find resolutions buried within the unrecognizable tales of antiquity.

She parked in clear view of the cemetery. Inside were the bones of her father. A lonely resting place that harkened rich, haunted feelings. Soon, her sister would be one of their number. Reunited with her paterfamilias beneath the soil. A marble monument proclaiming her forever nineteen. The rusty gate leading to the hallowed ground stood ajar and bobbed back and forth in the wind. Making shape for something vanished like the outbreak of an apparition. Superstition chilled her, and Anna quickly looked away. Dare not look death in the eyes for too long.

Anna swung open the car door almost without choice. Like some other force controlled her. Perhaps it was God. She needed answers for everything and a little more. This seemed like the best place to start. As she walked across the pavement, her sneakers echoed of desolation. Her teeth clicked with the inadvertent pressure of the frosty air. She wasn't wearing a coat and finally started to feel the effects. Before, the rage had warmed her, but that burden was released and replaced by something far worse. Despite wearing none, her cheeks felt layered as if wearing too much makeup. For her, the church looked like a warm refuge of the heart.

Anna opened the door. The vestibule was brightly lit, and she heard a ruckus from down the hall. It sounded like a fierce argument. A woman's voice rose above the others like the roaring of a ceremonious grand inquisitor. Approaching, Anna tried to single out the thread of Ruth's dictation. Words and phrases reverberated in her head like mystery, fear, and the taking charge of the world. Standing outside, Anna heard the soft and distinct sound of someone crying. Without thinking, she knocked on the door. The room hushed but for a stinging set of vitriolic whispers. Heavy feet plodded toward her.

Pastor Hinson opened the door to his office. Inside, Daniel was sitting in a chair sobbing. His face was damp, and snot ran. They made eye contact, and he rose with his arms out. Both extended like the actions of the newly blind. A pleading look of hopelessness plastered across his face. He wanted to embrace Anna and share in her sorrow. That was easy enough to recognize. Oddly, she felt it too. He took several steps. Then his mother snatched him by the arm and held him back. Strong hands grasping. Quick and forceful. Ruth pointed toward the door, and Pastor Hinson suddenly blocked Anna's view. She tried to look over his shoulder inside, but he quickly took up all the space in the frame. She'd not noticed how big the pastor was. His expression morphed from panic to fatherly in a millisecond. His smile became the vestibule of a false witness.

"Hello, Anna," the pastor said. "Please, follow me." He stepped into the hallway and closed the door behind him. "Let's talk in the sanctuary." He held out his hand and pointed down the corridor. He spoke purposefully as they walked. "I want you to know how terribly sorry I am for your loss. Word reached us just moments ago, and my heart aches for your family." He placed a hand on her shoulder. "At least we can rejoice in the fact that Samantha is with God and singing amongst the angels."

At first, Anna didn't respond. What would you say? Her heart still hurt with bizarre physical manifestations. An awful stench and bitter taste that never left her mouth. Sat in the back of her jaw like the onset of a deadly cancer.

"I was planning on going to your home to speak with your mother. Still do. Counsel and support in this time of woe is very important. It's imperative that we all remember God's love. He will always guide us. We can find comfort in the rod and staff."

The pastor flipped on the lights of the sanctuary and led Anna toward the front pews. The stained-glass window surrounding the ambulatory depicted the ascension and bathed the retrochoir in a rainbow of light. The chancel was lit by a huge and particularly ornate chandelier that hung above the altar. Her eyes were drawn to the dais whereon lay an enormous and ancient-looking Bible. It was wide open, and Anna wondered if on the page was written some hidden clue that explained everything. *Nothing's ever that simple*, Anna thought.

They sat together, and the pastor faced her. Hinson placed a hand on her shoulder. "Do you mind if I pray over you?"

"No," Anna said, despite having no faith in God, or now, humanity.

"Okay, heavenly Father, please look after Anna and her family during this time of great grief. We do not understand your almighty plan, but we take consolation in knowing that you are here. Please, grant us the serenity to accept the things we cannot change, and the courage to change the things we can. Ours is not to wonder why. Ours is but to worship unconditionally. Just like your son's love for us. Despite this tragedy, blessed are the Renfro family. In Jesus's name. Amen."

"Amen," Anna whispered.

The pastor leaned in close and hugged her tightly. Unlike her embrace with Brokeback, this felt strange. Long and awkward. Forced and uncomfortable.

"There, child," he said, sitting back. "Tell me how you feel. Remember, we are in God's house. Everything is sacred, and one need not fear."

Anna rocked slightly. She was staring at an ancient stain on the maroon carpet. It looked like Eucharist grape juice or old speckles of blood. She tried to remember those tales from her youth. Somewhere in the back of her mind, a voice told her that they were meant to be the same thing. "I really don't know how I feel," Anna said. "This doesn't seem real. Like it's happened to someone else. I never expected this. Not in a million years."

"Yes, the ways of the Almighty are shadowed in mystery. We don't know his plan and aren't supposed to. It would be an insult if we did. Playing God."

"What could God possibly want with her? Taking her now?"

"Again, that's not for us to know. We must share strength in this time of sorrow and realize that all will be revealed in the fullness of time."

"I don't agree with that nor accept it. There was no reason for her to be taken from us. Not in such a horrible way."

"I understand you feel that way, but we mustn't run from the shadow of death. We must fear not. Because paradise awaits."

That old verse ran through her head. "Why did God lead her into that valley? You don't just wander there on your own."

"Ah, that wonderful verse. 'Yea, though I walk.'" The pastor leaned back in the pew, and it creaked of old wood and protest. "People misunderstand that verse. In truth, at first, I did as well. The valley of the shadow of death isn't a place one is drawn to. Nor do we get taken there." He exhaled and inhaled heavily as if preparing a long oration. "The valley of the shadow of death is our existence. We are born into it, and our whole lives we traverse it. It's that way and won't be any other."

Pastor Hinson leaned close and placed his arm around the back of the pew. Anna felt the warmth of his breath on her neck. Pulsating chills vibrated up her spine. "Think of it as the valley of life that the shadow of death stalks," he said. "The moment we come screaming into this world, until we take our last breath. The wraith haunts us, wants us, and stalks us. Pleading and yearning for just one chance. All it takes is just one tiny touch and that's it. What matters is the worth and merit we place in our time on the road. What we make of our brief existence."

He paused and sniffed deeply. As if inhaling her very scent, soul, or a thing far beyond her very understanding. He shifted and began to whisper. Like a man harboring some secret or divining a new thread of discourse. Possibly hinting at what that might be. "We've spoken about roads before, and you disagreed. That's fine, but hear me now, please, I beg of you. This is a matter of great importance. There is protection with God. His rod and staff, as the verse continues, they are meant for comfort . . . Now, this also gets misinterpreted. That God is somehow going to shield us from the evils of the world and keep us from death. No."

Pastor Hinson wiped the corner of his mouth with the back of his hand. There was saliva glistening off his knuckles, and sweat beaded across his forehead. When he opened his mouth, she noticed that he was missing several teeth. Probably from grinding during his many zealous sermons. Anna looked him square in the eyes and noted that he spoke through her. Like she wasn't even there.

He paused briefly and then continued his lecture unabated, his voice rising feverishly and gaining momentum. "The rod and staff are meant as a security. It's for keeping us from going astray and nothing more. As long as you have faith, you mustn't fear. Because heaven nears. If you haven't asked Jesus into your heart, then you should be terrified. Horrors await you beyond all Christian reckoning. We can't even imagine it—"

"Pardon me, Pastor," Anna interjected. "But what does this have to do with my sister?"

The spell was broken. Hinson shook his head and smiled. "Yes, yes." His eyes restored to this realm. Comforting and compassionate. How he turned the switch was utterly unnerving. Almost like switching a mask. Which one was real? "Your sister asked Jesus into her heart. She was saved; all glory be to God. So, no matter how badly she was disfigured, know that she is whole again and in heaven. She's an angel now. Doesn't that give you comfort?"

"What? Comfort?"

"Yes, knowing that she's with God and no longer on this earth that's filled with such suffering and sin."

A wave of fury washed over Anna. "Are you fucking serious?" she asked. "None of this superstitious bullshit gives me any comfort . . . You are just some shyster or gullible—I don't know which is worse. My twin sister is dead. That's it. If God is real, I say fuck him." She stood. "You hear that, God!" she shouted in his house. "Fuck you!"

"That's quite enough," Hinson said, calmly yet forcefully.

"Yeah," Anna said, breathing heavily. "You are right. That is enough." She spun on her heels and marched toward the exit. She wasn't going to wait around to hear any more. Anna was angry. Mostly, though, with herself. Because deep down, she knew that this false prophet spoke words of substance. Perhaps even truth.

Yet something else tugged at her as she stormed out of the Cove Road Baptist Church. She slammed the door, brokering a loud crack that echoed like a percussion against the mountains. Everywhere was an afternoon smoky haze in the valley. The grayness broken up by spotlight rays of fire. Each step was angrier. A million ideas spiraled in her mind, yet one kept pausing before flight. Frail and almost incomprehensible. Anna couldn't shake what the pastor had said. *Disfigured*. How in the fuck did he know about that? The mutilation? The sheriff and coroner weren't releasing that information. Besides those two, only Anna and Brokeback were supposed to know.

Chapter 24

Anna, her mother, and Brokeback sat in various forms of strained relaxation around the trailer's living room. The TV screen flickered with one of the *Fast & Furious* movies. Anna wasn't sure which. Each just a replication of idiocy that was made palatable by race cars and gorgeous women. Anna sipped a beer and relished the bitter taste. The alcohol did its job. She felt her cells expand and the mechanisms locked deep in her brain slow to a crawl. Her mother lay in the fetal position on the couch and hummed softly. Opaque and empty eyes. Across the room, Brokeback sat catty-corner to the television and fiddled with his hands. Rubbing them over and over. His knuckles had finally stopped bleeding.

When Brokeback arrived at the trailer, Anna had been shocked but not surprised. Her uncle was stained with blood, and his eyes burned like the destruction of a thousand suns. Brokeback's hands were deep red and caked over. He held them under the faucet for a long time. As he did, he filled her in on his own inquiry. Right after Anna had left his trailer, the sheriff and GBI agent had arrived and grilled him for over an hour. It was standard investigative bullshit. They didn't know anything and were grasping at straws. For a change, Brokeback was completely honest with them. His miniature dope empire was insignificant compared to finding out what happened to Sam. He even told them that. The sheriff understood and was of the same mind. The GBI agent seemed not to care and just wanted her uncle's scalp. Brokeback and the sheriff formed a bizarre alliance in keeping focus on the task at hand. Eventually they left, and Anna's uncle divested himself of everything but his own quest to find the truth.

Then Brokeback told Anna about driving to Smith's Hardware and finding Redbone behind the counter. Her uncle, with a huge smile on his face, asked the toothless dope addict to help him with something around back. Always in hope of free meth, Redbone hustled around the side of the shop. No such luck. Her uncle hit the addict in the face half a dozen times before asking the first question. Despite protesting his innocence, Redbone gave up names, saying anything to make the pain stop. Brokeback left him crying in the alley with more missing teeth and a broken nose.

Anna had listened as Brokeback recounted it all. "Names, names," he'd said. "Names, blood, bonemeal, and more names." Spud with his girls were next, and then all the others who orbited Brokeback's meth-filled world. Her uncle questioned them and checked off each. A visitation with all the meth addicts who held a sufficient stake of possible guilt. Justified or unjustified. The lot equitably bound together in a bizarre trial. The irrationally condemned proclaimed through blood and tears a host of false evidence to make the pain stop. After a long time, Brokeback grew tired. Even he knew that this was indeed trivial and finally admitted to his innermost self the real reason for it. Purely a manifestation of release. And it worked.

While her uncle spoke, Anna's phone kept ringing. It was Trevor. He kept inundating her with calls and messages. Only one reason for this. She sadly reckoned that news of her sister's death had reached Athens. Again, he was trying to ingratiate himself with her for his own perverse gain. She kept on ignoring him. Finally, there was a rambling string of texts that were a peculiar milieu of insincere apology and frustrated anger. Anna politely told him to eat shit and die, then powered off her cell phone.

The sadness in the trailer reached a stasis beyond measure or bound. For a long time, no one said anything. Anna watched her mother. One eye was crusted shut, and the other looked nearly dead but for a few sporadic twitches. Her hair wild and spread across the couch pillow, like a minstrel wig made up with wire. The gulf between them as wide as the River Styx. Perhaps each hearing Sam call to them from the other side. Half-muted and fading more every time. Life now providential to itself. Anna tried to think of ways to keep her twin's memory alive, but she didn't know how. Maybe living on as an ill-conceived ghost. After what seemed like an eternity of purely unadulterated nothingness, there came the distinct sound of a knock on the trailer door.

Brokeback was up in a flash. Nimble as a cat despite his advanced age. He stared long and hard at the partition and waited. Today he'd made enemies. His hand wrapped around the small of his back. A small protrusion where Anna guessed he carried a gun. Moments turned to centuries turned to instants that slowly passed. Perhaps it was just the wind. That possibility was squashed when another salvo rapped on the wood, followed by a call from the other side. It was the sheriff and he needed to talk.

Her uncle quickly turned his shirt inside out and unbolted the door. Blood still visible, but there was nothing to be done about that. As he opened it, Brokeback blocked the sheriff from entering. Anna stood behind his enormous frame and listened intently.

"Can I come in and talk to y'all for a second?" the sheriff asked. "It's about Samantha and real important. I've got an update on the case."

"Not inside," Brokeback said as he stepped out onto the porch. "Jenny ain't well, and she's finally calmed down a bit. I don't wanna get her all worked up again." He shook his head. "She's in a real bad way."

"Fair enough," the sheriff said. He stepped back and waited for Anna to join them outside. This news was for her as well.

Sleet blew sideways against the closing of day. Stinging wind that smelled slightly of snow. That, or a prequel for the cannonading of a hard rain. Already, wet wood underfoot. A host of seemingly deliberate advents. She thought about her sister. They finally knew what became of her, and she was no longer missing. Small blessings. Sam was stiff and dead, but that was infinitely better than the alternative. Yet Anna took little comfort in that.

They stood in a circle like some haunted powwow. The sheriff took off his hat and ran his fingers through his thinning hair. Anna could tell that Sam's death was taking its toll. Not just on her family, but on everyone. This was breaching the known boundaries of small-town life.

"Well, Brokeback," said the sheriff, "I know you won't take no comfort in this, but we ain't looking at you. We're gonna keep our eyes on your doper friends as suspects, but the coroner found something that's blown the lid off this here thing."

"What is it, Sheriff?" Anna asked fearfully.

"All right . . . Samantha was pregnant."

Anna gasped audibly. Then went mute as a stone. She covered her mouth, and her knees buckled. Therein lay a host of dreaded possibilities.

"Coroner said that she was seven weeks pregnant. We aren't sure if she even knew. Her blood alcohol level was so high that . . ." The sheriff paused, catching himself. He tried to take on the aura of support but failed. "That doesn't fucking matter. What I'm trying to get at is that we've been looking at this shit sideways. I've got a gut feeling that it's someone she knew. I mean, most likely this . . . this kid's father."

Anna felt Brokeback's arm drape across her shoulder. Strong and taut. This man of unspeakable violence provided support and comfort. She looked out at the newness of full dark. Nothing to see but absolute blackness without feature. A scene no different if she shut her eyes.

"We've sent the DNA down to Atlanta for testing. Should be back in a day or so. It's been given top priority. In the meantime, do either of you have any idea who the father might be?" the sheriff asked.

Brokeback shook his head. Anna rolled through her memory like a deck. Countless nights while she was at the University of Georgia and talking to Sam on the phone. She'd never mentioned anyone. No dates or secret rendezvous. Not even the slightest hint. Twin intuition didn't pick up on the tiniest possibility. Yet news of the pregnancy was absolute proof. *What about now?* Anna thought. She retraced interactions since the disappearance. Checking names off a mental list. Over and over it went.

Then her mind came to a screeching halt.

Daniel. The pastor's son.

At the press conference and then today at the church, he was overly upset. Sobbing and crying. Even reaching out to her for comfort. This she'd taken for the sad exuberance of a good young Christian man. Perhaps there was more. In fact, Anna was nearing the absolute conclusion that it was him. She wanted to speak, but there was a constriction in her throat that stymied her. Perhaps her own trepidation. The pastor's son? The most respected man in the community's child might've committed a cardinal sin. Or sins. Sex? Murder? Both? Unlikely to some, yet not entirely beyond the pale. A story as old as time. Just open the pastor's revered book.

"Daniel Hinson," Anna croaked. "Might be Daniel."

The sheriff's eyes widened then narrowed. Absurdity and truth rolled into one. Like some solitary Janus of lore. About his head was the faint pluming of breath where he'd exhaled. Ratcheted and shuddering.

"All right," the sheriff said. "I'll talk to him. Can you think of anyone else? Or anyone who might know besides you? Your momma?"

"Sheriff, she was my twin sister. We were best friends before entering this world. If anyone was to know, it would be me. And I think you ought to go talk to Daniel."

There was a strange moment of trepidation. The sheriff wasn't thrilled at the prospect. Finally, he nodded. "I'll go see him here directly." He took a step to turn around but paused and looked at Brokeback. "I'm sorry for today. Hell, I'm plumb sorry about all this shit." He raised his hand and waved it about. Almost like he was referring to the world at large. "When I ran for sheriff . . ." He paused to collect himself. Tears filled his eyes. "I've always wanted to help people . . . Put away the bad guys. But this . . . this is something new. I never signed up for dead girls. I know it's my job. But this is the most horrible thing I've ever had to deal with in my life. I don't think I'll ever get over it . . ." His voice croaked. "You have my word, Anna. I'm gonna find the son of a bitch who did this."

Just then, a gust of wind blew through the mountains. In the yard, the first droplets of cold rain smacked onto the gravel driveway. The sheriff raised a hand in farewell and descended the steps toward his cruiser. Anna and Brokeback stood together and watched him drive away. The headlights blinking through the trees. Stark color, then nothing. She followed it with her eyes until it vanished in the distance. Tracing its movements until there was only blackness.

"Come on, kid," Brokeback said. "Let's go check on your momma."

Chapter 25

One day turned into two with no news from anyone. Brokeback, Anna, and her mother remained cloistered in the trailer like latter-day redneck penitents. Inside whiffed with the stench of undisturbed air, ragged and lasting. Her uncle sallied forth only once to pick up liquor and a little food. The absolute necessities to escape reality. Disappear from the land of the living. Solace in nothingness.

They waited for the sheriff to call, but he didn't. They watched the local news, but there was nothing new to report. No discussion of Sam being field dressed in the woods like some pathetic animal. Thankfully, her pregnancy wasn't chronicled either. Anna's mother still didn't know. Nor was there any need to tell her. At least not yet. The investigators were keeping certain facts close to their chests. This gave Anna heart, but that was overshadowed by a cruel omission. Nowhere was there a discussion of suspects. No investigative leak providing names. A vision of Daniel outlined in red flashed through Anna's mind. Perhaps this man of God held more sway in the community than she imagined. Left unquestioned and unmoved.

They spoke little and stayed in the living room. Anna couldn't sleep in the bedroom. Too many ghosts lingered there. And her sleep was wracked with horrible nightmares beyond her previous understanding. Like a legion of awful had moved in and taken the place of her sister to taunt Anna. Specters laughing and pointing at all of her twin's things. Telling tales only Sam would know.

She's burning in hell, the phantoms whispered. *And she wants you to join her.*

Come on down, wombmate, Sam's voice harkened. *Please.*

Anna screamed for it to stop. Bloodcurdling and filled with agony. Supported by rage. Brokeback burst into the living room with pistol in hand, a protective and murderous look etched across his face. The silver barrel looked like a small cannon reflecting mirrored light. Brokeback saw that Anna was failing and falling back to sleep. Shivering and sick with fear, anger, and exhaustion. But there was warmth in his embrace. He didn't say a single word. No need.

Hold on tightly to the good memories, she thought. *Please, for dear life. For eventually they will go the way of all things.*

Time fluctuated between stasis and speed. Anything but normal. Anna's mother remained mute as a stone. Only moving to use more drink and drugs and return to silent sorrow. When she did, her mother tottered like a mawkish madwoman through intoxication, shifting fleetingly in and out of unawareness. Hopefully, she thought, her family hadn't hit some sort of fairy-tale loop where they'd be locked in this rotting trailer for eternity. Forever swallowed up in the spoiling stench of offal and perpetually ravaged by drafts of brutal mountain air. Moving among the weakening plywood floorboards screaming in a cacophony of agony like lost souls. Anna couldn't shake the comforting siren song of suicide. A burning sense of satisfaction in taking her own life.

Suddenly, these thoughts were shorn away with the abrupt shrieking sound of Brokeback's cell phone. Anna looked up but seemed briefly unaware. She was shivering violently. Like some other thing was in command. Good or bad, she didn't know.

Her uncle answered. "Hello," he said. "Yeah, Sheriff . . . We all here together . . . All right, I'm listening . . . Great God Almighty . . . What does that mean? . . . No, no, you're right . . . Of course not . . . Okay, I'll let them know . . . Thanks."

Brokeback hung up the phone and placed it next to his gun on the cheap coffee table. He ran his fingers through his hair and sighed, then he stood and motioned for Anna to follow him. He took two strides and was at the trailer door. Brokeback held it open and waited for her. Anna moved uncertainly and paused a time or two. Outside, the temperature sank with the sun, but she didn't feel it. Pricks of adrenaline raced through her. She walked across the soaked deck where her uncle waited.

The scene about was blue-looking from the pale moonlight. The trash-strewn yard shrouded in dense fog. Anna wondered at the time but remembered that it didn't matter. She stood uneasily with anticipation and dread next to her uncle. She felt like a soldier waiting for sunrise and the commencement of battle. Check your powder and ball. Keep it dry.

"They've arrested the goddamn pastor . . ."

Anna felt her left knee give out, but she righted herself at the last second.

"He's admitted to knocking up Sam. Can you fucking believe it? That heathen lying hypocrite no-good motherfucker." Brokeback was breathing heavily, and blood rushed to his face. He looked like he was about to explode. "I'll kill him. Graveyard motherfucking dead. Then I'mma burn that fucking church to the ground. Man of God, my fucking ass."

Anna stood paralyzed.

"Sheriff said he done admitted to being the one. The father. But denied killing her. Can you fucking believe it? Saying it's a coincidence. Ain't no such fucking thing as a goddamn coincidence. Even so, that'd be some crazy one at that. It's all bullshit."

Something tugged at Anna's heart. A small voice sounded. No truth to that. Despite what the pastor had confessed to, she knew it wasn't him. Unsure why or how, but there it was. She'd have to consider that when the shock wore off.

"I don't think—" Anna started to say but was cut off by a piercing scream from inside the trailer. Agony in its purest form. A tremendous cacophony followed. Stamping feet, flying debris, and shattering glass.

Brokeback tore through the trailer door with Anna right on his heels. The television news showed video of the pastor being led down the church steps flanked by two deputies. His hands were manacled, but he paraded with head held aloft. Like some lofty Christian martyr being persecuted by secular authorities. Believing that redemption was nigh. Anna turned away in disgust. A wave of bile rose in her gut. Then she looked over her uncle's shoulder and saw that her mother was gone. And so was the gun.

Her uncle was down the hall. Anna followed and screamed for her mother. The lights were on in the bedroom. Brokeback ran and tried to open the door, but it was locked. His enormous hand slapped on the wooden frame, and splinters sounded. He reared back and punched just above the lock. The sound of cheap metal and plastic ratcheted, but the knob still wouldn't turn.

Brokeback screamed, "Jenny, open the door! Please! Jenny, don't do anything stupid! For fuck's sake, open the fucking door!"

Nothing.

Anna was crying and screaming for her mother to come out.

"Jenny, I'll bash this fucking thing in! You know I will!" Anna's uncle looked back just for a moment and then kicked the door in.

Shards of wood went flying, and they both practically dove into the room. The scene took Anna's breath. Her mother had the pistol in her mouth and was sobbing uncontrollably. She was against the far wall with her hand out in protest. Brokeback slapped the gun away. The noise of skin on metal echoed throughout the room. He was just in time. The gun fired wildly by her mother's head and opened up a large hole in the roof. Black soot covered the side of her face. The shot sounded enormous in that tiny, enclosed space. The stench of discharged gunpowder filled the room.

Anna blinked several times in rapid succession to clear her vision. When that was righted, she beheld her mother and uncle locked in an embrace. Her mother hugged Brokeback tightly, using every ounce of her strength. Brokeback's enormous arms engulfed his sister with a hybrid of love and fear. Her mother gibbering indecipherable words with snot dangling from her chin.

Brokeback squeezed his sister and whispered softly in her ear. "Jenny, it will be all right. I love you so much. You and Anna are the only family I got. Only family *we* got." Then he looked up at Anna. His eyes were wet and full. This huge, manly man. Toughest in the whole county.

A person who struck fear with his mere presence. He was brokenhearted and shaking violently. First, tears tracked slowly down his face. Then he started to sob. He turned completely to his sister and laid his head upon her shoulder. "We have to stay strong for each other . . . We are the last remaining Renfros." Then he whispered something in his sister's ear that Anna couldn't decipher. For them and them alone. Sibling camaraderie. A thing Anna once knew but would never experience again.

There was a wet smell that Anna recognized as mountain rain. She looked up and saw the hole in the ceiling. The size of a golf ball. Already, droplets of water were trickling down onto the filthy carpet. A damp stench permeated. Anna walked over to the pistol. It reflected the yellow overhead light. The silver revolver was the most beautiful thing she'd ever seen. A sign of the world to be. Hopeful release from all to come. She cast a sideways look at her family. Such unmitigated sorrow. Neither seemed to notice her. Like she wasn't there. Or a phantom survivor of some great tragedy.

Anna picked up the pistol and held it in her hand. She was shocked by the weight of the thing. Four or five pounds of tangible fatality. A twisted image of what mortality seemed to be. The gun mirrored the darker recesses of her heart. Hers would be a collective death. Only right to join her sister. Ushered almost simultaneously into the world. Why not be carried off? Anna placed her finger on the trigger. Tight and ready. She clamped her eyes shut and pressed the frozen steel under her chin. Hole in her head to match the hole in her heart. Seemed fair.

Anna, don't, said Sam's ghost. The voice was clear and calm, powerful and steady. *You are needed here. Not just for Momma and Brokeback.* Earnestness rising. Anna seemed stung by the clarity. *But to find out what really happened. The world they've painted. It's all wrong, and only you can help make it right.*

Anna lowered the pistol to the soundtrack of her family crying. She looked over at them consoling each other in hopeless grief. Neither saw Anna's flirtation with death, nor heard the siren truth of her twin. Anna quickly pushed the cylinder release and opened up the revolver. Inside were six enormous bullets that looked like rifle cartridges. She dumped them out into her hand. Beautiful in lethality. Anna shook her head slowly and pocketed them. Then she closed the cylinder and tossed the gun to the ground.

Anna scrutinized Brokeback and her mother, both still fastened in a tight embrace. She watched them for a long time as they rocked back and forth gently. Not even death can undo, Anna thought. Even sweet oblivion will turn away. And it mustn't come back.

Chapter 26

The rain finally stopped, and the dawn burned like the rising of a thousand suns. Claret and orange and everything in between. Small bits of hope amid the turmoil. Implacably gone was the nightmare desolation. The mountains in the distance took on the mien of an alien land, a world unheard of. Cold wind still shifted and blew through the valley.

Yet something had changed. Anna couldn't place it. The trees formed dancing shadows across the gravel driveway like nature's marionette. Was God now pulling the strings?

Sweat pooled on her mother's forehead, but she was finally eating and sleeping. Anna wiped away the perspiration with a damp cloth. Her mother stayed on the couch and, in her dreamland, seemed to chase something. She kicked and whimpered like a dog. A bizarre leer upon her face. Perhaps she was reliving memories of chasing baby Sam around the trailer. The child giggling with rapturous delight. Always the more active of the two. Being reminded of a precious light that was. Hopefully, forever would be.

Love in its purest form.

Hold on to it, Mom, Anna thought. *If you don't, it'll slip away. Just like sand through your fingers. Just, please, do not envy the dead. They want us with them enough as it is.*

They did not watch the news on purpose. No idea what was going on with the investigation. The sheriff never called. Doubtful that he would. Brokeback grew restless but managed to swallow his anger. He seemed ready to destroy, ravage, or kill anyone and anything. Anna knew that he just felt helpless. Everyone did.

She'd lost all track of time. Now, a useless luxury. The days had trudged past innumerable and uncountable. The only demarcation was the rising and setting sun. Anna was on the porch, mindlessly watching the world about when her cell phone rang. She almost let it go to voicemail, but on the fourth ring she picked it up off the couch. Billy Travis's name flashed on the screen.

"Hey, Billy."

"Hi, Anna," he said. "How are y'all making it?"

"We are holding on," she said. "Barely . . . Momma's in a bad way but is getting a little better."

"What about you? How are you doing?"

"Gosh, me? I don't even know. Everything's happening so fast, and I'm just trying to stay above water."

"That makes sense. I'm sorry. I know it's hard."

"Thanks. I think I'm going stir-crazy"

"Well, let's get you out of there. Want to get a drink?" he asked.

"Um." She paused. "Do you mind if I think about it and call you back? Just here in a few."

"Absolutely, yeah."

"All right, thanks, bye."

Anna stood and weighed his query. She stared out at the burnt-looking terrain. The sun was setting in the west. The last of the light seeping like melted wax upon the known world, fading farther and farther away. Soon darkness would catch her, and she worried about her heart. Already broken beyond measure or bound. How much worse could it get? She knew the answer. Things can always get worse. Anonymous life seethed in the outer dusk. Hidden, nearly breathless, and waiting. Hooded but for death's eyes searching for more.

I am of you, she thought. *And you of me.*

Anna looked at her phone. There was only one place to get a drink in Marble Hill. Yellow Creek Bar. The last known location where Sam was seen alive. Anna thought about that. Instead of a deterrent, she felt compelled. Like inside those walls were truths yet spoken. Sam's ghost or spirit or a thing beyond comprehension had asked her to find out what really happened. She was still her twin sister. Not even death would change that. How could it?

She called Billy back. He answered on the first ring.

"Sure, I'll meet you there," she told him. "I probably won't be any fun, but it'll be nice to get out."

They spoke for a minute more and finalized their plans. Then she hung up.

Anna looked down. She wore a long-sleeve T-shirt, but there was little warmth to it. She couldn't stop shivering. Was it the cold or something else?

Anna found herself in the bedroom. She stood before the tiny closet and stared at Sam's things. Much of it passed or exchanged between the two. Her eyes were drawn to Sam's favorite dress. It was a wrap design, and the deep-set maroon color seemed to block out her strange feeling of unease. Anna held it up and stood before the full-length mirror. She remembered Sam wearing it at a bonfire party. The last night before high school friends went their separate ways. Beer was passed around, and everyone drank to the past and well-wishes for the future. A crystal-clear visage of Sam laughing and hugging everyone goodbye. So full of love and life. Now, dead and gone. Anna feared the haunting of old, happy dreams. Dangerous and pleasing. Fully encroaching on this life. She clenched her eyes shut and felt a stinging pain in her chest.

That's all right, she thought. *Fear time, because it accelerates at a different pace. Remember to feel this way. Live in it. Perhaps it's the new normal. Or at the very least, you'll always be on guard. Make a list. Keep alert. Watch everything.*

Anna quickly changed into the dress. She couldn't remember the last time she showered. Her dull skin and stringy hair in stark contrast to what she wore. She stood before the mirror like someone under scrutiny. Everything accountable. Her soul burned, and she knelt before the bed. She looked at the filthy floor and back up at her reflection. Blood-shot-red and water-filled eyes staring back. She was crying and couldn't stop. She continued for a long time. Finally, she just whimpered and thought about the very nature of evil. Minding its very forms.

A few minutes later, Anna stood outside the trailer wearing the dress and a coat. The temperature had plummeted with the sun, and the ground looked craterous and frozen. Off in the blackness a lonely whip-poorwill cried out just once. No response and there never would be. Everything seemed like a sylvan wilderness. A place unknown of human habitation. Anna knew that going to the bar was random, senseless, and almost uncontrollable. The whole endeavor a curious and unbalanced coincidence that reeked of inevitability. Like a horrible ancient proph-ecy about to fulfill itself.

She drove toward the crossroads of Marble Hill. The turns and move-ments were familiar. She passed the haunted Baptist church where the devil resided. Malignancy postulated over everything, and she shivered at the sight. The ground saturated with corpses and the sacristy a place of unmined evil. She placed her foot down hard on the accelerator and surged onward. Anna watched the blackened country slip past beyond her headlights. Along a descending stretch of highway, she saw a vulture picking at some dead thing. Mean avian eyes glaring at her. Bloody beak red with the stain of viscera. Offal hanging down. As Anna bared down upon the perverse feast, the bird took flight into nothingness. There and gone. She kept driving. A flash in the rearview mirror showed the soar-ing scavenger return to gorge some more.

A short time later, Anna parked outside Yellow Creek Bar and pulled into the same spot her sister did on the last day of her life. She shut off the engine and placed her head on the steering wheel, bouncing it against the cheap fake leather a time or two. Finally, she heard a vibra-tion from inside her purse. Anna took out her cell phone and saw that it was a text from Billy. He was inside and waiting. She opened up the visor mirror and scrutinized her appearance. Nothing out of the ordi-nary, yet nothing to account for. Gone was the look of defenselessness and vulnerability. If only Anna had paid attention, she would've seen the tinge of uneasiness in her eyes. Her reflection posed a strange form of likeness. Yet a fraction out of place, a hidden imbalance beyond her knowing, and therein a jarring juxtaposition whereby the world seemed slightly unlevel.

The bar was practically empty. An old-timer from the retirement development sat slouched atop a stool with elbows perched upon the timeworn bar, nursing a drink. The Christmas lights and stale cigarette smoke created a thick rainbow of ghostly afterglow. Swaying phantom figures on the ceiling. The rafters flooded with garish colors twitching in subtle changes. Like a thing alive and undergone a vibrant metamorphosis. The air was cool, and there was a distinct stench of stale beer, warm sick, and disinfectant. Her nose crinkled from the scent. Anna observed everything around the room with an air of discovery. She looked over at the barman, who watched her with somnolent eyes. His entire attention focused on Anna, and he studied her with the intensity of a painter. A shockwave of disquiet and unheedful disconcert raced up her spine. She blinked several times and pushed the feeling away.

Billy was across the room at a booth. When he saw Anna, he rose and walked over, striding across the dance floor with a cool niceness. Gone were the oil-stained and dirty hands. He wore a seemingly new button-down shirt and strangely pressed corduroy pants. Ironed and clean but pockmarked with deep-set grease spots. Unbroken and uncomfortable-looking shoes. Anna found it somewhat odd. Out of proportion and ungainly. Ostensibly dressed to impress a brokenhearted twin sister during the worst days of her life.

Stop, Anna thought. *Don't unravel.* There was no need to constantly reevaluate the world's imbalance. It just was.

"Hi, Anna," Billy said. "How are you holding up?" The query was placed in all earnestness. She saw in his eyes truly imbued concern. Now, Anna felt a little guilty for questioning his sympathies.

"Not well," she said. "I'm just barely making it."

"Yeah, I can't even imagine. I'm so sorry." He reached out and hugged her. "Goddamn, I'm so sorry," he whispered in her ear. She felt his strong arms and his comforting embrace. She leaned into him, reached around his waist, and reciprocated in kind. Billy rocked her back and forth slowly. It felt right.

"Come on," he said. "Let's get a drink."

"Yes, please. Let's."

They walked over, and the bartender took their orders. Billy ordered a pitcher of beer, and Anna asked for two shots of tequila and a margarita chaser. She tried to pay for her drinks, but Billy shook his head. He held a circular tray with the drinks and precariously led Anna toward a booth in the corner.

They sat down across from each other, and Anna noticed apprehension on his face. He was nervous. Billy's hand shook as he poured a glass of beer from the pitcher. Anna smiled. She took one of the shot glasses and downed the tequila. It burned her throat, and she sipped from the margarita to drive it away. The alcohol electrified her brain, and she tried to understand Billy's configurations. All but a stranger a week ago. Now, someone she felt a strong connection with. She sat back and watched him as she nursed the frozen drink in her hands.

Billy took out a pack of cigarettes and offered Anna one. She shook her head. He lit his and inhaled deeply. The tip burned fiery red, and he exhaled a huge stream of smoke out of the corner of his mouth. The little booth looked opaque with fog for a moment. Anna saw his face return from the shadows. For the briefest of moments, she noticed something circuitous and conspiratorial. Then, in a flash, his warm smile returned. A look of caring animation.

They sat in prolonged silence. Both mutedly steering away from small talk. He'd ordered whiskey for himself and took the shot. He grimaced, paused, and rapped his knuckles atop the table. The incandescent illumination above seemed to swallow him whole. Dark to light shadows that timestamped different reflections. Merging into something profoundly alien. Perhaps that was just the alcohol, she thought. There was a pained expression etched across his face. She recognized that Billy was going to say something that he shouldn't.

"I bet this seems pretty weird. Being here, I mean. I didn't think about it being the last pla—"

"No," Anna cut him off. "I don't want to talk about it. Let me just be here with you." Her heart was pounding. She practically felt the physical pulsation from deep in her chest. "Is that okay? I just wanna sit here and think of anything else."

"Of course," Billy said. "I'll get us some more drinks."

He rose, and she watched him walk unsteadily toward the bar. Anna stared down at the shot glass filled with light amber liquid. She took the second shot and thought about having more. It would, at least momentarily, erase her feelings. Or, more likely, mask her sorrow for at least a span of time. But the alcohol wasn't exactly doing the trick. Just the thought of it wired her full of adrenaline. The idea threw her off-balance. Already, her cheeks were flush with warmth. Sweat dampened her skin. Nervous perspiration started to seep out from nearly every pore. Irregularly breathing in the smoky air.

All of a sudden, the multicolored Christmas lights strung from the ceiling began to blink. The roof at irregular intervals seemed drained of color, then flickered with burnished electricity. Like neon-colored fire. She sensed a change in the air. Standing atop a balancing wire between fretfulness and prodigious consideration. Something was going to happen. But justifiable concerns vanished completely. She stepped headlong into another realm, perhaps finding peace at last.

Billy returned with the tray.

"Got us some more of the good ole mother's ruin," he said.

Anna looked in front of her and saw two more shots. She'd hoped that coming here would provide some insight into her sister. Some understanding of what had happened. Instead, she felt just a miasma of confusion mixed with a small dose of fear. All she'd done was sit. Like a being possessed, she drained one and then the other and sat back with her eyes closed. They burned going down, and she forgot all about her chaser.

"Let's get out of here. I want to go," Anna said matter-of-factly. She'd been there for only a short time, but Anna felt like she had to leave. "Can we go to your place? Mine is haunted and I can't stand it. Let me follow you in my car."

"Sure. Absolutely. That's no problem at all."

Anna got up slowly and held Billy's hand to steady herself. Her legs almost gave out, and she felt momentarily faint. She understood that this was probably a mistake. Yet being with him might fill the literal and figurative hole inside, save her from the deepest recesses of her heart. Anna seemed giddy like someone in full anticipation of a long-awaited visitor. Truly, though, this judgment felt right. Like she'd been in conflict with herself and finally raised the white flag of surrender. Just resigning to this decision soothed the dull aching that resided just behind her eyes.

Billy placed his arm around her shoulder, and they walked toward the exit. As Anna neared the door, she heard a voice from behind. She'd grown accustomed to ethereal visitations from her sister, yet this was terrestrial. She turned and saw the barman waving his towel. He was calling her name and shaking his head.

Anna kept going, raised her hand in farewell, and walked out the door.

Chapter 27

Anna woke with a thunderous pain in her temple and was momentarily disoriented regarding her location. The storm clouds had vanished sometime in the night, and bloodred rays of sunlight burned through the cheap plastic blinds. She shifted her head out of the direct light and watched dust pirouette in the air. Shade passed every so often with the advent of running clouds. It took Anna a few moments to recognize where she was. It was bone-chillingly cold in Billy's trailer. She was nearly naked and huddled like a newborn under a threadbare blanket. He slept beside her and breathed heavily off rhythm. A slight whistling in his nostrils that told her he was fast asleep.

The night before, she'd reached a certain stage of drunkenness where she seemed possessed by some other life force. She'd unleashed a manner of beast that surprised herself. Pent-up frustration, loneliness, and wretched sadness found salvation wrapped in his strong arms. Flesh pressing flesh drove the demons away. Their sex incubated something within her close to religious frenzy. Remoteness left, and for the first time since her sister's disappearance, she didn't feel utterly alone. Anna relished it even though she knew it was just temporary.

She tried to go back to sleep, but she feared her nightmares. Instead, she just stared at the urine-colored walls and thought about absolutely nothing. Abject blankness felt like a sweet gift. Slowly, brief visions of the night before came back. Parking at a small turnaround in the woods. Traipsing across a fallow field. Holding hands and hurrying toward the destination. He was lying, she remembered thinking. He did live far back on his parents' property. She loped drunkenly toward a darkened mass that was the primal trailer he called home. Looking like some ancient obelisk of depression set in the ground hundreds of years before. Yet it was far more than that. Filthy but cozy and sickly sweet.

Everything else was shrouded in a fluid blur. Bits and pieces she recognized, but more proceedings were completely locked in her unconscious. The harder she tried to remember, the more elusive it became. The enormous cry of a crow outside startled Anna, and she nearly jumped out of bed. Instead, she slid out from under the covers and planted her feet firmly on the carpet. She clenched her toes into the flooring and rubbed her thighs. Goose bumps jutted from her skin, and she stood uneasily.

Anna exited the tiny bedroom and walked down the hallway toward the kitchenette. Billy was snoring still, and it sounded louder in the enclosed space. She moved silent as a mouse. Watching her feet and stepping around various obstacles. Nowhere in sight did she see her clothing. At the moment, she could not care less. She'd not had a hangover of this type in a very long time. All she wanted was water and perhaps something to drive away the pounding headache that seemed to burn the backs of her eyeballs.

She found a moderately clean-looking mason jar on the counter. It would have to do, she thought. Anna walked over to the sink and turned on the tap. The water sputtered beet red and slowly turned lighter until it cleared. She put the glass down and turned away in revulsion.

"Yeah," she whispered. "That's not gonna happen."

Anna opened the refrigerator and looked inside. Curdled milk, spoiled food, and fifty-odd cans of cheap beer. She grabbed hold of the nearest and popped the top. Sniffing the contents, Anna fought back the rising taste of bile. She leaned back and felt the cool plastic counter chill the small of her back. After taking a deep breath, Anna turned up the beer and chugged it with several strong gulps. She twitched involuntarily but managed to keep it down.

Great God Almighty, she thought. *Hair of the dog. I hope this works.*

Despite how shitty she felt, the beer actually seemed to do its job. She drank several more mouthfuls and realized that it tasted strangely good. It made her feel slightly better and softened the blow of her brutal headache. Her vision tried to right itself, and the pounding in her eye sockets drifted slowly away. She heard coughing followed by a few irregular snores. Anna paused in an attitude of listening. Billy was still sound asleep. She wondered what to make of the night. How safe he made her feel. The disappearance of her impending sense of dread.

What now? Anna asked herself. *What the fuck now?*

She was shivering in the kitchen, and the beer only made it worse. The drafty trailer dug the cold to the bone. She'd be better off outside. Anna needed something warm and walked quietly down the hall toward a closet. She opened it soundlessly and looked inside. Hanging across the metal bar were various coats and sweatshirts. She looked them over with an inquisitive eye. Halfway through the lineup she saw a hoodie from their high school. A Pickens High School dragon on the front. It was deeply stained with oil marks but, at the same time, seemed so inviting. Comforting like the way Billy made her feel. Anna didn't know what this was, but she felt a connection to him so profoundly that it made her simultaneously happy and frightened.

She tugged the hooded sweatshirt off the rack and slid it over her head. The hoodie smelled slightly musky and pumped with pheromones. The mixture acted as an intoxicant. Anna breathed deeply into the fabric and shuddered involuntarily.

Then she took a step back and was about to close the closet door when something on the floor caught her eye. It looked like a picture frame propped sideways against the back wall. She reached down and picked it up. Turning it to face her, she saw her sister's missing poster. Her exact replica staring back. Thoughts began to bombard her at a blinding rate of speed. Disembodied and surreal intramural voices drifted through her thoughts without coherence. She felt a rush of light-headedness and finally realized that she'd forgotten to breathe. A bizarre spring of outrage welled up inside. *Why? What the fuck, and why?*

Anna was about to turn down the hall toward the bedroom when she saw something else on the ground. A rush of cold struck her with a forcefulness of almost biblical wildness. There, lying on the dark and partially shrouded closet floor, was a pair of shoes that Anna would recognize anywhere. Imitation black leather pumps with a crack in one heel. Her sister's missing shoes.

Anna was about to scream when a brutal shock of pain exploded on the side of her head. A blinding flash of white light obscured her vision. That was the last thing she remembered before blacking out and entering nothingness.

Chapter 28

Out of the almost inescapable blackness crawled a memory from ten years prior. Their family had taken a rare trip to Lake Lanier. Momma had saved up just enough money from her meager salary to take the girls to the park's little man-made beach. The outing was planned long in advance, and the twins anxiously awaited the day. When it finally arrived, the trio packed up the car with bath towels, government cheese sandwiches, and knock-off sodas. A pot from the kitchen was brought along for the girls to make sandcastles. It was a brutally muggy morning and promised to be a scorcher by midday. That was all right, their mother promised, the lake would cool them off. The whole adventure seeming so foreign that it took on the aura of a fairy tale. Neither of the twins had ever known excitement quite like this.

The man-made beach was full of commuters. The three struggled through the basking crowd and hunted for an open spot. Anna looked around in wonderment at all the toys, food, and bright-colored umbrellas. Floats and balls and huge trays of food that seemed like an embarrassment of riches. Quick pangs of desire sprang forth then were quickly pushed away after they'd found a clearing in the far corner. Their mother set down their meager possessions and laid out the stained and frayed bath towels.

The twins ran down to the water, completely unaware of the unspoken protocols about flying sand. Neither owned a swimsuit and went in the brown water wearing shorts and dark T-shirts. They were the only ones without. Their mother unable to afford such luxuries, which was just fine. In many ways, abject poverty keeps you from wanting things to which you can never aspire. You don't miss what you can't have.

For a while, the sisters splashed and swam in the warm lake while their mother watched from the shore. She waved every so often at her daughters and drank deeply from a liquor bottle. After a time, the sisters went back to the bath towels and basked in the sunshine. Their mother had already passed out and was snoring loudly. They sat cross-legged facing each other and ate their cheese sandwiches. Anna finished all of hers while Sam wrapped up the crust in a paper towel to take home and give to the new puppy she'd named Rufus.

Anna remembered sitting there with her eyes closed and feeling a delicate hand clasp around her wrist. Momentum pulling her up. She opened her eyes wide and saw her sister smiling and pointing to the trees beyond the sand. Tall and swaying in the breeze. Not unlike the ones surrounding their home. Anna rose and ran with her twin toward the dense, lush green, Sam pulling her along. Her sister spoke with earnestness about seeing a beautiful and majestic monster from the sky swoop down and enter. A netherworld creature of yore. All the while exclaiming its virtues and immensity.

The sisters hurtled through the brush and swatted errant limbs out of the way. There was no trail, but the girls were used to that. Quick bare feet through the woods slapped against pine needles, twigs, and baked clay. Rough feet felt nothing by years of practice. Calloused and dainty. Hints of a rumored childhood. Anna was giggling uncontrollably when her sister grabbed her tight around the waist at an abrupt clearing. She looked over and saw Sam holding a finger up to her mouth and then pointing to a slow-moving stream ahead. There, in all its glory, was an enormous heron.

A jarring slam and violent rattling brought Anna to. She tried to open her eyes, but found the left was swollen shut. Her one good eye spied the surroundings and recognized that she was in her own car's back seat. Her mouth tasted of metal, and she knew that wasn't a good sign. She ran her tongue along the back of her teeth and tasted bitter blood. Her head ached in a way that was nearly impossible to describe. Like needles

thrust in her forehead. She'd never experienced pain this bad. At least
not physically.

She tried to move her hands, but they were stuck behind her back.
After tugging on them for a time, Anna realized that she was bound at
the wrists. Moving her legs, Anna found that she was fastened in the
same way at her ankles. The ropes were tight, taut, and unmoving. She
groaned inaudibly at this recent turn of events.

Anna was unsure of the time, but the day had perceptibly bright-
ened. With her one good eye, she spied out the window and watched the
tops of pine trees sprint past. The sound of the road altered for a second,
and she recognized crossing over a wooden bridge. Anna tried to count
the number of bridges in the county but grew mentally exhausted and
gave up. She laid her head down on the seat and tried to discern recent
events. Vaguely aware of the facts.

Then a vision of Billy flashed through her mind. Next, her sister's
shoes. The ones she wore the night of her death. Only one person could
have them. There was no other explanation.

The sound of her tires changed, and the road turned violently rough.
They were off the tarmac. *They*. Anna felt a sudden wave of nausea pass
over her. She'd slept with the very creature who had carried her sister off.
Murdered Sam and kept a trophy.

Anna shifted her weight and inched her way down for a better view.
She noticed the front seat and saw Billy behind the wheel. He was tap-
ping his fingers on the steering wheel to a song in his head. Like he didn't
have a care in the world. That today wasn't a surprise and just part of a
diabolical routine. Anna shook all over at the prospect. The truth laid
bare. She was about to die. The only good being that she'd be reunited
with her sister. Killed by the same man. Twins in everything to the very
last.

The sun through the car window sporadically flashed from faint to
blinding. Dead trees surrounded everything, and she felt locked in an
apocalyptic nightmare. All she knew was that they were moving deep

into the woods. The shifting depths of timber converging into a forest. Taking her away. Making sure she was never going to be found. The environment made sense; she was in the presence of a madman.

Fuck him, Anna thought. *To kill me, he's gonna have to fucking kill me.*

She heard him whistling. A whimsical musing that managed to accomplish only one thing. It just pissed her off. Leaning back, she studied him with something beyond homicidal rage. Staring into his soul. Reading the thoughts therein. Inner resilience bloomed. A thing long buried or finally incubated after all this time. She wasn't going to become a victim. He might do his worst, but she'd never give him that.

Outside the car and in was a vast, slow-moving ritual of incremental catastrophe. A baffling world of the horrible made real. She still felt a little bewildered. The very identities of folks she knew were in constant flux. Anna took stock of her situation. She was bound at the wrists and ankles, but she was in the back seat of her own car. Slowly and cautiously, Anna inched her way toward the passenger-side door. Wiggling from side to side and hoping not to draw attention from the monster behind the wheel. Her plan was fatalistic, but she had no other choice. The jump and landing would hurt like hell, Anna realized, but it was a risk she'd have to take. She knew this was a stupid plan with an infinite number of variables for failure, yet what else could she do?

Anna placed her foot on the door and hooked her big toe behind the handle. The door would automatically unlock when she yanked it forward. She was breathing hard and perspiring. The intense jarring of the car and trees passing took on the air of a ceremony. Tick tock. It all seemed like an eternity, but that was a relative term.

Anna started talking to God, then found the conversation shifting to her sister. A still, small voice answered back: *I love you, Anna.*

"I love you, too," she whispered.

She opened her eyes and felt a flickering, burning sensation in her heart that she took for conviction. *It's now or never*, she thought. Just as she was about to open the door, something shiny caught her attention. Bright sun reflected off metal. Anna turned toward it. The last thing she remembered was seeing a steel pipe closing down rapidly toward her head.

Chapter 29

When Anna came to, she realized that she was strapped down to a long wooden bench with no back. The ropes were so tight around her chest that they constricted her breathing. Every inhale and exhale was a struggle, making her even more lightheaded. With each gasp she felt like she was drowning. Oddly, her head didn't hurt anymore. Perhaps the latest blow had knocked out the previous pain and she was returning to normal. At least somewhat. Added to that, Anna was freezing cold. Her skin pricked painfully where her body fought to keep its temperature up. She looked straight ahead at a stone hearth and saw a small flame. A tiny fire that only vaguely hinted at warmth.

Anna closed her eyes tightly for just a moment. A flood of images assailed her in a flash. *Stop*, she thought. *Stop it right now.* Now wasn't the time. She needed to focus. Take an accounting. Try and figure out where she was, what might be happening, and how to get out. It appeared that she was in a cabin of sorts, but besides that, for all she knew, she might've been on the moon. Besides the cold, Anna noted the stench. The whole room smelled of decay and rot mixed with old, damp wood. Anna didn't know what was coming down the pike, but that sure wasn't a good sign.

She moved her limbs and found that her legs weren't bound anymore. Spread open in an inviting manner that made her sick. She recognized that she was wearing shorts and a T-shirt and was secured chest down on a slab of wood. Her arms were tied under the bench, and she saw a nightmare vision of a pig twirling on a spit. Another rope around her waist was affixed to the bench. She tried to find the knot, but that came to nothing. It was likely behind her. Anna placed her feet firmly on the floor and tried to rise, but the bench was too heavy. All that attempt did was burn the rope painfully into her skin. She decided not to try that again.

Then came Billy's voice from the darkness. "You cold, bitch?" Anna didn't say a word. "I bet you're cold. Lemme help you."

Loud thudding steps approached her from behind. Then, all of a sudden, the bench rocked wildly and skidded across the wood floor toward the fire. He had kicked it with such force that when the bench slammed into the hearth, Anna heard wood splinter. Her hip smashed against the stone, and a blast of pain raced up her side. She let out a small shriek. The fire was close to her left side, and it burned in a good way.

"That any better?" Billy asked.

Anna didn't respond. She was tight-lipped and focused on a million calculations of how to get out of her current situation. A weird sort of strength entered her soul. It was a mixture of blinding wrath and resiliency. *Let this son of a bitch yap*, she thought. *Just wait and see.*

"Keepin' your mouth shut, huh?" Billy asked. "That's all right. Won't last for long."

A sound in the darkness was followed by agonizing pain. He'd booted her forcefully in the fleshy part of her thigh and she felt teardrops of blood drip from her wound. Pins and needles raced down her leg and bit to the bone. She moaned from behind gritted teeth.

"How about I try this," he said. She heard the boards creak and his steps grow nearer. A hand from the darkness reached out and pulled a red-hot poker from the flames. "This is gonna hurt really fucking bad. So, get ready." The burning metal disappeared from sight. Then nothing but intense pain. He'd laid the metal across the fleshy top of her exposed back. She smelled something burning and realized immediately that it was her flesh. Anna let out a bloodcurdling scream that would've awakened the dead. It echoed long after.

"Now will you talk?"

Tears were streaming down her face. She didn't want to give him the satisfaction but feared the poker even more. She pounded her head on the wood to displace the pain. After a few seconds, she spoke with a raspy, broken, but indignant voice. "Why did you kill my sister?"

"Ah," he said sarcastically. "The million-dollar question. I'm glad you jumped right into it." There was a pause. Footsteps on the dry, rotted boards. "Lemme get some light in here. Too dark. I can hardly see what I'm doing."

Anna turned her head and watched as brilliant light shone through one window after another. Billy had unlatched the wooden shutters and illuminated the nightmare room. Across the room, she saw a table filled with various mean-looking tools. Things that were probably used for anything but their intended purposes. Beneath the table was an orange hardware store bucket with a towel draped across the top. A legion of flies circled the opening and tried repeatedly to enter but their efforts were in vain.

She heard a scraping sound and saw Billy pull up a wooden stool right beside her. "There, that's much better," he said. "Now, back to your question. Why did I kill your sister? Well, I actually didn't kill your sister. She was already dead before I got ahold of her. Shame, though. I woulda loved it." There was a cold pause, then Billy chuckled hauntingly. "Luckily, I've got my chance with you. And I'm gonna make the most of it."

Anna watched his cold, blackeyes. Sickness and rage flowed through her.

"My role in that thing was getting rid of the body." A shit-eating grin formed across his face. "Basically, I did it for the money. And, well, some extra benefits beforehand that I most certainly enjoyed." Anna watched closely as Billy absently picked at dirt under his fingernails with a long, wood-handled, rusty-looking ice pick. A mundane task turned ominous and diabolical. Anna felt herself shaking uncontrollably with utter fear. "So, you see," Billy said, "it was all just a mop-up job on my end."

He quit picking his nails. "Now's my turn. Did you ever suspect that I had anything to do with this? Or was I completely off your radar?"

Anna's torso and neck hurt from lying strapped down to the bench. There was no give, but she did notice one change. When he'd kicked her across the room, the knot from the rope around her waist had moved to the side of the bench. Just within easy reach. Anna tried to play it cool and not give herself away. She remained silent and pretended to contemplate his query. She didn't want to give him the satisfaction of answering, but she needed to stall him until she could figure out what to do next. "No, never. I thought you were a nice guy. I had no idea you were evil."

Billy chuckled. "Well, that sure does make me feel better. I was starting to worry that I was playing my hand a little too loose. I don't have to worry about you. At least not before the hour is out."

"What did you do with the rest of her?"

"Excellent question!" Billy exclaimed. Anna watched as he rose from his stool and walked toward the torture table. He tugged at the bucket underneath and pulled it clear. The flies rose and returned. He removed the cloth from the top and reached inside.

"Here she is," Billy said, and hauled forth her sister's severed head. He held it by her golden hair that was stained in splotches with dark red blood. It swung from side to side like a nightmare pendulum. Anna saw her sister's matching face rotate into view. Sam's mouth was frozen open as if in mid-scream. Howling in protest against the horrendous act of defilement. Her eyes were crossed in such a way that they looked like mismatched, glassy doll's eyes. The flies kept circling the head and landing to taste decaying flesh. Billy laughed and shook the head up and down. Bits of serrated skin flapped, and Anna saw the tonsured pearl bone that was once connected to her sister's spine. After a few more shakes for good measure, Billy returned Sam's head to the bucket and covered it again.

Anna vomited across the bench but didn't cry. She was all out of tears. All she wanted was revenge. She no longer felt the searing pain of the fire. Something far fiercer burned within her. She thought about beating him to death, and that made her smile.

"You little bitch! You threw up all over the place. I'm going to make you eat that shit." Billy sighed. "Well, enough chit chat. I've got to make a

couple of calls and get some more wood. I'll be back. Don't go nowhere."
He cackled idiotically and turned to leave. She heard him walk with a
light air, and it pissed her off.

When Billy opened the door, the whole interior was awash in light.
She looked around and thought how the inside of the cabin looked like
the remnants of a home many times plundered. Some evil predator's
lair. There were many ideas swirling in her head. She just needed to settle on one. After he slammed the door shut, she decided and set that
plan into motion.

Chapter 30

Although her hands were bound, she managed to twist the knot around to her stomach. The rope seared into her skin, but Anna didn't have time to think about that. Like a woman possessed, she began picking at the knot. She finally got one strand loose, but at the cost of a fingernail. It dangled precariously, but Anna didn't hesitate, ripped it off, and continued her work. Blood streaked her hands as she struggled with the rope and time. That last part was the most important. She had no idea how long Billy would be gone.

Quicker than she imagined, Anna had the rope unraveled. It dangled loosely on either side. She arched her back to stretch and felt a burst of agonizing pain. Her hips undulated like a woman in the throes of contractions. After two pulsating spasms, she returned to the task at hand. For a few quick moments, she tried to reach the knot tied around her wrists, but it was impossible. She wouldn't give up, though. She'd already thought about what she needed to do. Had to do. It didn't make the prospect any easier. Less than a foot away were red-hot coals. Just enough room for her to place the rope against the fire. It would scorch her hand, but Anna had little alternative. Do nothing and die, or burn and live. She chose the latter.

With a sort of unexplainable conviction, Anna slammed her left wrist against the coals. She smelled burning and cooked meat but strangely felt no pain. That wouldn't last. Just the shock of the act kept her conscious. The stench was completely unimaginable, but she kept pushing. She had no idea how much of the rope was burnt. All she needed was for it to fray and weaken. *Just keep going.* She knew that this was her one and only chance, so she had to make it worthwhile.

After a few more seconds, Anna pulled her wrists from the red-hot coals and inspected them briefly. Both wrists were burnt, but the left one looked like something out of a horror movie. Blistered red all around the outside. She watched bubbles form before her very eyes. The main pressure point was black as ink, and her skin drooped where it had melted. There was still no pain, and her hand felt stiff. Rock hard and she couldn't move several fingers on her left hand. Like it had cooked the muscles and ligaments within.

At this point, she didn't care. Buried somewhere amid the skin and soot was the rope. Anna couldn't discern it in the light, so she could only pray. Which she did. *God, please help me kill this motherfucker. That's all I fucking ask. Amen.* Then she placed her head flat against the bench and started to pull. Now came the pain. The rope felt like it forged through the fleshy part of her char-grilled skin and scraped bone. Anna clenched her teeth to keep from screaming. She bit part of her tongue and tasted warm blood. Yet there was singleness to her purpose. She had to break the rope and free herself before Billy returned.

Anna paused and took several deep breaths. Her myriad of thoughts was tangled in an almost dreamlike landscape. No more nightmares, just the faintest glimmer of hope. Strength from somewhere. For a moment, Anna thought she heard her name called out several times in an echo. Sounding like a muffled warning through cotton. Her eyes darted toward the orange bucket. Could it be Sam?

No, those cries weren't from a ghost. They were from that son of a bitch. Evil personified in human form. It was time. Now or never. She pulled her arms in opposite directions as hard as she could. A wondrous inner strength overcame her and Anna felt something give. A gap formed, and the ties loosened. She redoubled her efforts and finally tore the rope clear apart. Her hands were unbound. The cord was still deeply embedded in her skin, and she managed to painfully extract it. Her adrenaline pumped through every cell in her body. Here she was, nineteen and reborn.

She stood up and quickly looked around the room. Over on the table was a claw hammer that she zeroed in on. Limping painfully, she snatched the tool up and moved behind the door. She did this not a moment too soon. There was the distinct sound of boots on boards. Steps approaching the door. Then it swung open. Anna sidestepped out of the way and took a position behind him.

"Howdy, honey, I'm home!" Billy hollered. He stood with an armload of split wood and paused, looking directly at the now empty bench in front of the fire. "Oh, fuck—"

Anna didn't let him finish the sentence. She brought the hammer down squarely on the crown of his head. The thud it made was both sickening and exhilarating. She figured that would've knocked him out cold, but it didn't. Billy dropped the wood at his feet and turned around to face her. Their eyes locked.

"I'm gonna hurt you so bad for that," he said. Billy's nostrils were flaring and his eyes were wide with murderous rage etched across his face. "You're gonna beg me to die."

Despite his words, Anna noticed something else locked deep within his eyes: fear. She raised the hammer, turned it claw side out, and brought it down again. He caught it just in time. Billy snatched the hammer from her grasp and threw it across the room. Now she was defenseless, vulnerable, yet unafraid. The fear in her was shrinking, so tiny now that Anna could hardly sense it. She reared back and was about to hit him in the face when the briefest glimmer of light flashed across her vision. Anna looked down and watched in slow motion as Billy drove the metal ice pick into her stomach. It entered with almost surgical precision. A pin going through fabric. She stared dumbfounded at the wooden handle that protruded from her skin. The weapon had penetrated her up to the hilt.

It took her breath. The wind rushed out of her, and she staggered, almost falling. Anna watched as Billy reached for the handle, but she stumbled a few steps just out of reach. He clutched at nothing, and she saw an opportunity. He was off-balance as well. Using all her strength, she shoved him in the chest. Billy rocked backward and tripped over a piece of his spilled firewood. He fell with eyes full of terror. Arms outstretched and clawing wildly at the air. Searching for an invisible purchase that was never to be. There was nothing to slow him down. Gravity only accelerated his descent.

The base of his neck cracked against the jutted corner of the bench, and Anna watched it all with delighted bemusement.

Chapter 31

She imagined something like in the movies. A small snap and then instant death. Instead, when Billy's neck broke, it sounded enormous in the small cabin. It reminded her of a huge oak breaking in two. She saw a vision of Brokeback out in the woods with a chainsaw felling massive trees for firewood. Billy didn't scream or cry, and neither did he die. He just lay on the floor with his head cocked at an ungodly and unnatural angle. Chest rising and falling weakly. His eyes were wild and filled with confusion, fear, and dread.

Then he let out a moan of outrage.

Anna turned away. She feared what she might find if she looked down at Billy. Her adrenaline was still flowing, but she knew that wouldn't last. The pain from the ice pick would come shortly. But she knew that it had to come out. Anna took a deep breath and then stared at the protruding tool. There wasn't any blood. It seemed almost like a toy taped onto her skin.

Anna walked cautiously over to the table. The ice pick bobbed up and down, and she felt the metal inside her shifting. She spied a roll of duct tape and set it in front of her. After catching her breath, she peeled off a six-inch portion and tore it with her teeth. She laid it on top of the spool with the sticky side up. She paused and looked over her shoulder at Billy. There was no change. Anna turned back to the task at hand. She sadly scrutinized the handle and the tape. *This is gonna suck*, she thought. *Like, really fucking suck.*

Anna took her badly burned left hand and grabbed the table as best she could. Gripping it with all her might. Her other hand held the ice pick. She took several deep breaths and counted down from three. At zero, she pulled the tool out of her stomach and was surprised at how easy it was. No tugging or yanking. Just retracting from whence it came. Her lower back muscles constricted several times, but that was the extent of the pain. She tossed the ice pick across the table and inspected the wound. A line of blood poured gently from it. Anna understood that wasn't the potential problem. What mattered was internal damage. The extent, she had no way of knowing.

She took up the piece of duct tape and placed it flat against her skin over the wound. It wouldn't hold for long, but she didn't need it to. Just long enough to get out of here. Her first order of business was finding warm clothes. Anna looked around the room and saw a jacket in the corner. She hobbled over and picked it up and slid her arms through. Now, she was at least covered. Warming up was enough. Already feeling less dirty, less violated, and more courageous. She was going to survive, she knew the truth, and, most importantly, she would reunite and reassemble her twin sister.

Anna cautiously approached Billy. He seemed to mumble something incoherent to himself. As she neared him, he followed her with his eyes. His mouth opened and closed like he was trying to drink the air.

"Get me some help," he gasped. "I think my neck's broke." She noted that those few words fatigued him. Like he had to fight for each one. She ignored his request. "Please, I've got money. Ten thousand in cash at my trailer. In a shoebox under the bed. It's all yours. Just get me to a hospital." His pathetic breathing was painfully labored. "And I'll confess to everything. The whole goddamn thing. I swear it on my mother's life."

Anna stood over him and patted the left side of his jeans with the palm of her hand. Nothing. She grabbed his hips and twisted his body around. His head remained flat against the floor, and his body moved as if on a swivel. She reached into the right-side pocket and found her car keys. Pulling them out, she heard him crying. Anna stood up and looked him in the eyes. Staring down at this now useless would-be killer, she couldn't help but smile. He started to wail at the sight of her rapture, but she'd already turned away.

Anna's heart was pounding, and she felt sweat run down her rib cage. She knew that staying focused would keep her from passing out. Left foot, right foot. She walked unsteadily toward the orange bucket that held the remains of her sister. She bent down to pick it up, and a stabbing pain rocked her lower back. A thousand brutal pangs jabbed into her kidneys. Anna let out a guttural moan but managed to gather up the metal handle and lift the horrible container.

The bizarre cistern wasn't as heavy as she imagined, and she was incredibly thankful for that fact. She trudged laboriously toward the open door. Her movements felt robotic, and then it finally happened. The infusion of pain Anna feared struck her all at once. Her left hand was all but ruined, and her waist hurt in a way that was nearly indescribable. *It's okay*, she thought. She was alive, the rest of her sister was now found, and Billy was about to die.

This short period of discomfort Anna faced was absolutely worth it.

Anna limped toward the open door and stepped outside. She was partially blinded and squeezed her eyes shut. She kept having to adjust her grip on the handle to keep it from slipping and spilling out. Something terminal gripped her heart, and she held on to the bucket for dear life.

After a few moments of standing on the porch, she finally opened her eyes to the world about. She'd never seen anything so beautiful in her whole life. The light spread out and looked like a yellow gauze painted across the sky. Everything took on the aura of a picturesque wasteland. No animals. No wind. Just the crowded sense of nothingness. Surrounding the cabin was a crudely made split-rail fence. Earthen-looking wood that was almost decayed. Finally, a sudden maelstrom of wind blew through the forest like it had a mind of its own. Sounding like lost souls begging for salvation.

Anna moved across the scrabble yard with jerks and stops. Walking like a woman attached to strings being led along by a crazed puppeteer. Her tongue was swollen in her mouth and dry like ashes. She no longer felt any pain and was strangely mournful of that fact. The day was either winding up or down. Anna wasn't really sure. Time seemed held in an abeyance. A suspect thing that was still in question. There was so much she desperately wanted but felt strayed beyond the grasp of mankind.

A few more steps and Anna carefully set her sister's remains in the middle of the yard and took off limping toward the woods. She looked down and watched a warm runnel of blood track down her leg from where Billy had booted her. With winter, the forest floor was covered in pine needles, brittle leaves, and a host of twigs. She bent down and scooped up a huge armful. Resolute and unwavering, Anna trudged back toward the cabin. She was slow going, but her inner resilience outweighed everything else. Anna climbed the steps and paused outside for just a moment, then stepped inside.

She carried her armload of fire starter toward Billy. She smiled at him, and he followed her with his eyes. He mumbled something vaguely coherent about the unfairness of life. His words meant nothing. Fear and disbelief etched across his face. She ignored it and dropped the pile of leaves and sticks atop him.

She went up and down the steps half a dozen times, hauling armfuls of dry kindling. Mechanically retracing herself like a woman possessed. Each time she entered the shack, Billy cried out to her. Pleading for salvation and cursing her soul at each interval. Anna paid him no mind and continued to cover him with debris.

Finally, she nearly gave out. There was a wave of pain from her stomach, and she nearly fainted and dropped her pine straw. She stopped and looked about. The world looked altered and blurred in the mixed light bounding through the trees. Despite being clear of mind, Anna felt like she was locked in a smoky haze. She retched several times and focused on placing one foot in front of the other. Even in her state, she moved with resignation. Almost stoic.

Anna entered the cabin for the last time. She looked around at the torture table, the bench, and Billy. All of it about to go up in flames. She slowly trudged over to the hearth and was about to cast the straw into the flames when a buzzing sound stopped her dead in her tracks. The humming was coming from Billy's pants. Anna shifted the bundle to her hip and reached down to rummage through his pocket. She pulled out his vibrating cell phone and stared at the screen.

The phone flashed the name Hinson. She froze and tried to understand what she was seeing. This was impossible. The pastor was in jail. The phone vibrated a second time and then stopped. Anna was so baffled by this that she waited a second too long to answer. She needed to call the number back. Anna tapped the screen several times, but only a numerical password notification popped up. How could this be?

"What's your fucking password," Anna demanded.

Billy didn't answer. Anna knew he wouldn't. She had a moment of clarity and realized it had to be the son. The pastor was taking the fall. There was no other explanation. It gave her a new purposefulness. Anna knew where she had to go. She'd confront the murdering bastard in his home and make this right. This final judgment he won't escape.

Taking careful steps, she approached the smoldering fire. Red-hot coals lay staring menacingly back at her. She'd formed a trail of straw from Billy's broken body to the hearth. All she needed to do was cast this last armful into the embers. She turned around and stared at the crumpled body of Billy. His eyes were wide with unqualified terror, yet at the very last he seemed resigned to death. There was no pause. She'd traveled so far down the path of her own iniquity, Anna figured she might as well see it through.

With that, she tossed the last armload of the straw into the fireplace. The dry leaves and straw flashed a blinding yellow light, and the blaze began to spread. Billy was screaming the whole time. Seeing the foreshadowing of things to come. Anna just turned around and calmly left the small cabin. On her way out, she shut the door.

Cautiously, she walked down the steps and over toward her sister's remains. Flies circled the bucket, and Anna wished she'd remembered the cloth. Too late now. That was all right, she thought. Better to have her coming home. No matter the shape Sam was in.

Finally, Anna paused unsteadily by the bucket and watched the cabin.

She stood with her hips cocked away from the wound in her stomach for what seemed like an eternity. Nothing happened and then more of the same. She watched it with growing annoyance. Just as she was about to venture forth for more fuel, Anna saw smoke rising from the ancient roof. Then black soot seeped out of the open windows. She knew that all was well when Billy began screaming and swearing oaths against her soul. These proclamations made sense at first. All the horrible things he'd do to her. Anna just shook her head at these last declarations. This part was over. But there was much more to be done.

Gray and black smoke billowed out of the open windows. Bloodcurdling screams continued from inside. Soon, flames licked the window and the cabin was an inferno. The wretched shouts, pleas, and curses from inside were gone, and the only sound was wood splitting from the intense heat. She watched the small log cabin until it was utterly consumed. His death helped quell her grotesque throes of unmitigated grief. The conflagration negated Billy to all but a distant memory. He was no more. Charred to nothingness. Ashes and dust. She couldn't stop smiling.

Chapter 32

The sun was moving farther to the west, and Anna knew it was time to leave. She picked up the bucket. Slowly, she began her trek barefoot down the treacherous dirt road. Or a rumor of road lying in wait. There was a reason why Billy hadn't driven all the way. This hike would be hard going. In her maledicted state, Anna followed a bend in the road and came out of a hollow. Calico bushes were thick on either side and were the only things that looked alive in the winter woodlands.

Her body was failing. At one point, she thought she heard distant revelry and music. Anna didn't know if this was the slow creep of death. Perhaps it was following her, but she didn't turn around. She didn't need to. Anna already knew. It was the wraith. Waiting to lay claim. *Please wait*, she thought. *I'm not done yet.* A flood of everything flashed across her vision, just ahead and out of reach. Things that should've been locked away, never to see the light of day. Yet there it was, and the line had been crossed. Come what may. Anna paused and listened to voices long dead rise and fall. She shook her head, spat, and continued on.

Tall ridgelines topped with outcroppings of dull yellow limestone towered above her. They were balds of escarpments and shelves, exposed places in the wood set happenstantial, with rocks covered in mosslike, gangrenous sores. She labored like a woman demented down the dirt path. A lone survivor holding on for dear life amid the rage of floodwaters. Anna seemed the very epitome of absolute misery, wandering lost, lonely, and afraid.

As she shuffled along, Anna looked down into the stinking bucket that held the decaying parts of her twin sister. Long past commiseration.

She spoke harshly to it and ended by telling Sam that she envied her. *It's the living who suffer*, Anna said. *And your time is over.*

Left foot. Right foot. Left foot. Right foot.

She found a sort of rhythm and was making good progress until an enormous noise disoriented her. Momentarily, she'd taken leave of her senses. Overhead, she heard the flapping of immense wings. A huge shadow passed over her and trailed off in the distance. A shifting malfunction in the heavens that was trailing away. Anna looked up into the crystal-clear blue sky and saw the outline. She recognized the bird almost immediately as a heron. Lost far in the mountains. Perhaps afraid and disoriented just like herself. Anna's mind calculated disjointedly the last time she'd seen one.

The memory of Lake Lanier stirred from the deep recesses of her mind like the dawning of some crazed hallucination. The bird was white and majestic. The pencil-like black legs bent backward, its S-shaped neck bobbing with each step. The heron looked over at the twins once but quickly continued its walk among the river stones. The yellow beak stood out in stark contrast with two pebble eyes as black as obsidian. Sam held a hand over her mouth and hugged her sister tightly. A look of shock and admiration on her face.

Movement shifted the focus of the twins. Out of the clearing across the creek came two boys. Not much older than themselves. Clad in fancy swimsuits, sunglasses, and sandals, this male duo looked like polar opposites to the poverty-stricken sisters. They stared at one another as if confused where the other had come from. The awkwardness of people crossing paths on a journey only to nod slightly and continue on.

Anna was about to whisper that they needed to leave when they both watched in shock and horror as the lead boy reached down, picked up a rock, and threw it at the heron. The projectile lobbed with no real velocity and arched slowly toward the bird. Finally, the stone came down and struck the heron flat on the back. The creature cawed in pain and lunged upward. Its huge wingspan flapped loudly, and the heron took flight. It swooped down the little river toward the lake, still cawing in outrage or fear, perhaps both. Anna watched it go and was awed by its grace and beauty. A free thing without measure or bound.

Out of the corner of her eye, Anna saw her sister reach down into the creek and pluck out a disk-shaped rock. She watched in shock as Sam hurled it at the two boys across the small river. Soaring with great speed, the stone looked like it flew on a wire, so precise was it. Anna watched, as if in slow motion, as the rock hit the offending boy square in the forehead. His eyes walled like the blind. Then he sank like a sack of potatoes into a heap. What Anna heard next was his compatriot squealing.

Sam snatched Anna by the hand, and the twins hurried off back through the woods toward the man-made beach. Her sister was laughing even louder this time. Once they cleared the brush and hurdled across the sand, Anna watched as Sam chortled and waved her fists crazily in the air, skipping across the sand and jumping with a triumphant exultation. Anna had recognized something in her sister almost immediately. Her twin's whole countenance had matched the free and eternally unique crane.

Anna's stomach burned, and she retched then vomited black blood down the front of her shirt. She wiped her mouth with the back of her hand and looked around. She followed the spectral roadway that wound along the base of a ridge. The other side led to bottomland, and Anna heard the unmistakable sound of rushing water. The bucket's weight seemed to magnify, and she slowed her pace. Anna looked up to see that the bird and all signs of it were gone. Perhaps it was a hallucination or visitation. Either way, she thought, *Thank you.*

The spine of the surrounding ridges sloped away toward the river. Everything seemed to lead to that. The land roving downward like a threat. Natural and malefic. Areas baked and fissured. What lay ahead? A trail leading to salvation or hell?

Salvation. Or so it seemed. Anna saw her car on the other side of a bridge made of wood and concrete and badly in need of repair. Ruined planks held together by disintegrating masonry. Anna paused and redoubled her grip. She studied her car from across the bridge and seemed frozen. Like she'd forgotten what to do. What were bridges or cars or anything for?

Anna's vision blurred, and she thought she saw ghosts wandering across the ruined bridge. In her half-crazed mind, she felt like an orphan set out on a path that led to a witch's cabin at the terminal end. She wondered if she and Sam were together in some other dimension. If so, she hoped her doppelgänger didn't waste a single moment.

She stepped onto the bridge, and there was a loud creak of pain. The other end of the board raised up precipitously and slammed back down when she shifted her weight. She placed her feet cautiously and tried to select strong-looking wood. Her already failing state made this dance all the more precarious. Anna's body seemed to fight her when she needed it most. She stopped and tried to catch her breath, but that only made it worse. A thundering pain racked her jaw and creeped slowly to the crown of her head. Nausea followed, and she tasted warm blood pool in her mouth. It hurt too bad to spit, so she let it dribble through her teeth and drool down her chin. She stared at her car, and it seemed to drift farther away as if floating through a tunnel. The distance threaded to a gulf and was gone.

Anna stumbled along, going in and out of consciousness. Her feet crossed, and she lost balance. Running sideways to catch herself, but there was no chance. As if it were a thing preordained. She went headlong over the side of the bridge, and the bucket went flying. Just before hitting the water, Anna had a moment of clarity. Leaving Marble Hill was supposed to make her life better. A new world without problems. Yet, she'd found, it had only multiplied them.

Anna's whole world shot to black when her head bashed against a jutted rock at the bottom of the river.

Chapter 33

Sam twirled before the mirror, and the bottom hem of her dress circled like a dervish. She wore a red dress with spaghetti straps and a deep V-neck dipping below her cleavage. It cinched at the waist. The long skirt was slit at her thigh and ended with a floor-sweeping train. She'd spent nearly all her money, over two hundred dollars, on the whole outfit, including the three-inch metallic silver pumps. Sam beamed with joy for the night ahead.

Anna felt a mixture of jealousy—because Sam looked unimpeach-ably beautiful—and irritation. She couldn't understand why this dance captivated her twin so profoundly. Both had gone the year before and were of a consensus that it was no fun. Sam's obsession this time irked Anna, and she was glad the night wouldn't be forever. Anna wore last year's dress and, in truth, didn't want to go, but her sister begged and pleaded, so she acquiesced. No new fancy dress or shoes. She was saving up for her freshman year at college, and the subject was still raw between them. For the first time in their life, the twins would be separated. Half of a whole left behind.

"Well, woombie?" Sam asked. "What do you think?"

"You're gorgeous as usual," Anna said. "But I still don't think this stu-pid dance is worth two hundred dollars."

"Well, I don't understand why you're not wanting to party."

Anna laughed sarcastically. A sort of sardonic amusement. "It's just a dance. Prom is not that big of a deal, and you know I have to save my money."

Sam shot Anna a look of outrage and pained desolation. "Maybe not for you. But for me it's really important. You're going to be leaving *me* in the fall!" She hissed. "God forbid if I want to spend a special night out with you!" Sam's eyes were wet. She spun on her high heels and exited their bedroom, slamming the door behind her.

Anna woke on a little sandbar cut out from a curve in the river. She was still in shock. Every part of her hurt, and she was confused as to how she'd gotten there and unsure of her continued existence. Eventually, she looked over and stared at a twirling leaf trapped in a pool. It swept and almost escaped the endless cycles but was pulled back in. Staring in bemused wonder, Anna felt the completely rational fear that she'd lost her mind. All of the colors were strangely saturated, bleeding into awkward and unknown hues. Overall, nothing made sense.

After a time, her mind settled down to a dull roar of diminished intensity. The waving trees created shadow monsters with surreal clarity. Anna knew that she was among their number now. She looked all about, and her vision distorted and blurred, then vanished. It took her a few moments to realize she'd just closed her eyes.

She was disoriented like someone from a dream or dreamer's dream. Her eyelids blinking occasionally and out of tune like an ancient person on their last day on earth. Thunder plagued her head. Misshapen and immovable things racked her mind. Finally, her brain slowed into the truth of what she had done. And what she needed to do. All else were threads of insignificance that didn't matter.

Anna moved her arms around the sand in search of purpose. She dug her fingers down deep and tried to pull herself out of the water. No movement from her legs. An intense fear crept over her that she was crippled like her toasty compatriot. Using all her strength, she sat up and looked down. Her legs moved when she told them to, and relief overcame her. She wasn't paralyzed. Just numb. A sinister laugh boiled up from within, and she felt like a madwoman finally viewing a brief moment of transparency. Wait too long and it'll be gone.

Everything around the creek looked spectral and insubstantial. Slow moving and viscous. She kept prodding her hands into the sand for purchase and crab-walked out of the river. Sitting up, Anna looked over her still-intact body and felt dizzy with relief. *Little miracles*, she thought. Moving her hands and feet, she smiled with a strange, feckless grin.

The air was practically electric with sound. Quick-moving water surrounding everything on both sides. Anna looked around and couldn't see the bucket. That was long gone. Perhaps that was for the best. Let Sam have these mountains. She deserved this beautiful and natural kingdom. *I'll always know where she is. Perhaps here, Sam will find peace.*

Anna slowly took another accounting of her body. The hole in her stomach was the size of a pencil head, but the hurt was nearly indescribable. Her cooked wrist had felt so good in the frozen water. Now the pain quickly returned. *Bleak times ahead*, she thought. "That's okay, God," she whispered. "Bring down your worst and be damned."

Standing painfully, Anna thought she heard a low rumbling in the distance and decided that was the way to go. It came from far away and across the creek. Anna understood what she needed to do. She stumbled into the creek and found herself in waist-deep water. One side of the river was filled with mean-looking, jutted rocks. On the other were several sluices of silver mountain stream. Anna shook her head. She tried to concentrate on her steps. Slipping on a rock would most certainly end her lucky streak. A few feet away was a small shoal with dead reeds and ankle-high water. It took her several minutes to reach the other side and crawl out of the creek.

Anna was shivering again and hugged her knees against her chest. She heard her name echo off in the distance. She rose painfully and set off into the woods. The river was at her back, and she walked on barefoot through the trees in search of any sign of civilization. None.

The warm sun began to dry the shirt on her back. She feared a long purple dusk because she knew she'd never survive the night. This painful realization spurred her on. Nerves so frayed and taut that they seemed to hum. She shivered uncontrollably, but surprisingly didn't feel the least bit cold. The day burned in her, and she kept walking. The world of form seemed to vanish, and Anna realized that she'd momentarily blacked out. *Focus*, Anna prayed. *Please, God, just let me focus.*

She marched on through the woods as if daring death to take her. She had no idea how far she'd gone or in which direction, but she knew the creek was behind her. The foliage crunched underneath her bare feet. She continued on drunkenly. Anna was nearly overcome with exhaustion. She thought she'd known tiredness before, but she was badly mistaken. The profound sound of silence kept her awake. Anna paused and looked around and saw nothing but her own shadow following her. Then, from off in the distance, a dove called out mournfully. *Of them and them me*, she thought. Anna redoubled her will to live and kept going.

There was a steep rise that led to what looked like a clearing. She cut upward and fell twice but managed to keep on. Loud noises that sounded like trucks kept racing past, and she figured atop the hill was a road. That realization gave her a strength she didn't know existed. Anna used trees to propel herself forward. Swore harshly at the pain in her stomach that burned ferociously as tears tracked down her cheeks. Her vision burning blinding white with each step. All the trees looked like a consort of ghosts in revival.

You aren't going to die here, Anna thought. *You might think so, but you're not.* "Fuck this," she screamed. "Not today."

There was a final steep incline that Anna crawled on all fours to get up. It sapped all her strength, but she finally managed to hit level ground. She lay down in the grass and stared at the asphalt. A bubbling feeling of relief welled, and she laughed and cried intermittently for several minutes. Finally, Anna pushed herself up and walked out into the road. She stood for a moment and tried to catch her bearings. It looked like Highway 53, but Anna didn't know for sure. She tried to gauge her location with the sun but still didn't know if it was morning or evening. Waxing or waning. Finally, Anna let out a sigh of exacerbation and turned right. Slowly and methodically, she set off down the road.

It wasn't long before she heard the sound of a car coming down the pike. She turned and held her hand out to flag it down. It was a cherry-red BMW and the driver didn't even tap the brakes. The convertible raced past and out of sight. Anna raised two birds and cursed the driver's soul. Undeterred, she continued her slow and methodical walk along the white line. *Mustard and mayonnaise, mustard and mayonnaise,* she heard Brokeback spectrally say.

After what seemed like a long time, a sputtering automobile that sounded like a wounded animal came into view. Anna walked out into the middle of the road and held her hands out wide. As it came closer, she recognized the ancient truck and driver. Old Man Stallings slowed and stopped beside her. He reached across the seat and rolled down the passenger window. Anna took a step back and hugged herself tightly. A ruddering and yammering murmur fluttered from within that was almost like a hallucination. She fought back the urge to vomit and swallowed several times in rapid succession. She was ill at ease and uncertain what her next movements should be. Anna was certain of only one thing. *This ends today.*

Chapter 34

The old man sat behind the steering wheel and watched Anna with sad and burnt-looking eyes. He reached across and opened the door. His face was full of understanding and reverence. Stallings's eyes were fixed on her. Lids heavy, but ever watchful. He looked behind her and took several deep breaths. His expression was that of recognition. Something followed her that only the near-dead see. Or perhaps those who've killed. Anna was both. The old man blinked several times as if trying to drive away the nearly invisible dead that obediently trailed her. Now, Anna wandered into that strange and darker world.

She stood awkwardly as if waiting for an invitation. Anna recognized that she put off the aura of someone at a way station and nowhere near her final destination. She was ragged, tattered, and shoeless, yet unencumbered by the mindless violence that she'd crudely commenced. She had come to terms with the fact that she'd murdered someone and was going to do it again. Probably go straight to hell for it, but so what?

Stallings motioned with his head for her to enter and patted the passenger seat. Anna slid in slowly and shut the door.

Suddenly, Anna reached over and clasped Old Man Stallings's arm. She shook it heavily back and forth.

"Whaddya do that for?" he asked. If the wounded and blood-slicked girl in his cab caused him fear or apprehension, he hid it well.

Anna started laughing. Strong and painful. Finally saying, "I just wanted to make sure you were real." She placed her head back against the cool glass of the cab. "I think I might've gone a little crazy." She closed her eyes and stopped abruptly. She seemed temporarily immobilized and was frozen in an attitude of surprise.

"Well, darlin', we're all a little crazy to some extent," Old Man Stallings said. "Just some more than others." He kept the truck in park, and it idled with an occasional loud whoop and rumble of the big block engine. "I hope you don't mind me saying, but you look like death warmed over."

Anna started laughing all over again. "No," she managed to say between giggles. "Not me. Someone else, though. Warm and crispy." She braced her hands against her sides and took a few deep breaths to calm down. Now, Anna noticed Old Man Stallings looking at her with confusion and concern. Perhaps a bit of sympathy as well.

She knew she looked like shit. Without asking, Anna reached over and turned on the truck's heater, which crackled to life. The fan moaning slowly in rotation from under the dash. Clearly, a thing he never used. The smell of burning dust permeated the cab. The acrid stench brought her back to some form of sanity. Stallings had turned toward her with his back against the door. He stared at her. Soaking wet and shivering. A ruined hand and wrist with a stained, bloody shirt that clotted into black and maroon around her stomach.

Anna stared out the window and watched the world about. It rotated without her consent. She was a thing of insignificance. This made her mad. She felt a deep rage down to her marrow that she'd not let slip away. It coursed through her like electricity. A kaleidoscope view of the future flashed through her mind, and it wasn't good. A maelstrom of events that she couldn't control. The clouds made shifting designs of shadows on the blacktop. She knew what she had to do.

There was no other choice.

"So, home or hospital?" Old Man Stallings asked. "I reckon I'll choose for you and that's the latter." He took off his coat and handed it to her. She placed it around her shoulders and looked ahead. Stallings turned slowly back toward the steering wheel and grasped the gearshift.

"Neither, please," she responded.

"A'ight, well then, where to?" He shifted into drive.

Anna pointed toward town.

Stallings pulled back onto the highway and cut a U-turn. Anna was still disoriented and was unsure where the old man was taking her. The scenes went by in a familiar blur. Like she was seeing them but not seeing them. Either side of the road went for miles and miles. The whole world seemed uninhabited and rolled on forever. All of it new configurations of a restructured world.

Softly, Stallings spoke and partially reassured her. "That works. But you've gotta tell me what the hell happened to you."

So, Anna did. She started with her kidnapping, torture in the cabin, her escape, Billy's death, the fire, her sister's head, falling into the river, coming to, and finding him. Her speech was focused with a fierce intensity. There went the weight of the world. He just listened and drove on in silence. Slowing to hear the whole thing. Occasionally nodding or shaking his head.

There was a spot along the side of the road that allowed him to pull over. He stopped the truck and put it in park. He tapped the steering wheel several times with his thumb and stared out in the dead wilderness.

"Billy told me the preacher Hinson had nothing to do with it. Killing Sam." Anna took a deep, wincing breath. "I've got to find out the truth. I'll do whatever it takes."

Old Man Stallings took his hand off the steering wheel and rubbed his brow. Despite the cold, he was sweating.

"You don't have to drop me off. Just take me home. I'll get over there one way or another." She paused. "I don't want to get you tied up in all this."

"Remember when I told you about my time during the war? And I said it weren't the only bad thing I've done? And hat it wasn't something that I regret?"

Only a vague recollection, but Anna nodded anyway.

"Well, I'll give it to you straight. Might think less or more of me, but that's all right." He didn't look at her. Just stared straight ahead at the expanse of bare winter trees. Anna watched him closely. Despite his age, he cut an imposing figure. Big hands and wrists. A lifetime of hard work that didn't disappear with time. A man not put off by hardship.

Perhaps now she wasn't either.

"It was sometime in April of 1952. Spring had sprung, as the stupid saying goes. I was working at the marble mill. Hard work, I tell you. Pullin' in good money, so not much to complain about, I reckon. Life weren't all that bad, but I was still haunted by the shitstorm from the Pacific. Had a young wife who died but I won't talk about that . . ." He paused and shook his head. "It don't really matter."

Anna's wrist throbbed, a hydraulic pump of agony. She tasted something metallic set deep in the back of her teeth. Stinging pressure that hit her like a blow to the abdomen.

Stallings turned to face her. "This town used to be mighty rough. Full of poor folks and poorer ones on top of that. Mostly just tryna make it. Some did better than others. But with all this came some trash. People so sorry you can hardly find a word to describe 'em. Wouldn't if you didn't have to, I reckon."

Almost suddenly, an eighteen-wheeler roared past on the highway. The truck shook violently, but the old man paid it no mind and continued on. "Life was hard. For us working at the mill, you never knew what the next day might bring. Some of it was pretty dangerous, but we kept on. Money'll make you do some dumb things."

Spasms of pain raced up Anna's spine. The pulsations formed a deliberate pace as if set to music. Stallings tapped his fingers on the steering wheel. He turned to face Anna. "Things was a whole lot different back then. It was a lot better. Well, that's my opinion at least."

Anna looked out the window and watched the dance of shadow and light from the tree branches as they drifted back and forth. Vibratory motion. Seeming like a cursed thing set to continue endlessly. In almost religiously inspired repetition making crosses along the graying earth. A higher power? Perhaps no divination there. Solely random.

Stallings continued. "There was this fella, well, a piece of shit really, from somewheres else that worked at the mill. I think Alabama, but that don't really matter. He was a stranger. Not one of us." He reached into his pocket and pulled out a bag of pre-rolled cigarettes. He selected one and offered the bag to Anna, who shook her head. Stallings rolled the window down an inch and lit the crooked cigarette with his ancient Zippo lighter. "He raped a four-year-old girl. I ain't gonna say who 'cause she still lives here. But let me tell you, it was about as close to hell for that youngern as you can get without falling in. In fact, I hate to use that term to describe what he did to her, because it was a far cry worse than even that."

Old Man Stallings pulled on the cigarette, shook his head, and blew a stream of blue smoke out of his nose. "He snatched her right off the street and had his way with her. Knocked her around a good bit too. We saw her face the next day, and God was it a mess. Eyes swollen shut, nose broke, and front teeth gone. Luckily—I guess you can say that— they were her baby teeth, so that turned out all right. She had bite marks all over her too. Why? Damned if I know." He shuddered, inhaled, and continued. "He 'bout near destroyed her. Her momma had to tend to her. Can you believe that? Imagine having to doctor your own daughter after such a thing. Goddamn, I still hurt for that woman, and she's been dead on five years or so."

He tapped on the steering wheel and tossed the cigarette out the window. "Me and some other fellas from the mill were drinking at a bar just outside town. It weren't a bar-bar like we got now. This was a dry county. It was just the bootlegger's house where you'd drink your beer. I've had bad whiskey in my day, but some of 'em places sold the worst. That was pretty normal around here. Some old folks around here sitting high and mighty in churches, business, and government spent many an hour there."

Along the highway, two cars sped past in rapid succession, and Anna watched intently as Stallings followed them with his eyes. One was a Crown Victoria with SHERIFF'S DEPARTMENT written along the side. It sped out of sight around the curve.

Stallings went on, "That baby's aunt come up in the place just hol-

lering bloody murder. Ragin' and cryin' at the same time. Told us everything that happened. Most awfullest thing I ever heard. To imagine it
would happen to a child. I'd hate to think you could. It still chills me to
remember what all she said. How she said it." Stallings lifted his hand
and showed it was shaking. "Even now . . ."

He paused for a moment before continuing. "There were eight of us,
and we all pretty quick decided what needed to be done. Weren't a lag-
gard amid the group. It was catch 'em and kill 'em. I might misremember,
but we might've thought about lawing him for a second or two. Then
again, I think altogether we wanted to kill him, so that's what we done."

The world looked barren and dead. This little cab seemed like the
last outcropping of humanity. The earth appeared slightly tilted upon its
axis and set askew. Anna almost felt its lopsided spin.

"Well, we snatched that fella up like he done her and hauled him
deep into the pineys. We had a rope, a host of weapons, and vengeance
in our hearts. I tell you what, ever' man in our company knew that son
of a bitch weren't gonna leave that place alive. We marched him out for
miles into Copperhead Valley and tied him up. Pulled him real taut from
the tree. Ever' man took turns beating him. I hit him until my hands hurt
and then hit him some more. When it's real cold out, I feel the ache in
my knuckles still. He probably knew what was coming 'cause he was just
a squalling about his momma. Well, he should've thought about that
when he was raping that poor child." Stallings tapped his fingers on the
steering wheel. "When we got bored of it, we hauled him on up and hung
him there. He eventually died of it. We left him there. I figure bones are
probably the only things left if the scavengers haven't hauled 'em away."

As the old man talked, Anna looked at the reflection of his aged face
in the windshield. There was contemplation and desperation etched in
his features. She noticed that he was staring at her with a fiery gaze that
evoked something from an older time. It frightened her in a way that she
didn't understand. Or maybe she did. It was a feeling she'd known all her
life. Just acute now that her deliverance had come.

The sun hung with a glow in the distance like an incandescent fire. A thing beyond the realm of God and man. Woodlands smoking amid the barren trees. They were so stripped that they looked like the fingers of a skeleton. Everything tinged with gray like old metal. Come spring, all of that wasteland would turn stark green with hundreds of different hues. So thick it'd be impossible to see through.

Anna turned to the old man with amazed acceptance and momentary incredulity. They sat in silence for a long time. She feared the old man had spoken too much and his mouth had atrophied.

"When shit happens to you, they happen," the old man whispered. "A person's path through life seldom changes slowly. It'll change abruptly and change what you thought was visible from the beginning. Sometimes you've gotta take matters into your own hands. But know that it'll haunt you for the rest of your life . . . Look, just do what you think is right."

He reached across her to the glove compartment and dug around the strange collection of trash strewn inside. Brown receipts and dirty tissues tumbled onto the floorboard. She saw a mini brass picture frame with a weathered, sepia-stained photo of a young woman smiling for the camera. He moved aside a bag of candy orange slices and a pocket-sized dictionary. She watched his timeworn hand search among the clutter. Finally, he stopped and pulled out a hawkbill knife with a handle made of duct tape. He flipped it with a cool dexterity and caught the blade between his forefinger and thumb. The old man handed it to her with a mute gesture of his chin. A great tool for her malefaction. She took the handle and felt the warmth of immeasurable rage. It seemed to vibrate in her hand with ancient patience waiting just for her.

Anna held it with both hands and looked at her reflection. She saw someone preparing for a grim and austere endeavor.

The old man reached behind the wheel to the gearshift and put the truck in reverse. He slowly backed out onto the highway and placed it in drive. The truck shuddered for a moment as he pushed the gas. Then it lurched forward, and they headed off down the road.

Chapter 35

A few minutes later, the old man's truck pulled up in front of a long driveway that led to the pastor's house. It seemed to go on forever. Stallings
parked along the side of the road and left the car running. Anna kept
blinking, and her head hammered like she'd had it sat on by a fat man.
Her vision doubled, which created a duality of paths, but there was only
one. The driveway was steep and curved around a wooded thicket with
evergreen mountain laurel hiding the home from view.

Anna turned to the old man, but he stared straight ahead. The last
light reflected off Stallings's white hair, and it formed some prophetic
halo. His eyebrows bunched together, not in anger or pain, but absolute
sorrow for the peregrine turn of Anna's life. No need for a conversation.
He understood, and there was nothing left to talk about. He asked if she
needed him to stick around and give her a ride home, but Anna just
shook her head.

"Thanks," she whispered, and exited the truck. She took a step forward and closed the door. Anna heard the truck switch gears, and the
metal screamed like a being under torture. Struggling and clanking like
a thing on its last leg. Then it slowly pulled away and headed off down
the road.

She was in a sorry state. The only positive was that the puncture
wound in her stomach had stopped bleeding. She redoubled her grip
on the knife and started up the drive. Anna felt like she was in a trance.
She could no longer feel her feet—they were more like awkward clubs
banging onto the ground.

The driveway seemed unending, windingtoward an unfaltering,

inescapable oblivion. She was dazed with exhaustion and fought against the threat of unconsciousness.

After several yards, she stopped. The urge to vomit surged up her esophagus, and she ran sideways to a bush and began retching with hands on her knees. She remained in that position for a long time, spitting occasionally to get the taste out of her mouth. Her expelled filth pooled in the grass. She stopped and smelled an outrageous and awful stench. It seemed to settle over everything. Hung in the air.

Anna rose almost drunkenly, and she nearly toppled over. Her gut burned and tears burst to her eyes. Wetness rolled down her cheeks, and she swore at her recklessness.

The wind picked up, and it got very cold. The trees bent and swayed with cracking sounds, which evoked a hidden and natural form of incubated rapacity. The air smelled sweet with slight hints of snow. Anna stood listening. Everything was quiet. The gray sky above was full of running clouds. They sprinted above like flowing water.

Anna walked slowly through the trees to hide her progress. She moved like she was displaced from reality. All that mattered was this vengeful fixation. She made her way between the large trees. They served as markers. She slapped her hands against the trees for purchase as she climbed. They sounded oddly hollow. She had to stop often and will herself to the next. A bird's wings flapped above and echoed like applause. Leaves scattered across the yard, sounding like voices of warning. Anna watched them whirl away and kept on. They held no message that she'd heed.

The house stood solitary and stoic atop the hill. The driveway wound up to a detached garage that matched the iron-colored bricks of the home's façade. The house looked new but had an archaic quality among the oaks. The brown grass seemed frozen. Everything empty and evoking stinging abandonment. The area was windless, silent, and no one seemed about. The world was shadowed except for when Anna blinked, and she quickly realized how tired she was. A shape flickered past, and she hoped it was a bird and not buckshot.

Anna remained among the trees and watched everything with predator eyes. Every sound was made animate, and she registered it all like some inexplicable accountant of the natural world. Although there wasn't a place on her that didn't hurt, she managed to glide up the steep incline. She kept redoubling her grip on the hawkbill knife, a comfort object and dark harbinger. Anna reached the apex and hugged the side of the garage. She poked her head around and looked in through the window, but it was too dark to see inside.

Damn, Anna thought. *They might be gone.*

She thought about that for a minute. She could hole up and wait for them to return. Yet the prospect of standing in the cold for an extended amount of time meant that she'd probably die. Death itself wasn't really a concern. In fact, the opposite was true. Joining her sister held a certain allure that Anna couldn't shake. It called to her like sirens situated amid rocks in the middle of a vast sea. The only reason she hadn't succumbed to her yearning was the fact that she needed to kill at least one or all of the Hinsons.

She noticed a small light emanating from the house. Just in case, Anna quickly went up the stone steps toward the front door. She used the knife handle to smash the full-length window in the center. There was an eruption of cracking and then a rain of glass falling down. Hopefully if someone was in the house, the sound would distract them while she snuck around back.

The backyard was enclosed by an archaic-looking fence made from timber of the region. Off in the distance were blue-peaked mountains that flowed seamlessly into that paper sky and ascended forever.

Anna climbed the wooden porch steps and approached the back door. It looked strong and was made with oak and had no windows. She had a terrible moment of fear. Would it be locked? As she slowly reached for the knob, the door shot open. Anna lost her footing in surprise and hit the deck hard. A shadowed figure stood just within the doorframe. Anna rolled over on her stomach and found herself breathing heavily from panic. There was a horrible moment of silence that sent shocks of blistering cold up and down her spine like reckless pandemonium. The chill forced her into inarticulation. Clattering teeth that rendered her mute. Rising to her knees, Anna watched as a delicate hand reached out and steadied her as she stood. Then the other appeared from the dark. It held a small revolver.

The sight of the pistol made Anna's hands clammy. Her eyes skittered about and instantaneously studied everything like it might be her last view of the world.

She felt for the knife and realized in horror that it was gone. She must've dropped it when she fell. Perhaps somewhere near her feet.

Do not bend down, she thought. *Don't even try to look.*

Anna saw Ruth and noticed the woman looked haggard. The gaunt appearance of a vulture. She was ghost white. Ruth reminded Anna of a living and breathing papier-mâché doll set loose upon the world. The gun shook in her hand.

The pastor's wife spoke slowly and evenly. "Come inside, please." The gun hadn't really been the thing that worried Anna. It was Ruth's eyes. They had an atavistic look. Like she'd planned this from the beginning.

Anna entered the kitchen. She quivered and jerked as she walked through the house. It was so dense with silence that it seemed like a monastery. There was a cool gloom to everything. She felt like she was entering a cave, and her eyes took a long time to adjust. The only sound, Ruth's soft whispers directing Anna toward the living room. A small cylinder poked into the middle of Anna's back. Just enough pressure to make her aware that it was there. Anna's footsteps were amplified in the emptiness. She sensed the shadowed and armed figure close to her side. There was a cold draft in the house that Anna knew wasn't there, only imagined. Off to the right, she spied through the windows and saw a purple dusk forming. Soon, the sky would take on a beautiful cyan that would move with darkness upon the earth's curve.

Anna was told to stop in a bland living room. There was a tiny television set upon a stand, and the place looked like something out of a 1950s movie. Huge-backed chairs and an ugly couch that was beige and stamped with multicolored flowers. Inside the blossoms were brown Bibles. All of these stood atop red plush carpet. Anna noticed dusty light that came through the window. There was a huge picture of Jesus looming over the mantel. A replica of the Last Supper on the far wall. Everything else held a barren air. A flash of movement and Anna followed the gun that pointed toward the couch. She walked over and sat underneath an ornate wooden cross. The crucified Christ dangling in unobstructed agony. It took Anna a long time to finally look at Ruth fully. See into her eyes. Soul.

The pastor's wife had lost her former grandeur and stood strangely with the gun, like an imposter. Anna saw that Ruth was vulnerable and transparent. The equanimity of a victim instead of a victor. A person detained against her will. Anna knew the eyes of a killer because she was now one. Not a transient or fellow traveler. She'd killed and would gladly kill again.

Ruth sat in a chair opposite Anna, placed the gun on her knee, and pointed it at her captive. She took several deep breaths and tried to feign a smile. "It's all so strange, isn't it? I feel like someone who belongs in an institution. Perhaps that's what this is." Ruth waved her hand around at the breadth of iconography scattered about as if asking Anna to take in the whole bizarre scene of this living room trapped in time.

"I know you must think that I'm evil or crazy," she went on. "I offend your sensibilities. Yet he is my only son. His well-being must reach to the heavens. I won't apologize for that. I know you won't ask me to because, deep down, you know that I'm right. You know how important it is to get away from here. You even succeeded." Ruth nodded as if thinking this might compare the two.

Her eyes seemed to rupture into madness. There was arrogance there too that Anna found terrifying. Like this person was on quicksand and might lash out in a horrific way.

"He's my only child and deserves so much more than this. When your sister told me that she was pregnant, I knew he'd be stuck here. That is all. That is why." Ruth sighed and held her free hand up, feigning exacerbation. "You don't have to speak. From the looks of you, you seem to be in a form of shock. That's all right." Ruth seemed to look past Anna. Like perhaps she was all alone. Yet, the gun never wavered from Anna's direction.

"I'll tell you a little about my history. Perhaps that will reveal my actions. I'm not making excuses, but perhaps this might evoke some form of closure. Or understanding. Yet, before continuing, I must confess that I don't plan on killing you." She waved the gun slightly back and forth atop her knee. "This is just to make sure you don't leave before I have my say."

Anna nodded slightly.

"Good. So, I never wanted to come here . . . I was a young and intelligent woman, you see. Fell in love with an intelligent man. Everything was perfect until he brought me to this place. Now my life is purely a shadow of what I'd long desired. A country pastor's wife amid a bunch of hillbillies. That's okay. I'd long resigned myself to that fact."

A loud exhale. "But I'll never let that happen to my son. My only child. I brought him into this world for something more. He has scholarships to the best schools in the south. Yet, sadly, he is principled like his father. Blind to all else but what he deems right. I tried to get your sister to have an abortion. Promised her money, a car, jewelry. She said no. She assured me that she'd have his child. Then he'd be stuck here. Here." With her free hand, she pointed at the ground. "I know you understand."

Anna didn't respond. She realized that the pastor's wife had been lying all along. About Sam needing spiritual guidance. Every time the two met, Ruth was just pressuring her sister to get an abortion. Anna tried to steady her boiling emotions, and she breathed in and out slowly and listened with growing anger to this horrible confession.

"I don't regret it at all. True, she was desecrated, but I had nothing to do with that. The boy went . . . well, he got carried away." Ruth closed her eyes and shook her head. "But take heart. Hers will be a cautionary tale for the realities of the world."

"Billy's dead." Anna had not spoken in so long that her voice startled her. "He's dead now. I broke his neck and set him on fire. Burned his ass alive. That's your fault . . . Did you plan for him to kill me too?" Anna asked.

"No, and I don't care," Ruth said. She shrugged like this news was irrelevant. "As I said, I don't regret what happened. You see, it was necessary. Now that she's gone, my son will get to live his life. It wasn't personal. I took no pleasure in being the architect of death. It was her or my son. And I'd choose him every single time. I will do the same now . . ." Ruth shook the gun for emphasis.

"You made the comment to my husband about there being just one road, and you are quite right. It takes many shapes, and it changes with each step, but there is only one. And along it is contained all that's ever needed. Here is just more of that . . . I wanted you as a witness. Here and now. Because to engage in an enterprise without one truly calls into question everything. Your sister's death would be nothing without one."

"You bitch," Anna said through clenched teeth. "You're a goddamn bitch. The thing about Sam was that she was faster, louder, and brighter than the rest of the world. And you fucking ruined it."

"Well, even so," Ruth said.

"Everything you've been saying is complete bullshit. Your condescension and self-righteousness are astounding. Now what do you want? Admonishment? Absolution? You get none. Damn you to hell. You die."

Ruth shook her head. "No, I want none of those things. Well, not from you at least. This is all your kind's fault. White trash. Bad blood. But be thankful. Those who suffer misfortune are set apart. It's actually a gift because you must either perish or fight back into the realm of humankind. The deepest community is that of sorrow. Bonds that can never be broken. Yours and mine." She pointed her finger back and forth.

"You can perhaps see," Ruth said, "the hand of God in destruction. Just like you can in miracles. God is quite wrathful, and if you inquire sufficiently, you can find evidence of his nameless rage. Your desire has to be strong enough. But you must be careful. God does not destroy without reason. The joinery is not completely hidden. No, you just need to know where to look . . . The past cannot be mended. In many ways it doesn't exist. Some think it's all that matters, but there is no such truth there. The past is dead. The future a question. All that matters is the present." She finally left Anna's gaze and stared at the floor. A woman defeated before the game was out.

Anna felt like she was lost in a conversation that was completely haywire. Everything a little off-balance and unaccountable. "What the fuck are you talking about? Do it then," Anna said. "Just fucking do it."

Ruth appeared to be weighing Anna's words like someone trying to accommodate their meaning. She whispered something. Prayer. Benediction. Absolute blasphemy.

Then Ruth nodded and placed the barrel of the pistol under her chin. Anna turned away. The explosion was immense in that small space. The acrid smell of gun smoke assaulted Anna's senses and billowed from where Ruth sat. She made a noise like some malign beast dying. Her rasping breath grew fainter and fainter until the final rattle that sounded like the last falling leaves from a frozen winter. Perhaps it was in Anna's mind, but already there was the stench of putrefaction and decay.

Anna stared at the wall behind the chair. There was a crucifix turned upside down. A bullet hole had shattered the cross and cleaved it in two. Christ seemed to watch Anna with incapable anger. Bleeding rage in the knowledge of his hammered impotence.

She stood painfully and spied old yellow photos scattered about the room of folks who looked long dead. Their sepia faces staring at the camera with expressions of benign goodwill. Ghosts of old circumstances like faded memories.

Anna limped into the kitchen toward the back door. She walked as if one leg had grown longer than the other. She passed her reflection in the glass and noticed that she looked wrong.

She'd always look wrong.

She knew the expression on her face. The same one that countless others have worn before. All common victims of loss, tragedy, and disaster. The sadness of it beyond speech or the literate world. Each second it got harder. Every breath heavier. Even her heartbeat felt like a razor.

Anna reached to turn the knob and saw her hand. It was near black with dried blood. She held out the other and saw the same. She was ragged and dirty, yet something else completely unspoken for. She hurried outside onto the porch. The evening dusk had turned the mountains into darkening colors and shapes against the purple sky. There was nothing but near silence and a faint wind. The seeming world completely depopulated from Anna's bearings. She knew that, in the dark, out past the long-shadowed twilight lay the valley of the shadow of death. The magnitude of everything hit her at once, and she fell on her knees and sobbed into her filthy hands.

She let the tears come. Anna wept in the way of an only and lonely child because, now, that was what she was. An acolyte of some new order. The fellowship of the damned. As above, so below. This was the ending of a cycle. All closing in. The sanctity was inchoate. Anna let the images of all she'd done and lost pass before her. She grieved her griefs. At long last, they came.

Chapter 36

After leaving the Hinson house, Anna stumbled down the driveway and collapsed in the middle of the road. A passing motorist stopped, lifted her into the back seat, and took her to the hospital. The next few days were a blur. The doctors patched up her wrists, which they promised would heal over time. The nerves and charred muscles would completely repair themselves, leaving only a scar. As if by some miracle, the ice pick wound was superficial. The tip was so honed and sharp that it had slid between the vital organs. The wound only needed to be cleaned and covered to stave off infection. Anna was in the hospital for a day for cleaning and dressing her burns. The physical marks would eventually repair, yet the psychological damages might never mend. Perhaps they weren't supposed to.

After Anna was discharged from the hospital, the sheriff and GBI went to her mother's trailer and interviewed her about Ruth and Billy. She told them everything that happened from start to finish, except for killing Billy and seeing Old Man Stallings. She showed them the bruises that covered her body and the burns that communicated a story of their own. Finally, she ended by lying that Billy had had second thoughts, let her go, and must've run off. The officers listened and took notes without interrupting her. When she finished, they thanked her, and the sheriff promised to update them once all the details were hammered down and the paperwork was filled out.

While this went on, Anna's mother lay curled up in the fetal position. She stared absently at the blank television and was silent as a stone. Anna tried to get her to eat or drink something, but it was no use. She grieved her thousand griefs and would continue to do so until the day she died. Anna understood that better than anyone and finally left her mother alone.

As Anna slowly healed, Brokeback came and went bringing bags of supplies that were filled with random objects and mostly unhelpful. One bag was full of pencil erasers and chicken broth. Another holding men's underwear two sizes too small and a box of kitty litter. The last held a puzzle of a cheese pizza and nail polish remover. When asked about the bizarre gifts, he just shook his head and began to cry. Overall, Sam's disappearance and murder had left him completely unhinged. For hours, he'd either sit in silence and drink Wild Turkey straight from the bottle or march outside the trailer, fire his pistol into the air, and curse God to hell. As with her mother, Anna left him to mourn in peace. They each suffered in their own way.

Anna remembered hearing that time heals all wounds, but she knew that was a lie. Each day, the weight of her sorrow seemed to grow heavier. Like she was struck with a new form of a Sisyphean curse of everlasting grief. Every step and each breath from dawn to dusk was harder than the one before. Perhaps, Anna hoped, she would learn to superficially exist with the pain, or at least live long enough to die trying.

Three days later, the sheriff arrived at their trailer early in the morning and updated the family on what the detectives had uncovered. He went through each piece of evidence in methodical detail. They'd found the cabin where Billy's charred remains were located among the ashes. Upon further investigation of his single-wide, the detectives and sheriff located enough concrete evidence to back up Anna's claim and directly tie Billy to Sam's disappearance and the disposal of her body. In addition to the clothing, the authorities uncovered the ten thousand dollars paid by Ruth lazily hidden under his bed.

Along with Anna's account of what happened at the Hinson residence, the investigators found the wife's burner phone that provided confirmation and spelled out in intricate detail the crimes committed against Sam. The phone log showed her in constant contact with Billy through calls and texts in the days leading up to the murder. Also, hidden in her dresser was a receipt for ten thousand dollars, which Ruth was seen on surveillance camera withdrawing from her personal savings account a week prior to Sam's disappearance. These bits and pieces finally threaded together to provide a coherent narrative.

The sheriff also updated them on the search for the last of Sam's remains. The police had combed the river for several miles from where Anna had fallen off the bridge but were unable to locate the missing head. Although Anna didn't say anything out loud, she was glad of this fact. She knew where her sister was and would forever be. Had the investigators found the rest of her body, she thought, that might've been the end of Sam's story. Like dried flowers pressed between the pages of an aged family Bible, she'd be put up and forgotten.

The sheriff went on to explain that Pastor Hinson was going to be released later that day without charge. Their investigation found no evidence that he was involved or knew about his wife's actions. Brokeback pounded his fists hard on his knees and shouted a string of expletives. "He tried to cover up for the boy," Brokeback yelled. "What more proof do you need? He knew something, goddamn it!" But the sheriff just shook his head and raised his hands in utter finality. Off the record, he agreed with Anna's uncle, but there was nothing else he could do.

Listening to the sheriff, Anna didn't know how much bad news she could absorb without going crazy, nor how much she had to absorb in order to survive in the world as she found it to be. She had no notion at all of what would be left when all her innocence was finally gone.

The sheriff rose to leave. Tears filled his eyes, and Anna understood that this tragedy affected more than just her family. Up until this point, she'd considered this misfortune theirs alone. Yet looking at the sheriff's face, Anna saw unmitigated grief. This case would haunt him every day until he died. And not just him. Her sister's murder was burned into the very fabric of the community. Never again would Marble Hill be the same. Now, their identity was forever infused with Sam's death. The town with the murdered headless twin. It was at this moment that Anna knew she'd have to leave and never return.

Later that day, Anna received a call on her cell phone from a number that she didn't recognize. She almost let it go straight to voicemail, but something gave her pause, and she answered on the fourth ring. "Hello?" she said. There was silence on the other end. "Hello? This is Anna . . ."

"Anna," a muffled and broken voice said. "Anna, it's Daniel. Daniel Hinson."

The name felt like daggers piercing her heart, and she almost threw the phone against the wall. Instead, she stayed on the line. Perhaps she felt the pain of this fellow traveler. Anna heard his stifled sobs and understood that his heart was breaking as well. His cries reminded her that ultimately pain enslaves completely. It is the one god before which we bow without reservation or question. Daniel loved her sister and needed someone to share in his misery. Understand his grief in the knowledge that the dead don't turn in their tracks and follow their own footprints home.

"Yes?" she said.

"Can I talk to you?" he asked. "In person?"

She paused and was greeted by a long silence on the other end. Finally, she said yes. "Let's meet at Big Brew Coffee," she said. "Today at four o'clock."

"Thank you," Daniel said. He was sobbing now. "My God, thank you so much."

Anna got to the coffee shop fifteen minutes early, and Daniel was already there. He was at a small table near the window staring at his lap. He didn't look up when she entered and only lifted his head when she pulled back her chair to sit down. His eyes were bloodshot, his blood-red capillaries like a spider's web, and he appeared like the shell of a broken young man. He'd lost so much for no other reason but that he'd fallen in love.

They sat in silence for a long time. Only the lonely sound of commerce from the coffee shop working like a soundtrack. Finally, Daniel looked up and faced the mirrored image of the woman who was his ever-abiding world. He swallowed hard several times and finally spoke. "I loved Sam. And she loved me."

"I know," Anna said softly.

"We had plans. Once I graduated, we were going to get married. She was going to go off with me to Emory and take classes at Perimeter College. It was important for her to get a degree. I wanted that for her as well."

Anna just shook her head. This was something she didn't know about her sister, like things whose very consequences lend them ambiguity. Things so charged with meaning that their forms are dimmed. She had no idea Sam had fallen in love and wanted to get married. There was a whole different side to her sister. What else didn't Anna know? What else would she never know?

"I'm broken," he choked. "Lost. I don't know what to do."

"I know," Anna repeated. She said no more. Anna knew that you don't talk someone off the ledge by telling them that what sent them out there in the first place is true. Tomorrow is going to be worse, and the day after, unimaginable.

Everything is a lesson. This is the way the world is. Happiness is just what you have before the sorrow sets in. And she finally learned that evil is real. The basic stuff. You can't turn off the dark. You can only turn on the light.

There would be no funeral for Sam. Anna and her mother made plans with the coroner to cremate Sam's remains. After several distraught days of discussion, Anna's mother decided that she couldn't live in Marble Hill anymore. There were too many terrors, both real and imagined.

It didn't take long for Anna's mother to pack her meager belongings. Except for a black garbage bag full of clothes, her mother planned to leave everything else behind. She'd find a job and try to start anew. The trailer was stalked by the ghost of her dead husband and now her daughter. Lost souls without rest. An overdose and a murder swirling amid the pungent odor of neglect and poverty. Anna knew her mother would gladly burn the place down in an effort to expunge the haunted souls, yet they needed to try to sell the trailer and get what money they could.

Brokeback was staying behind and promised to watch the trailer until it sold. He couldn't and wouldn't leave Marble Hill. There was too much money in his dope business. He was the big man in a small town where he peddled fear and misery along with crystal meth. He claimed to understand and promised to visit, but that was yet to be seen. Perhaps just as they needed to leave, he had to stay.

Christmas and New Year's passed without mention. The house was still encumbered in heartache, and there was nothing to celebrate. The plan was for Anna to go back to college and get her degree while her mother worked at an Athens Pancake House. It was a cold day in late January when mother and daughter packed up the car and prepared to leave. Brokeback stood awkwardly in the yard with Rufus and watched the solemn procession of his sister and niece with sad eyes. When they were done, Anna held open the passenger door and called for Rufus. He ran over and jumped into the car with a look of confusion and excitement rolled into one. Finally, everything was ready, and it was time for them to go.

Anna's mother wrapped her arms around her brother and wept. He rocked her back and forth and whispered softly in her ear. His eyes were wet. He looked to Anna and beckoned her over with the toss of his head. She jumped into his arms, and he spun her around like he had when she was a child. He set her down gently and regarded her with a smile.

"Remember, baby girl," he said, "keep it between the mustard and the mayonnaise and you'll be all right."

"I will, Brokeback. I will."

Epilogue

The shiny black Cadillac drove quick and smooth around a bend on Cove Road. Blinding light from the callous sun flashed off the waxed exterior. All the windows were rolled down, and inside sat a solitary man. Hank Williams Sr.'s rendition of "I Saw the Light" blared over the stereo, and Pastor Hinson tapped his middle finger on the steering wheel and hummed along to the music as the wind blew through his thinning hair. The huge silver cross that hung from the rearview mirror sparkled and blinked reflected light along with the music. The sun baked the Georgia asphalt and sent dancing waves of shimmering heat off the blacktop.

The Cadillac effortlessly sailed around a hard bend in the road. Ahead was an old Chevy truck straddling the line in the middle of the thoroughfare. It was a rusty-looking cream color without a license plate. The hood was propped open, and, at first glance, the truck looked abandoned.

As the Cadillac slowed to a stop, there was an unmistakable flash of movement from the other side of the upturned hood. Someone was trying to breathe new life into the old truck and was clearly in need of help. Pastor Hinson put his vehicle in park and exited. He smiled broadly and helloed his unfortunate neighbor.

"Howdy!" he hollered. "Do you need some help?"

A loud grunt and a string of curses rang out from the other side of the hood.

The pastor walked toward the truck and was slowly rolling up the sleeves of his starched white dress shirt. He'd already tucked his tie below the third button. "Not only am I a purveyor of lost souls, but I also know my way around the internal combustion engine. The terrestrial gifts dispersed by the Almighty are as confusing as they are majestic." He chuckled. "My brother in Christ, let me be your Good Samaritan."

Brokeback stepped from behind the upturned hood with an automatic shotgun raised at his shoulder. Before Hinson had time to register the mortal danger he was in, he had been shot twice in the chest. The reports were so rapid that it sounded like one long explosion. The pastor's arms flailed wildly as he toppled backward and fell wounded onto the roasting concrete. Dark red blood bloomed, spread, and stained his white shirt.

With the shotgun still at his shoulder, Brokeback calmly walked toward the writhing pastor. He watched Hinson struggle to breathe with his mouth agape. Brokeback was struck by a pain of sadness that he couldn't kill the man every day for the rest of his life. Just today would have to do, he thought.

He placed the barrel against the man's forehead and fired. A welter of gore vomited across the pavement. Bits of brain, skull, skin, and hair were embedded into the asphalt. The pastor slumped awkwardly, and blood pooled around his head. Brokeback lowered the shotgun and looked over the scene. This heretic dead and no living soul in sight.

He reached down and picked up the spent casing from the ground and put the steaming shell in his pocket. He retraced his steps and gathered up the remaining casings. Then he went back to the body and nudged the pastor's upended foot and watched it fall helplessly to the side. Content, he walked back to the truck, got behind the wheel.

Brokeback pulled out his cell phone and called Anna. "It's done," he said. There was silence on the other end of the line. He ended the call and started the engine and set off down the road.

There wasn't a cloud in the cobalt sky. Gone were the miseries of winter and the encumbered horrors of the recent past. Gone were the naked trees that looked like fingers on a skeleton. The landscape sprouted bits of greenery signaling the advance of spring and the dawning of a new season, year, life.

Clay Anderson is an author and bookstore owner. He holds a Master of Arts in History along with a Master of Fine Arts in Creative Writing. He authored the novel *The Palms*, for which he was nominated Georgia Author of the Year in 2019.

http://www.dclayanderson.com
Facebook: @AndersonClayAuthor
Instagram: @clayanderson_author
Twitter: @DClayAnderson

Springer Mountain Press
Instagram: @springernountainpress
Twitter: @SpringerMtPress
Facebook: @springermountainpress

Made in the USA
Columbia, SC
30 September 2023

23524413R00136